Where Angels Roost

By

Larry C. Scallons

Xulon Press

Copyright © 2009 by Larry C. Scallons

Where Angels Roost
by Larry C. Scallons

Printed in the United States of America

Library of Congress Catalog Number:
TXu001227421 / 2005-03-14

ISBN 978-1-60791-411-2

All rights reserved solely by the author. The author guarantees all contents are original and do not infringe upon the legal rights of any other person or work. No part of this book may be reproduced in any form without the permission of the author. The views expressed in this book are not necessarily those of the publisher.

www.xulonpress.com

*Dedicated to my family and friends.
The reasons why are in this story.*

Chapter 1

January 1945

Our positions are overrun as the Germans' last-gasp offensive begins. I grab a bazooka, a rack of six projectiles and start blasting. After knocking out six tanks, I climb up and begin machine gunning Nazis. Running from one knocked-out tank to the next, I finally run out of ammo. This stops the Germans cold, so I start running after them screaming, "Kapitulate! Kapitulate!"

The first Nazi surrender creates a domino effect so the others start throwing down their weapons and raising their arms. We count 623 bodies and more than 4,000 prisoners. Fighting and killing make me tired so I lay down and fall asleep under my poncho.

October 1945

After a nonstop seven hour flight from Washington, D.C., an Air Force C-54 four-engine military air transport taxis up to the passenger terminal at Love Field Airport in Dallas, Texas. The unloading ramp is pushed to the door, clamped in place and the wheels are locked. When the door opens passengers commence deplaning.

Last off the plane is a young slender Army officer with weary look on his pale face. On his right shoulder is a patch of an arrowhead with the letter "T" inside. This shoulder patch of the Texas National Guard Thirty-sixth Division, or Texas Army, is considered by most military experts the best infantry division of World War II.

The young officer walks into the terminal and up to a USO booth. The young lady at the booth asks, "Coffee?"

"Yes ma'am. I appreciate that."

She smiles big, "East Texas? On your way home? For good? The tune coming through the speakers is very appropriate now — 'Sentimental Journey Home.'"

"Yes ma'am, it sure is."

A two-star Army general standing with a three-star general says, "See that young colonel sipping coffee over there? If the meek inherit the earth, he won't be around. He's the most outrageous, vicious, ruthless killer imaginable. His name's Jonothan Jackson Quinn but we know him as Killer Wolverine."

"In southern France in January I watched him almost single-handedly stop more than 5,000 Nazis. He collapsed afterward. When we got to him he was peacefully asleep under his poncho. We roused him and he simply remarked that fighting made him sleepy. Doctors say he has such an enormous amount of adrenalin when in action that it makes him a physical freak. His explanation is that Jehova gives him the power. He's one of the top five youngest colonels of this war."

I walk out of the terminal and get into a Yellow Cab. The driver asks, "Where to, soldier?"

"Continental Bus Station."

"Going Home, huh?"

"Yes sir! Yes sirree Bob!"

The driver chuckles and says, "I like the way you talk. Are you Audie Murphy?"

"No but we come from the same neck of the woods."

"Must be something in the air," he says.

"Could be," I say.

I walk into the bus station, buy a ticket for home, and check my bag. I have 45 minutes before departure and will be arriving home at four in the afternoon so decide to call Rachel and tell her I'm on my way. Surprises are nice, but in this situation, maybe too much of a surprise.

I get some change, then decide to just call collect. I can hear the operator ask Rachel if she'll accept charges, then the operator says, "Go ahead."

"Rachel, it's Sonny. I'll be home on the four o'clock bus from Dallas."

She screams, "Oh Sonny, I could have met you in Dallas!" I can tell she's crying.

"It's been so long a little longer won't matter. I need to prepare myself. The bus ride will allow me to get myself pulled together. Give you time too. Tell Mama and Papa, Grandma, Grandpa, just the family. See you soon." I hang up the phone.

I fear I'll break down. I need mental preparation. I haven't seen my four-and-a-half year old baby daughter, Annabelle Mary, in nearly four years.

I go into the washroom and look in the mirror. Not too bad. I need to shave, freshen up, so hang my coat, shirt and hat on coat hooks. The restroom attendant furnishes towels and various smell-good lotions. He also shines shoes.

As I wipe my face with a towel, three big burly guys come in. "Well, well. Lookie here. We got us one of them bonie-fide war heroes. Heck, I seen more action in the honky tonks of South Dallas, more blood spilled than you ever seen. Ain't that right, sojer boy?" one of them says.

"If you say so," I reply.

"Well, I say so," he says. "I aim to prove you ain't a bit tough. I is gonna take off yo pants and make you my maid."

I can feel the surge coming. He makes a big round house swing. I kick him in the crotch, then stiffen my fingers and jam them in the left eye of the guy on his right. They scream and fall down. The flat heel of the palm of my right hand upper cuts the chin of the guy on his left. He drops like a pole-axed steer.

The big leader lays on the floor in a fetal position holding his crotch. I kick his head like a soccer ball. I grab the one blubbering and holding his head by his hair, slam him into the wall.

My blood boils up but I can hear a dim voice crying out, "Please, Mr. Soldier, no mo. You killin' them!"

It's the restroom attendant. "Lawd God. I ain't nevah seed any such thing in all my life. You didn't even double up yo fist."

I dress, grab my coat and start for the door. I call the attendant over, run my hand through my pocket, and pull out all the money I have — about $100.00. I give it to him. "For the mess I made."

"Don't let anyone in for five minutes then call an ambulance. Tell the police you seen nothing. I'm on my way home and don't want to be delayed."

"I sho will tell the police a big six foot six, 280 pound bully man done this. Go 'head on. I got you covered," he said.

"Thank you, sir."

Boarding the bus, I head for the back hoping no one will sit next to me. I'm not antisocial, just don't feel like talking.

As we ease out of the terminal, I feel a nagging regret. It's all over — a time for celebration, rejoicing, happiness and giving thanks.

I've seen and heard some of the soldiers, not many, complain about their suffering, their sacrifice, what they are owed, wallowing in self-pity. I know the time for tears and grieving is over for the sick ones with fever, the GIs, the rotten feet, the bleeding wounded, the dead men sleeping beneath the ground forever. I'll somehow miss the close comradeship that only men in battle understand. I have to readjust.

I push my hat down over my eyes and in a dreamy trance think back to the spring of 1932 and my first ride on a Continental bus to my new East Texas home.

CHAPTER 2

My first morning at the farm, after a fitful night of tossing and turning and wondering where I am, I hear people talking and moving in the kitchen.

Uncle Joe says, "He sure is a sickly, puny fellow."

I dress and walk into the kitchen. Grandpa Will and Uncle Joe drink coffee while Grandma and Aunt Willie fry meat and eggs at the stove. The kitchen smells of hickory and oak wood smoke. A coal oil lamp burns brightly in the center of a large bench-style table.

Grandma hands me a pan of water and tells me to wash my face and hands, then sit at the table and she'll pour me a cup of coffee.

I've never drunk coffee before. Half coffee and milk with lots of sugar isn't bad.

"We ain't got no high class breakfast food like *Post Toasties*," Uncle Joe says. "You'll have to eat country folks' breakfast."

Big platters of thick sliced bacon, fried eggs, hot biscuits and a big bowl of cream gravy appear on the table along with butter, ribbon cane syrup, plum jelly, pear preserves and other such good things.

Uncle Joe forks a piece of thick bacon which he calls sow belly and rakes about four eggs off the platter. He spoons gravy over all of it.

"Now you can see how poor country folks live," he says.

It's turning gray outside and will soon be daylight. Out on the porch, I hear cows mooing, mules braying, turkeys gobbling, roosters crowing, dogs barking, and a horse whinnying. I love it. I never liked silence. This noise sounds different from sirens, streetcars, trucks and plain city noise. This is wonderful noise.

Grandpa and Uncle Joe scald buckets to go milk the twelve Jersey cows anxiously awaiting them. Cream, butter and milk are an important source of cash money, so are 200 laying hens. If things go well, turkeys will be brought in about mid-November. Cotton, 25 acres, provides the main income starting around September, depending on the weather. An unbelievable amount of backbreaking toil involves making a living.

When I hear the horse whinny, my heart flutters. I didn't know a horse lived on the farm, only mules. I ask about the horse, "The Belle of Richmond," Uncle Joe replies. "That's Ma's pet thoroughbred mare."

Jumping Jehosaphat! A thoroughbred racehorse! I think.

"No one ever rides the Belle," he says. "She ain't never had a bridle or saddle on her. She's a runty little old horse that Ma raised on cow's milk, love and prayers. That horse slept by Ma's bed for a month."

I explode with curiosity. Uncle Joe says for me to get Grandma to tell the story about the Belle. I run out to the barn where the Belle stands at the gate with her head up looking toward the house. The prettiest, gentlest, big brown eyes are staring right at me. She looks more like a big Shetland pony than a thoroughbred racehorse. She is a brown color called bay, with black mane and tail, and black stockings.

I'm excited beyond myself. I run for Grandma and she says she'll tell me all about the Belle while we're following turkeys.

"The turkeys have to be followed," she says, "so we can gather their eggs to bring them to the house for setting. Turkeys don't hatch good on their own. They hide their nests so the toms won't break the eggs."

Strange, I think.

About 40 hens and two toms start down a long slope running into a distant line of trees. We trail about 100 yards behind.

We carry a syrup bucket with bacon and fried-eggs-between-biscuits for our dinner. There are several clear good springs in the woods for drinking water. Grandma also has a sack with glass eggs to replace the eggs we collect from the nests so the hens wouldn't abandon their nests. We watch the hens separate from the flock to lie in hidden nests, though Grandma already has most of the nests marked and located.

Later in the afternoon we start back to the house, gathering eggs as we go. I work at this pleasant chore and get a special thrill from finding the nests and collecting the eggs.

I pester Grandma to tell me about the Belle when we start back. She tells me, pointing in the direction of the house, "The adjoining property is a racehorse farm owned by Dr. Quinn. He's not only a horse doctor, but a human doctor as well."

"I knew his mama and papa. His papa was a doctor and delivered your mama and Joe. He became a big World War I hero. Dr. Quinn went to Harvard and Boston for his human doctor training and to Texas A&M for his vet skills. Unusual to be a medical doctor and a vet combined. He owns a clinic founded by his papa in town for people and his animal clinic is at his farm. He mainly treats horses."

"He has a regular thoroughbred breeding farm well known for its quality horses. It's considered a winning stable. He trains and races horses in Hot Springs, Florida, all over, and even some interest in the Kentucky Derby," she explains.

"One morning four years ago, I delivered eggs, butter and milk to the farm. Dr. Quinn and a few other people were running around the barn excited and talking loud. I went into the barn where a mare laid stretched out, moaning and groaning, in one of the stalls. A bloody little baby lay there in the straw."

"I heard Dr. Quinn say 'She's aborted, there's no way to save her. The foal won't make it. It's too early.'"

I shouted, "I'll buy the foal!"

"Miz Annie," Dr. Quinn says, "That foal will die. You can't save this little filly."

Grandma insists saying, "Not for free. I'll give you $50.00, and if I save her, I want her bred to Gallant Hood. The $50.00 is for her and the stud fee."

Dr. Quinn replies, "The odds of your saving the little filly are a million to one, but if you beat the odds, it's a deal."

She beat the odds, and Grandma had the Belle bred in February. This is April, and God willing, Belle will foal come January.

I beg her to let me ride the Belle and she reluctantly agrees with stipulations of no running and of being extremely gentle. Even with that, the Belle might not let me ride her she adds.

"Make haste! We have to gather hen eggs, feed chickens, slop hogs, and get feed ready for the turkeys," Grandma says.

I can see Uncle Joe and Grandpa in the distance plowing and planting corn and cotton while we shell a five-gallon lard can of corn with a hand cranked corn sheller for the chickens and turkeys. We fill large wooden troughs with buckets of clabber and pour it into five and ten-gallon crocks.

When we see the turkeys coming out of the woods, Grandma cups her hands and lets out a piercing scream, "Turk! Oooh, turk! Oooh, turk!"

The hogs start squealing. "Grandma," I say, "You should enter a hog calling contest."

"I won it two years in a row, but it's not ladylike, so I don't enter anymore."

The birds start running toward the house for their supper of corn and clabber. After they dine, we shut them in their roosting quarters for the night.

My first day seems like heaven, though my feet are so sore and painful, I can hardly walk. I'd gone barefoot and the cockle burrs, rocks and sticks had about crippled me. I sit with my feet in a pan of coal oil for a while then rub rosebud salve on them. They'll toughen up.

Aunt Willie sits at the kitchen table with a tablespoon in one hand and a quart bottle of clear liquid in the other. She gulps down three or four spoonfuls and makes a face, explaining it to be her appendicitis medicine. I ask her if she has appendicitis, and if it is catching. She says she takes a daily dose of mineral oil to prevent it.

She says the word so mournfully and sadly it almost brings tears to your eyes: "A-pin-dee-citis."

Uncle Joe walks in. "Willie, you so greased up inside with all that oil you gonna go to the outhouse some morning and grunt your gizzard right out," he says.

"When you have to go to emergency and the doctor cuts out your appendix," she says, "you'll wish you'd been taking mineral oil."

Uncle Joe and Aunt Willie are about 30 years old and never had any kids. Uncle Joe says it's because of all the mineral oil she keeps her innards saturated with.

Later that evening, everyone sits on the porch — Grandpa smoking his pipe, Aunt Willie patching clothes, and Grandma fooling with quilt scraps. I sneak into the kitchen, rummage around in the cupboard to find some brown sugar and dried apples then run for the barn to find the Belle.

She stands out in the pasture. I walk up with my dried apples in my palm. Belle looks at me, walks up, stretches her neck out, sniffs, snuffles and nuzzles her lips onto my hand. She takes a piece of dried apple, starts chewing with great relish and nuzzles for more. The brown sugar comes next.

We're going to be special friends. I find a boar's hog bristle brush in the barn and begin to brush the Belle. She loves to be brushed, rubbed, petted and talked to. As I ease up on her back, she looks around at me and just stands there.

I move my body and knees to let her know I want to move and she walks across the pasture. I don't know how to turn her without a bridle so I reach forward and push her head to one side, and she turns and walks back toward the barn.

I hear Uncle Joe holler out, "That fool Sonny is riding the Belle!"

After that, I ride the Belle nearly every day with an adjusted mule bridle. I give her apples, sugar and brush her until she glows. She'll nicker and call me every evening for our ride and treats.

"I declare. I believe Sonny would sleep with the Belle if he could manage it," remarks Grandpa.

CHAPTER 3

Spring and turkey-laying season soon ends. We have turkey hens sitting on about 300 eggs and a lot of chicken hens sitting on turkey eggs. It's hard on the chickens because turkey eggs take 28 days to hatch and chicken eggs take only 21 days. Grandma prays every night for a good turkey crop.

We make two trips to town each week to deliver butter and eggs direct to several families. We use large containers of cold spring water to keep the butter from melting. In the hottest part of the summer, our first stop is the icehouse.

We make deliveries in a buggy pulled by one mule. Any surplus cream and eggs we sell at Mr. Levi's General Store. I always get a moon pie and red soda water on these trips. It seems we are always churning and putting butter in square wooden molds, salting it, then scalding and cleaning crocks, churns, buckets, and anything to do with milk and butter. Grandma is strict about everything being sterilized and clean.

One of our best customers is the Quinn Racehorse Farm. No matter how much I plead, Grandma never lets me go to the Quinn Farm.

Grandma puts all money in a gallon cookie jar that she keeps on her chester drawers. She constantly counts and figures on how much we have. She pores over her ledger three or four times a week.

Uncle Joe always asks, "Are we there yet, Ma?"

The goal is $250.00 for a good used truck. With boll weevils, low prices, bad weather and all the calamities farmers have to endure, there has never been enough money for a truck.

Grandpa and Uncle Joe proudly call us poor, honest rednecks. If a truck could be had, the turkey crop could be hauled all the way to Dallas for top prices and we wouldn't be at the mercy of the buyers who come to small towns every November. Deliveries of cotton to the gin, along with faster transportation for other things, would mean better money.

Uncle Joe also dreams of a Poppin' Johnny Iron Mule for all the other farm work and of retiring our mules Ruth, Esther and Bathsheba.

"We gonna get there this year!" Uncle Joe shouts. "We got the best stand of cotton and corn we ever had."

The Quinn Farm has a small mountain of three- and four-year-old horse manure that has accumulated from cleaning out stalls. Dr. Quinn fears contaminating any of his pastures and oat crops with it so he gives it to us.

Every day Uncle Joe and Grandpa haul wagonloads of it to spread on the cotton and corn crops. Along with the turkey house and chicken house droppings, we have loads of good fertilizer. Uncle Joe built a homemade spray rig out of a 55 gallon oil drum and he sprays what he calls tobacco juice on the cotton for boll weevils.

Grandma ponders and puzzles over her ledgers one night. "I been studying these books," she says, "And for the life of me I can't figure why our coal oil and rosebud salve use has got so high. It's nearly doubled in the last month."

"It's Sonny and his feet," Grandpa says. "Every day he's been sitting with his feet in a pan of coal oil and rubbing salve on 'em."

"Let me see your feet," says Grandma. "Sake's alive, Sonny! Why didn't you tell me your feet was in such pitiful condition? Both your big toenails are black and about to fall off. I read somewhere going barefoot causes pinworms." Cuts and scratches are all over my feet.

"Well, come Saturday, after our butter and egg deliveries, we'll get you a pair of bull hide brogans at Dillard's Dry Goods Store," she says.

"Bull hide?" I ask.

"They're made of old bull hides, hard as iron. You can't wear them out," Grandma says.

That Saturday, at Mr. Dillard's, Grandma tells him we need a pair of bull hide brogans. "A very fine choice of shoes for a growing boy," he says. He measures my feet. "Size seven," he says, "but get eights for extra growing room."

I look over and see a pair of knee-high, lace-up boots with a little holster on the side for your Barlow knife. "Too expensive," Grandma says.

I'd broken the blade out of my knife practicing knife throwing against the side of the barn anyway. Someone had also broken the handle off the hatchet we use for splitting stove kindling, practicing his tomahawk throwing against the old post oak tree behind the barn. I hope nobody guessed who.

I get to studying them bull hides, and the more I study them, the more I like what I see. *Why these are perfect stomping and kicking shoes, especially with the extra room in the toe. I can probably even kick five-gallon cans with these, plus rocks and other such things needing kicking. I can stomp scorpions, centipedes, spiders, and even small snakes if I see any.*

Grandma buys six pair of white cotton socks for 50 cents and I get in the stomping and kicking business.

As we leave, Mr. Dillard says, "Miz Annie, if you had took Sonny down to the blacksmith and had him fitted with a pair of iron shoes, they would not outlast these bull hides. They're indestructible."

One morning, two months later, I start pulling them on and they disintegrate.

Any free time I have I spend riding and petting the Belle and slipping her various treats. She comes running and nickering every time I step out of the house. Lots of times I ride her way down in the pasture and just sit under a shade tree and talk to her while she eats grass. I dream of winning races.

Every few days Uncle Joe asks, "Ma, we gittin' close?"

"Soon, Joe, before turkey crop time."

"Hot dawg!" he hollers. "Nearly in high cotton!"

Into the summer I help thin cotton and corn, and relentlessly hunt turkey nests. I gather eggs two and three times a day. Egg production has fallen off and some of the hens are starting to molt. We now have nearly 400 baby turkeys to look after.

Every time a dark cloud blows up, Grandma looks worried and goes out with the young turkeys. Rain and young turkeys don't go well together since young turkeys drown in rainstorms.

We have a big pen of young fryers we're feeding only clabber and milk so we can sell them as milk-fed fryers, bringing premium prices. Grandma puts some medicine in the chicken and turkey drinking water that turns it purple. Prevents limber neck, she says. We brush coal oil on the poultry house walls and roosts, and put lime all around the houses. Stops blue bugs, she says.

What with a big garden, canning, jelly making, washing, patching, cooking and scrubbing, Aunt Willie, Grandma and I stay busy every day. Uncle Joe and Grandpa farm cotton, corn and hay, as well as do the milking twice a day. We usually go to bed shortly after dark. We have all the beds out on our mosquiter-proof screened-in sleeping porch. Even in the hottest part of the summer, it stays cool.

One morning as I'm going through the henhouse checking the nests for eggs, I see a big black chicken snake in one of the nests. I run for the house hollering, "Snake!"

Grandma comes out and I scream, "There's a whopper black snake in one of the nests!"

"Big snake calls for big remedy," she answers.

She goes into the storeroom off the kitchen and comes out with a monster long-barreled shotgun. "Ole big ten-gauge will fix that rascal soon as I find some shells." She finds two, loads up and away we go after the big rascal. When we get to the chicken house, she stands on tiptoe and can barely see into the nest.

"I see him," she says. "I need something to stand on." I run out and find a five-gallon lard can. She climbs on it then ears the hammers of Ole Ten back, puts two fingers on the triggers, sticks it in the nest and pulls.

BLAAARRROOOM!!!

I see snake pieces and chicken nest flying through the side of the chicken house out a hole big as a number three washtub. I'm nearly deafened by the blast as Grandma lies on the floor with her head against the wall.

I begin to hear a little better and her moaning and mumbling sounds like, "Leaving goshin'…hold the vipers…goin' to the Promised Land…oh Sweet Redeemer!"

I help her up while she mutters, "My, my! I blew half the chicken house down when I blew that big rascal to pieces."

We slowly make it to the house then Grandma eases down into a cowhide rocking chair in her bedroom. Aunt Willie is at a neighbor's house. Grandma tells me to open her trunk, feel underneath and way back in the corner for a bottle of nerve tonic. I do as she asks and she takes two big swallows, waits a minute, takes three more big swallows, then tells me to put it back.

"How 'bout my nerves?" I ask.

"I'm the one pulled the trigger and fell off the lard can. Sonny, look in my chester drawers. Back in the top drawer there's a little brown bottle. Fetch it here."

The label on the bottle reads "Honest Garrett's Snuff." She tilts her head back, puts the opening in her mouth and taps it on the bottom, kind of like a chug-a-lug.

"I didn't know you dipped snuff, Grandma."

"Well, you do now," she says. "It's our secret. I've studied the Bible from the first page to the last page and there ain't one word in it against snuff dipping. So there."

She rubs her right shoulder and frowns. I notice the right side of her face turning purple.

"Sonny," she says, "Go out to the barn and fetch me the hoss liniment while I sit here and let the nerve tonic and snuff calm my nerves." After an application of rosebud salve and hoss liniment, she seems much better.

That night at the supper table, everybody starts talking about snakes. A hoop snake puts its tail in its mouth and rolls along the ground like a hoop. A milk snake rears up to a cow's teat and helps itself to dinner. A coach whip can run as fast as a trotting team of horses pulling a buggy. A blue racer can run along the ground as fast as a running horse. And so it goes.

The talk turns to discovering snakes in the bedclothes and my skin begins to crawl. When we go to bed on the sleeping porch, I carefully check my small half-bed — seems okay. I barely doze off when I feel something slithering across my feet. I jump out of bed screaming, "Snake in my bed!"

Everyone gets up and pulls off the covers, looks under the mattress and under the bed and convinces me I dreamed it. No wonder with all that talk at supper. Sometime later in the middle of the night a shrill scream wakes me up. Aunt Willie screams, "Snake in the bed!"

We all go through the same looking and shaking of covers and finally settle back down. I doze off again, and in a while, I hear, "Oh my Lord!"

Grandpa Will stomps and hollers that he knows there's a snake in the bed. After another while we settle back to sleep.

Shortly, Uncle Joe starts wailing, "It's time to get up and start the day and I ain't had a wink of sleep all night. How can a man do a day's work with no sleep?"

After a night or two, we settle back down into a normal sleep routine.

Chapter 4

～⌒

My mama, back in Dallas, writes me a letter every week with one or two dollars in it. She is always cheerful, says her job is satisfying, and that she'll see me soon. I think it strange and puzzling her name never gets mentioned here and no one ever asks me about her. I think of her and pray for her every day. I worry about my mama.

At the same time I'm so excited with my strange new life that sometimes I forget my other life. I can hear the horses at the Quinn Farm neighing and nickering every day. Some days I can hear them running on their training track and a bell clanging from the starting gate. Grandma forbids me to ever set foot on that place, not under any circumstance. She says that if I do, the penalty will be severe.

I ride the Belle every single day, brush, rub, pet and talk to her. I've taught her to come at a whistle, to lie down, roll over, and other simple tricks. I've sent off for a book called *How To Train Horses*. The Belle's begun to bulge a little at her sides. Five more months before her foal will be due.

It is August now and the crop is what we call "laid by." The turkeys are growing and putting on size — what with grasshoppers, clabber, corn, and anything they gather in the woods. Grandma says it's her best turkey crop ever. Grandpa and Uncle Joe say it's the best corn and cotton crop they can remember.

Grandma declares, "Jehovah has sent an angel to watch over and bless us."

Grandma tells Uncle Joe that in two more weeks — the first week of September — we will have $250.00 for the truck.

"We soon be in high cotton!" he hollers out, "I'm a natural-born machinery man!"

We all put on a little extra spurt churning, scalding, scrubbing, and trying for that last little bit before the Saturday to buy the truck.

On September first, we hitch up our mules Ruth and Esther, load cream, butter, eggs, and a few hens and fryers to sell at Mr. Levi's store. We all stand around eating moon pies and drinking soda waters. It's a real pleasure doing business with Mr. Levi.

Some people in the store are talking about a carnival set up at the edge of town, and having never been to one, I ask if we could go.

"We can't be wasting money on such foolishness," says Grandma.

Grandpa is fixin' to start playing checkers with some men, and Grandma and Aunt Willie are going to visit a sick friend.

"Come on, Sonny," says Uncle Joe. "We'll go over to the carnival and look around."

I'm excited, my first carnival.

There's ball throwing at wooden bottles, ring tossing, shooting .22s at ducks moving across the back of a tent and other such games; candy apples, cotton candy and hot dogs. Uncle Joe spends ten cents for a big cone of cotton candy.

We stroll toward the back where there stands a row of tents they call "Freak Shows." A man bellows through a speaking tube to come see the Bearded Lady, Fat Lady, Alligator Man, the world's largest snake wrapped around a lady, and more. The tents have pictures painted on the sides describing what they hold inside.

"Come one, come all, only 25 cents!" the man shouts over and over.

We stand there looking, listening and eating our cotton candy when a tall, skinny-looking feller runs up to Uncle Joe and hollers, "Hey, Joe!"

"How do, Rufus? What you up to?"

His eyes are big as half dollars and kind of shiny.

"Joe, if I hadn't seen it with my own two eyes, I wouldn't have believed it. I have just witnessed the highest classed freak show in the history of the whole state of Texas, maybe the whole United States!"

He pulls out a sack of Bull Durham to roll a cigarette and his hands shake so bad he hands the makings to Uncle Joe and says, "Roll me one. I is so nervous, I can't keep my hands still."

In a loud voice, Rufus says, "What I seen was a geek show. They had this here little horseshoe shaped corral with a three-legged stool in the center and we all stood around the sides and looked over in it. A little white-faced booger came in and sat on that stool, looked around at all of us, and let out a heehaw kind of crazy laugh.

"Then some feller came up with a white-legged rooster and handed it to the little booger. He held the rooster up high so we could all see it, then he stuck that rooster's head into his mouth, and gave a little twist to his head, and spit that rooster's head out! That rooster flapped and jumped and squirted blood all over!

"Ole Ida Mae Simms stood next to me and she let out a squall and fell over and started kicking and squealing like a shot jack rabbit. She near showed everything she had. Hadn't been for them long-legged Gold Medal flour sack step-ins, I'd have seen it all.

"Joe, you orta go see it. Best two bits you'll ever spend. I gotta go and see can I find my wife and kids. I'll see you round," he says as he walks off.

"I don't want to see no such crazy things as that," Uncle Joe says. I'm disappointed.

Returning home late that night, we all lay on quilts in the wagon and try to sleep while Uncle Joe sits up high on the seat behind Ruth and Esther. He starts singing in a high tenor voice. Songs so sad just about make you cry — lovesick dying cowboy songs, woman done him wrong songs, being so lonesome about to die songs. I doze but hear something about kissing a cow song.

After a while he bellows out, "I'm a natural-born machinery man!" I know he's thinking about the truck.

Where Angels Roost

After church on Sunday, we eat dinner and Grandma gets the jar down and spreads money into separate little piles all over the table. We all stand around not making a sound, although Uncle Joe breathes awful loud. I don't know why Grandma runs the making of these decisions but Grandpa seems agreeable to working it that way.

She gets a small sack, puts most of the money into it and tells Uncle Joe, "There's $275.00 in the sack with an extra $25.00: $5.00 for a bus ticket to Tyler and eating money. Be careful Joe, don't get skimmed. We're depending on you. That leaves us less than $100.00."

"Do you want Sonny to ride Ruth or Esther to town to catch the bus in the morning and ride back, or what?" she asks.

"It's only four miles Ma, and the way I feel, I believe I could run the whole four miles on my own two feet. I'll leave about daylight and be back, I hope, by sundown. If not, Tuesday. Tyler is only about 40 miles and the road is good," Uncle Joe replies.

That evening, Uncle Joe sings happy songs about Taking Sally to the Dance, Camptown Races, DooDah, Yellow Rose of Texas and such. I never heard hear him sing another sad song.

Grandma and I help with the milking in Uncle Joe's place. I wash all the cows' teats with warm water and soap while Grandma and Grandpa do the milking. After the milking and feeding of chickens, hogs and turkeys, I spend time with the Belle.

Grandpa and I tighten all the bolts and grease all the wheels on the wagon, empty the nubbins out of a large corncrib, and prepare to gather corn. We hitch up Ruth and Esther to the wagon and drive down the hill to the bottomland where the ripened corn is ready for gathering. I notice the cotton has opened up and will be ripe for picking.

Ruth and Esther pull the wagon between the cornrows and Grandpa and I pull the ears, give a little twist, and throw them in the wagon with high sideboards.

When we need to move the wagon, one of us hollers, "Git up!" To stop, we holler, "Whoa!"

Where Angels Roost

When the wagon gets full, we drive up to the crib and unload, then go back for another load. After a day at this, we are plenty wore out.

After supper, we keep looking and listening for a truck coming since we're too excited to sleep. Along about nine, we see lights way down the road, must be two miles or more. In the country, it is always pitch black and you can see lights against the sky and clouds from a long distance. The lights are coming closer so we all stand up and look that way. We can make out two headlights turning into the lane coming up to the house.

Uncle Joe pulls up in a big truck and jumps out and screams, "We in cotton six feet tall! I'm a natural-born machinery man!"

"I'll make us a pot of rooster coffee," Grandma says, "and then we'll bring a lamp out and look at our truck."

Grandpa asks, "Joe, what breed is that truck?"

"Pa, it's a White."

Dead silence for a couple of minutes.

"Pa, I couldn't find no Henry Ford that weren't used up or one big enough. We need a stout work mule of a truck and them Fords looked awful puny to me."

"I ain't never heard of no White before," Grandpa says. "I always thought ole Henry made the best."

"Naw, Pa. Not the best, the cheapest. This White is stouter than a four-mule span. You'll see," replies Uncle Joe.

Grandma comes out to the truck with coffee and a bright gasoline lantern.

"Joe, how much did the truck cost?"

"Mother," I notice he calls her Mother instead of Ma, "the truck cost $237.50, and I bought a new battery, two new casings, a five-gallon can of lube oil, a 55-gallon drum of gasoline, a set of tools to fit this truck, grease gun and grease, rear-end grease, and a set of new plugs. I spent the whole $275.00, but I can keep this baby perfectly maintained. Gotta take care of it," he says.

Gasoline costs only seven cents a gallon. "You done good, Joe," says Grandma.

The rest of the week, Grandpa, Uncle Joe and I finish up the corn harvest. The next week we put up bundles of red-topped cane for winter feed for the cows and mules. Now it's time for cotton picking.

School doesn't open till mid-October and lots of kids don't start until December. They are the kids of families who go to West Texas to pull bolls.

Tarnation! Cotton picking proves the most awful job I've ever had. I bet the man who invented cotton never did any cotton picking else he wouldn't have invented it. I know now I will never be cut out to be no cotton farmer.

As I pick and drag my sack between the rows, I dream that if the Comanche had adopted me like I'd always wanted, all I'd have to do would be to sit around a fire and eat buffalo meat, smoke pipes, drink fire water, throw knives and tomahawks, shoot bows and arrows, and ride horses all the time while the squaws wait on me and do all the work. I decide my Comanche name will be "Iron Feet" because of what Mr. Dillard said about the blacksmith fixing me with iron shoes.

I turned 13 in August but people think I'm puny because I run small for my age. This makes me stubborn to prove that I might be small in size but big in hanging in there like some old bulldog. So I pick without complaining. All of us pick cotton because what is the use of making a record crop if you can't get it gathered and cashed in?

Our neighbor on the east has a 160 acre farm. Mr. and Mrs. Amos Jones have four younguns ranging from six to sixteen. We need some help picking our cotton so Grandma and I walk down the lane to their house to see if they're done with their cotton picking and can give us a hand.

Picking in real good cotton like we have pays 50 cents per 100 pounds. A big family can pick 1,000 to 1,200 pounds a day. In 1932, five or six dollars cash money a day is considered big money. We estimate our cotton crop will be 30 to 35 bales on 25 acres — more than a bale per acre. The horse stall manure from the Quinn Farm plus chicken and turkey droppings, along with thinning and spraying for boll weevils, is reaping us a bumper crop.

We walk up to the house where Amos, his wife Clare and their kids are sitting on the porch.

Where Angels Roost

"Come in, Miz Annie," Amos says. "How do, Sonny?"

"Amos, if you have your cotton picked, we could sure use some help," Grandma says. "Good cotton. You won't have to do no scrappin'."

"Shore, Miz Annie. We be there in the mornin'." He and Miz Clare look worn out and the kids look like they haven't been eating too good.

"Miz Annie, I'm plumb wore out," he says. "I made two bales of cotton on 20 acres. Boll weevils got in it. Johnson grass has got so thick in my corn land and the rest of the place, I cain't hardly farm it. We got a pair of ole wore out mules and a couple Jersey cows. Cain't sell no milk or butter, takes all the milk for the younguns. Clare and me been studyin' selling out and getting enough money to buy an old car, and head for Californy and a new start. I ain't made a bit of money out of this farm since 1918, the last year of the war."

"I been working cutting cord wood, digging ditches, working at the saw mill some, but that work is gone. We in debt to Levi's Store, Dillard's Dry Goods, feed store and hardware store. All told, we're in debt nearly $200.00. I is finished here so I'm sellin' out."

Grandma listens to all this and glances at me from time to time. I know what she is studying.

"How much you want for your place?" Grandma asks.

"Well, I had $1,500.00 in mind, but after studying about the Johnson grass taking over and this ole wore out land and the house and barn needing work, I'll take $1,200.00 and walk out — except for stuff Clare wants out of the house."

Grandma says, "Amos, let me and Sonny study on it. We may buy it from you. Give us about 45 days to give you an answer. We need to get our cotton in and sold before we'll know."

"That's good enough for me, Miz Annie."

We tell Amos we'll fix dinner for them all the next day and every day while they are picking. "See you in the morning," we say.

On the way back, Grandma says, "Sonny, $1,200.00 is a right smart amount of money. Study on it a minute and tell me what you think."

"Grandma," I say, "Johnson grass makes the best grazing ever and mighty good hay. We have twelve fresh milking cows now, and six coming on, makes 18. Two more from Amos. We have enough grazing and feed for 20 more easy. That Johnson grass is worth more than cotton land with less work. We can fix and patch up the house, have a good well of water, and hire a good hand for five dollars a week. His family can raise a garden and have a few chickens. Then we can hang in there until this doggone Depression lets up some."

"Sonny," she says, "I know you're only 13 years old, but first time I seen you in the spring, I got some kind of feeling about you. If you think we can handle it, I know we can. We were near about in the same fix as Amos before this year, barely hanging on. Now we all got hope. I don't know how to explain it. We'll see."

Aunt Willie cooks big pots of beans and potatoes. We make rooster chili and dumplings out of some old hens. We feed 'em all good. They eat like they're making up for lost eats. Uncle Joe sings and laughs and hauls cotton to the gin. We have him a load ready soon as he can unload and get back.

Every once in a while Uncle Joe yells, "We in high cotton, Sonny!" Sometimes he hollers, "We eatin' high on the hog!"

All the cotton gets picked, ginned and sold by the first week in November. Everywhere I go I hear "fair to middlin'", "strict middlin'", "low middlin'", "ordinary." Prices are based on the quality of the cotton. All our cotton gets judged fair to good middlin', but market prices are so low that we only average ten to eleven cents a pound.

A 500 pound bale brings from $50.00 to $55.00. The seed usually pays the ginning fee. We are gloriously happy when we finish with 36 bales, and count up nearly $1,800.00.

With our butter, cream, and egg money, we have about $2,000.00 — the turkeys still to go in a few days.

We're all sitting around the kitchen table and Uncle Joe carries on about a Poppin' Johnny Iron Mule when Grandma says, "The first thing is to buy Amos Jones's 160 acres, then we'll study on the Iron Mule."

Uncle Joe says we could borrow to buy the Jones farm, that we need a cream separator, six or eight more Jerseys, 600 high power white leghorn chicks and a baling machine. Among other things, we all need some clothes and money spent on the house and one of them new fangled butane systems.

I speak up and say, "No borrowing."

Total silence for about a minute.

Uncle Joe bellows out, "Why you little short-complected shrimp! Who you to be joining in this confab? You don't decide nothing about this family."

"Uncle Joe, I'm trying to help. What with you worrying about the truck and the Iron Mule and all the machinery, I figure you can't take on a worry about taking on debt."

I explain, "Grandma is going to put the Jones place in your and Aunt Willie's names. You gonna own it debt free."

Uncle Joe says, "Is that right, Ma?"

"Yes, Joe. It was Sonny's idea."

Uncle Joe gets up out of his chair, picks me up, hugs me up against him and says, "Sonny, I'm sorry for hollering at you. We ain't had nothing but good luck since you come here. I'm declaring now that I love you and you are included in any planning for our future."

I see Grandma smiling and Grandpa says, "Amen!"

Aunt Willie smiles showing all her pretty white teeth. My heart skips beats and I feel so good I near about burst.

When we start getting the turkeys ready, we string a temporary chicken wire fence around two acres, put shelled corn in a trough along with clabber and set up a bright Coleman pressure lantern on a platform right in the middle. We take turns staying up all night with the turkeys. Any critters coming around the pen can cause a stampede, so we have to be constantly on watch these last few days to put the finish on their growth.

At last we load 200 turkeys, half the crop, the other half will follow around the 10th of December. Turkeys are bringing a good price: 15 cents a pound. This first load will average about 14 to 15 pounds apiece, right at two dollars a turkey.

Grandma and I have taken Amos Jones's contract to the lawyer's office in town and we are going to close the deal around the first week in December. I have to start school but because so many kids haven't shown up yet, I get out at noon. I run all the way to and back from school, four miles. There's work to be done and I'm needed.

I've always liked school. Texas has an eleven-year school system. Since I'd already skipped the second grade, I'm way ahead of the other kids my age. I've just turned 13 and place in the ninth grade.

This month of November 1932, the voters go to the polls and elect a new president, Franklin D. Roosevelt, and a new governor for Texas, Ma Ferguson, which pleases Aunt Willie. A New Deal is promised.

We all hope the hard times for the country will soon get better. Right now our family here eats high on the hog. Jehovah loves us and we love Him.

At Thanksgiving, we invite Amos and Clare Jones and their kids to have dinner with us. We've just killed hogs and, with a big hen turkey and such, have more than plenty. We all stand around a loaded table and join hands.

Grandma says, "Will, say the blessing please."

Grandpa becomes quiet for about a minute, then says, "Our Father who art in Heaven...."

My head rings, and I hear the last part, "...the glory and the power forever. Amen."

Uncle Joe hollers out, "We love you, Jesus!"

Grandma has tears rolling down her cheeks. She looks at me and smiles the biggest smile. For being a secret snuff dipper, I think her teeth look pretty and white.

Grandma and I pore over the books, figure, cipher and study on how much we've got and what we need. The turkey crop has brought in near about $800.00. With our cotton money, butter, milk and egg money, we have $3,100.00. It doesn't seem possible.

Mr. Jones wants $1,200.00 for their farm, which in two years of the Depression market-values at only $800.00. This has no effect on us but the Depression doesn't end until 1941 and times get harder until then.

We have $1,900.00 left. Grandma asks Uncle Joe if he could buy a Poppin' Johnny Iron Mule, plows, planters and such as we need, for $1,000.00.

"A good one, now, Joe," she says.

Joe says, "Ma, for $1,000.00, I can get one near about new. I guarantee it. All the John Deere dealers have bunches of them for sale. A lot of farmers went bust. I can go up to Dallas in the morning and find one. I can pull a trailer and load Ole White Mule up." We've named our truck Ole White Mule.

Uncle Joe is right about the White truck. He has it running, as he puts it, like a scalded dog.

"While we're up there," he says, "I'll buy us one of them centrifugal cream separators and a big fifty-gallon crank churn. I need to order 600 of them high-powered laying white leghorn chicks and we'll try and buy four or five more jerseys for now. That will only leave us about $100.00 for emergencies. I believe with God's mercy we can manage."

Uncle Joe laughs and yells out, "We in cotton eight feet tall!"

Joe and Grandpa leave the next morning for Dallas. Soon as they leave, I tell Grandma we need one of them telephones put in for business reasons.

"We can call our customers and they can call their orders to us. With the increase in milk production, we can haul milk to Dallas in ten-gallon cans with Ole White Mule. Schepp's and Cabbell's dairy companies pay top money for whole milk. A telephone is only two dollars a month; it'll make us money.

"Hitch up one of the ladies to the buggy and we'll go to town and take care of it right now," says Grandma.

On the way, I say, "Grandma, let's stop by the butane gas place and check on what a big hot water tank and butane will cost. We need it for the milk utensils."

"Sonny, we runnin' out of cash money."

"Credit for things that makes us money is okay. It's not like borrowing money on the land. Let's do all this and keep it between us," I say.

"Sonny, you movin' my thinkin' so fast I can't keep up."

We arrange for the telephone and the butane and two fifty-gallon hot water tanks, and leave word at Mr. Levi's: Anybody looking for work, contact us.

Late that afternoon, Uncle Joe and Grandpa pull in with a lot of plows and equipment on the back of the truck and a big green tractor on a trailer behind.

Uncle Joe and all of us push and roll the tractor off the trailer. "For now," Uncle Joe says, "I gotta crank this Iron Mule to start. I'll rig up a battery start later. I didn't get no Poppin' Johnny. Still a Johnny, but four cylinders instead of one."

"Sonny, get up in that seat and let me show you what to do. See these little levers sticking out here by the steering wheel? When I say so, you pull 'em down."

He goes to the front of the tractor and jiggles with the crank, and turns. "Pull her ears down, Sonny!"

I pull down the levers, and he gives about two turns, and it fires and starts running and smoking. He runs back and moves the levers up and down till it smooths into a steady quiet idling.

Uncle Joe laughs. "I'm a natural-born machinery man!"

I believe so. I walk around the Johnny and it looks about new. It has a picture in yellow of a deer on the front and beneath it in small print, "John Deere Plow Company, Moline, Illinois." At that moment, I think Mr. John Deere is greater than any Comanche chief and decide I don't want to be a Comanche after all. Besides, they don't eat buffalo meat. They eat sowbelly, beans and cornbread just like we do.

Grandma and I walk over to Amos Jones' place to see them off to Californy. They have a big long Hudson touring sedan with the two-wheel trailer hitched behind, all loaded up. Looks like they are getting ready to pull out.

"We planned to stop by on our way out and talk to you about our mules and dogs," Amos says. "I've had the mules since they was babies. They just like kin. I got 'em in 1916, so they got some age on 'em. I couldn't stand to think they may end up as dog food. If you can see your way to keep 'em, soon as I can, I'll send some money for their keep."

"Amos," I say, "Don't worry and fret over your mules. I guarantee you they will always have a home here."

"Thank you, Sonny. I appreciate that."

"What are their names?" I ask.

"Laudie and Maudie," he says. "Now this big ole dog come here about five years ago. She's a bitch but the vet fixed her for five bushels of sweet taters so she won't be coming in heat or cause you no trouble. She gets her rabies shot once a year on account of the younguns and she's mighty good at bringing the cows up."

"She'll fit right in and we'll take good care of her," I say. "Amos, can you write?"

"Sure I can write."

"Will you write us and let us know how you are when you get to Californy?"

"I sure will."

We get a letter a month later. Amos and his family are in Burbank and Amos has a good job with the sanitation department of the City of Los Angeles.

I sit in school nearly all day now. I don't make friends easily and trot home soon as school lets out. This is a slack period for us at home, other than the milking and seeing after 600 baby chicks, which we have in a brooder house with coal oil heaters. We are mostly fixing: patching barns, turkey houses, fences and such.

The butane hot water tanks save us lots of work. Uncle Joe bought a big six burner double oven cook stove second hand on one of his milk trips to Dallas which saves lots of hard work sawing and splitting and hauling wood. We are moving on.

Christmas is about here and I think about going to Dallas and seeing my mama. I haven't said nothing about it yet. Belle is due to foal in three to four more weeks and she is bulged out fit to bust.

Uncle Joe, Grandpa and Aunt Willie leave with a load of milk for Schepp's Dairy in Dallas Saturday morning. Aunt Willie wants to see about some Christmas shopping and Grandma and I are sitting at the table when the phone rings — two shorts and a long.

"That's us," I say.

I pick the phone up and it's Mr. Levi, saying, "Sonny, I got a feller here what's looking for work."

"How does he look to you?" I ask.

"He looks healthy and strong, acts polite like he's had good raisin'," Mr. Levi says.

"Send him out and we'll talk to him."

About an hour later the dogs let us know someone is coming down the lane. It is cold and windy and he doesn't have a coat on. When he gets closer, I can see him to be a colored man, a young one.

My, I think. When he gets up to the porch, I say, "Come on in out of the cold."

We walk into the kitchen and he takes his hat off.

Grandma has a puzzled look on her face. "Grandma," I say, "Please get some coffee and some of that sweet tater pie for us."

As we walk to the table I start, "My name is Sonny Jackson and this is my grandma Annie Jackson."

He sticks out his hand. "I'm Booker Woods. They calls me Woody. I'm pleased to meet you, Mr. Sonny and Miz Annie." He is very dark and has prideful large brown eyes.

"Sit down, coffee and pie's coming up," I say.

"Thank you, suh."

Grandma pours three cups of coffee and sets three slices of pie out and we drink our coffee and eat our pie in total silence.

"Woody, you a Christian?" Grandma asks.

"I sho am, Miz Annie. Baptized when I was 14 — ten years ago."

"You Married?" she asks.

"Yessum, all legal like. Got the papers and the preacher say the words. My wife name Saree."

"Any kids?"

"No, ma'am. I ain't been married but about two months."

I have a good feeling about Woody. "Can you milk?" I ask.

"Yes, suh. I ain't braggin', but I can near 'bout knock the bottom out of a bucket and make that milk foam," he proudly reports.

"Woody," I say, "We don't kick or mistreat any of our animals, we don't cuss, we don't drink spirits, and we try to live by the Golden Rule. The pay is five dollars a week and a house and shares of the profit, once a year. Close to $150.00 or $200.00 bonus if things go well. We pay near Christmas. Think you'd make us a good hand?"

"Mr. Sonny, I sho will. All I wants is a chance."

"Where's your wife?" I ask.

"She's stayin' over Prairie Hill with her mama and papa. That's about ten miles from here."

"You want to hitch up a team and wagon and fetch her and your things? You can stay at her place overnight and move in tomorrow. Grandma, see can you find one of Uncle Joe's coats for Woody and give him one week's pay in advance."

"Come on, Woody. We'll walk down and I'll show you your house."

Grandma and me had cleaned and fixed Amos's house up nice and it didn't look bad at all. It looked fair to middlin'.

After Woody leaves, Grandma looks at me for what seems a long time.

"I declare, Sonny. Why the yearly shares of the profit?"

"Grandma, I read it in the Bible."

She looks at me and smiles. "If it's in the Good Book, you done good."

I get afraid Uncle Joe and Grandpa might get mad about Woody being colored and all, but Uncle Joe says, "I will declare my judgment after I see how he works."

After about a month, Uncle Joe and Woody are best of friends and as the years go by, Woody becomes a beloved member of our family.

CHAPTER 5

I tell Grandma I want to see Mama in Dallas during Christmas vacation from school. A look of anguish slides over her face as she says, "Sonny, I'm afeared."

"Afeared of what?"

"That you might not come back."

"I promise I'll come back. The Belle is going to foal soon and I need to be here for her in case she needs me."

When Grandma looks doubtful, I say, "Come with me please, Grandma."

On the bus to Dallas, I ask Grandma about Grandpa and some of our family.

"Are we any kin to Andrew Jackson, Ole Hickory, or Stonewall Jackson of the Confederate Army?"

"Not that I know of," she says. "But Grandpa Will has the same warrior streak. In 1898 he joined up in the Spanish American War. We had just gotten married. I was 15 and he was 18. He didn't come home from the Philippines until 1901. Then we had Mary, your mama, in 1902, and Joe, in 1903. We had two other babies but lost them to diphtheria and fevers. About near killed us."

"Your grandpa talked his way into the army in 1917. The old fool was too old and he came back from France in 1919. He had a terrible time and won't say much except that every day of his life

Where Angels Roost

now is God's blessing. He's a mighty good man, Sonny, and you can be proud."

"I was a Parker before I married Will," Grandma continues. "My papa and mama — your great grandpa and grandma — left me and Will the farm. Parkers are all over East Texas. Four of the Parker brothers fought under Sam Houston at San Jacinto. The Parkers are mighty important people in Texas history. You can be plenty proud of your blood. Cynthia Anne Parker, the mother of Quanah Parker, the great Comanche Chief, was my great aunt."

Grandma has already told me these stories. I ask about Mama and how come she lives in Dallas. Grandma studies the question a long time.

"In February 1919, after she graduated high school, she up and decided she didn't want any part of milking cows, feeding chickens, slopping hogs, working in the cotton, outdoor privies and no electricity. She went to Dallas, got married and got a job. Her husband, your papa, died in a flu epidemic. I never met him."

Grandma pauses for a moment remembering something, then adds, "You come early."

"Maybe that's why I'm scrawny for my age."

"Sonny, you small in size, but you big in things that count. Your mama give you good raisin'."

We get off the bus and ride a jitney not far from downtown Dallas out to Swiss Avenue, which is lined with elegant homes that look like castles we've seen pictures of in books. We ring the bell at the address Mama has given us. Mama opens the door, then hugs and laughs and kisses me. She kisses me about 20 times, then she looks at Grandma and starts crying.

Grandma spreads her arms and says, "Come here, girl!"

Mama does, and she says, "Mama, it's been so long and I love you so much."

Grandma cries too, and says, "My child, my child."

We go in and an elegant lady in a wheelchair rolls up and Mama says, "This is my son Jonathon and my mother Annabelle Jackson."

I have purt near forgotten my name and I didn't know Grandma's name is Annabelle. The elegant lady sticks her hand out and says, "My name is Frances Adams."

I don't know if I'm supposed to kiss her hand or shake it. I shake it.

Miz Adams says, "I have the same affliction as our new president — infantile paralysis, except we are not infants. Some people call it polio. Under these conditions, Mary is a blessing for me and I love her like a daughter. I don't believe I could manage without her. You are most welcome to stay here for a visit. Mary can have a day or two off to spend time with you; the maid can fill in for her."

We go downtown that night and have supper at the Adolphus Hotel, a swanky place. We go uptown to the Majestic movie show and see a picture called "The Champ" with Wallace Beery. I already want to get home to the farm as I worry and fret about Belle.

I've saved all the money Mama has sent me. I have it in my brogan. I walk uptown to Zale's Jewelry and buy Mama a little heart-shaped locket she can wear around her neck. I have my picture taken for a dime in a little photo booth and trim it to fit in the locket. The locket is fourteen-carat gold and costs twelve dollars and fifty cents. I give it to Mama for Christmas, and she squalls and carries on something awful.

I buy Uncle Joe a set of wrenches, Grandpa a new pipe, Aunt Willie some perfume, Woody a pocketknife and Saree some perfume. I want my big present to be for Grandma. I decide on an elegant looking wristwatch — a Bulova that costs $17.50.

Grandma cries. Women cry over anything.

I feel so proud and happy. Mama gives me a Barlow knife and Waltham pocket watch. Mama rides to the bus station with Grandma and me and waves as we pull out. She looks so small and purty and smiles, but still looks sorta sad.

Grandma and I hardly say anything on the way home. We are thinking our own thoughts.

Christmas morning I go to the kitchen where Uncle Joe, Grandpa, Aunt Willie and Grandma are all looking at me and smiling a secret sort of smile.

"Merry Christmas!" they shout.

I get a speck of dirt in my eye.

There's a hackamore bridle, a saddle blanket and a new beautiful saddle — a strange looking saddle. I've never seen one like it and am puzzled.

"It's what's called an English saddle," Grandma says. "I asked Henry, Dr. Quinn's trainer, what kind we ought to get you. He told me unless we were going to be roping steers off the Belle or her foal, which weren't likely, we shore didn't have any use for a cowboy saddle."

Cowboy saddles were the only kind I'd ever seen.

"We ain't cowboys," Grandma says. "And there's never been any cowboys in our family. We've always been farmers."

I can tell she's disappointed because I act like I wanted a cowboy saddle.

I hug her and say, "Grandma, you the smartest grandma ever. I'm shore glad you know'd what I wanted all along. Them old cowboy saddles are too heavy and we in the farming and thoroughbred horse business. We shore don't need any cow horses."

She brightens right up and says, "I 'preciate that, Sonny."

"You done good, Grandma."

I go back to school after January first in 1933. I check on the Belle every morning and run all the way home from school every afternoon to see her. On January tenth, something wakes me about two in the morning. I become wide awake and have a strange feeling. I dress, go to the kitchen, light a lamp then go to the barn to check the Belle.

I open the door to her stall and set the lamp on a shelf. Belle stands up and I can smell blood; a little bundle lies in the shadows. I stoop down and my heart starts beating so fast I feel like I'm dropping down one of them elevators in a tall building. It moves and raises its head up then I go to hugging and kissing the newborn little foal.

Belle nudges me aside and goes to licking her baby to clean and dry it off. In a few minutes, she nudges the baby and he starts trying to get up. I just stand there and let Belle take care of him. She is snuffling and giving out a real low nickering sound.

The baby manages to get up and wobbles around, then falls back down and gets up again. Belle licks him all over. In a few minutes, he sticks his little head back under her belly so he can get some milk.

He shows right off he's a colt, a little man horse. It's hard to tell his color yet but he looks like he will be a bay, like Belle.

I look him over real close and decide he's perfect. By this time, it is past four a.m. by my new pocket watch. I run to the house and wake Grandma and Grandpa and tell them Belle has foaled.

"Come quick!"

We go into the stall and Grandma just stands there and doesn't say a word for about five minutes. Then she looks at me. "Sonny, have you given thanks?"

"No, ma'am. I forgot."

"Get down on your knees and say what comes to mind."

Grandma, Grandpa and I drop to our knees. "Thank you, Loving Father, for blessing us with one of your creatures," I say. "Love and bless us always as we love you. Father we pray for our new baby to win two Derby races."

Grandpa adds, "Praise the Lord for his goodness. Amen."

I tell Grandma I have to go to school as I have tests in every subject and ask if she'll call Dr. Quinn to come check the Belle and her new baby. I need Uncle Joe to take me to school in Ole White Mule and to get about 100 pounds of white oats, about ten bales of good alfalfa hay, and five gallons of black strap molasses. Belle needs a little extra boost for good milk.

"Be sure to tell Dr. Quinn to make out the birth certificate and do the paperwork to get the foal registered in the National Thoroughbred Records. He'll know how to do it," I add.

"What you going to name the foal?" Grandma asks.

"I'm thinking on Thomas Jackson. That's our name and it's a wonderful name in our country's history."

"That's fine," Grandma says. "And I think it's a glorious name. I'm going to register the owners as Annabelle and Jonathon Jackson."

"That's us, Grandma! You're listing me as half owner?"

"I'm giving you half-interest in the new foal; we're partners." She puts her hand out and says, "Shake on it."

I float through all my tests in a dreamy sort of daze. School always comes easy for me.

I run the four miles home straight to the barn. Belle gives out a low nicker when I go into the stall. TJ — I start calling him by his initials right out — is laying down and I stroke, pet and talk to him. I'd been told that if you blow into a foal's nostrils, he'll always be tight with you. I don't know if this is true or not but I blow into TJ's nostrils anyway.

Belle has some white oats and corn and molasses mixed in her feed trough and plenty of alfalfa hay in the hayrack. I run to the house and ask Grandma about Dr. Quinn coming to see the Belle and TJ. She says he examined the Belle and flushed her out and said TJ was perfect, except for being small. He will take care of all the registration paperwork. After all, the Belle — bred to Gallant Hood — and TJ all come from his breeding farm. Up to this time, this is the happiest day of my life.

The year 1933 goes by like we are in two different worlds. We are working from "can to cain't" and prospering while all around us people are sinking deeper. Banks are failing. People are desperately seeking work. Orphanages are bulging full. We hope and pray our new president — FDR as he is called — can get some of his New Deal programs moving.

We work smart: all the added Jerseys, the Johnson grass and those white leghorns are the layingest chickens yet. We have our John Deere, Ole White Mule, a telephone and butane. We put a water closet in the house with a shower and bathtub; in Woody and Saree's house too.

Grandma declares, "It shore don't seem right 'going' indoors."

We pour a concrete slab and frame it up with six-inch walls, put rock wool insulation in and make us a big cooler house.

Uncle Joe hauls 300 to 400 hundred pounds of ice in the hot months so we have cold milk and butter and better eggs. We are hauling two loads of milk a week in ten-gallon cans to Schepp's Dairy in Dallas.

Grandma has her big flock of bronze turkeys and with the John Deere equipment, the cotton, corn and hay are paying off. The telephone makes us money too.

Uncle Joe hollers out near every day, "We in cotton ten feet tall!"

Electricity is due in the spring of 1934. Rural Electrification Agency — REA they call it — is one of the New Deal programs; we are already signed up. We have a Servel - a butane refrigerator. Aunt Willie needs a washing machine, lights and other labor saving things that electricity will bring. We will soon be in cotton all the way to the moon, I think.

The night of December 15, 1933, Grandma and I walk down to Woody's with his share money. Somehow, even though I am only four months past 14, I have kind of taken charge. Guess it is 'cause I am so scrawny. I'd always heard little men were bosses. I have to be careful with Uncle Joe and Grandpa, and even Grandma. I have to fool them into thinking it is their ideas all along.

We walk up to the door, knock, and Woody comes to it hollering, "Come in! Come in! I declare, Miz Annie and Mr. Sonny."

"Saree, make some coffee and get that 'tater pie out. We have honored guests."

All his white teeth show as he smiles so big. He sure knows how to make you feel welcome.

"Woody," I say, "Uncle Joe says you could do more work than two common hands. You good and easy with the cows and mules and the dogs all love you. I'm giving you a well-deserved pay hike to twelve dollars a week and a yearly share of our prosperity. We gonna put electricity in this house along with your water closet and butane. You gonna have a nice place."

I pull out $300.00 in $20.00 bills and hand it over to him.

"Lawd! Lawd! Mr. Sonny. I ain't never seen that much cash money in all my life."

"You deserve it. We've had our best year ever and you were part of it. Besides, you got a youngun coming you gotta think about."

Saree starts bawling.

"Dadgum women always bawling," he laughs. Woody looks right in my eyes for a long time and says, "Mr. Sonny, you the best white man I ever knew. No! That ain't right. You the best person I ever knew."

I get a speck in my eye.

As Grandma and I walk back home, I say, "I know, Grandma, it was a right smart amount of money."

She lets out a whoop.

Mama and I talk on the telephone about every week and I make trips with Uncle Joe on our milk runs to see her about once a month. One time Grandma and I went to Dallas to see Mama and stayed at Mrs. Frances's for five days. While we were at Mrs. Frances's elegant home on Swiss Avenue, some of her friends commented on the way we talked. One lady said it sounded East Texas Southern. I know proper grammar and vocabulary; I just talk East Texas Southern as it is our way of communicating.

I talk to Mama about coming to the farm to live. She kind of frowns saying, "I'll study on it."

It is 1934 and TJ's about a year old. He is just like the Belle: a small bay, black mane and tail, black stockings. I figure him about 15 hands full-grown. Right now he's just a yearling and I have him so spoiled he's bossing me around. He is sure loved. I ride the Belle about every day and stretch our rides out longer and further from home. TJ carries on so much that sometimes I lead him alongside for a five or six mile ride — ten or twelve miles round trip.

Belle has a nice, easy long lope, almost like floating. She loves to long lope; that's her breeding and she's happiest when moving out. She is fit, in good shape, and I have her feet trimmed and her shoes fit with some little caulks on the front.

The road going east from our place is mostly sand and we hardly ever see a car or truck on our rides. The road goes to Field Town, a sizeable town about 20 miles distant. There is a country store about every three or four miles and hardly any traffic other than wagons and teams, and people on horseback — a perfect way to ride the

Belle and let TJ come along. I hope the running will make him strong with good lungs.

I've heard about a brush track in Field Town, a straightaway track about 880 yards long — four furlongs. Mostly local people but some hustling gamblers from Louisiana also come. I've been told they have these match brush races purt near every Saturday. I am bad wantin' to go with Belle but she is so small and dainty I'm afraid I might hurt her.

We get hooked up to the REA in April 1934. Mr. Platter, the electrician, comes and wires the house, milking barn, the chicken and turkey houses — everywhere we need electricity — Woody's house and the barn at the old Jones's place too. Aunt Willie gets a new Maytag washing machine. We have a radio, a big electric refrigerator and a cooling unit put in the cooling house.

Our next big plan is to go to milking machines. We've painted the houses and barns and put new tin roofs on them. We have linoleum on the floors and are looking into sheet rocking inside the house.

Uncle Joe sings happy songs all the time. He says that if he can get Aunt Willie to quit her appendicitis medicine, and maybe take her down to Galveston and feed her four or five dozen oysters a day for a couple weeks, they might have a youngun before they get too old. He says if she could stomach that old mineral oil, she could sure fork some of them oysters right out of the shell. If it works on folks like he'd always been told, the trip would sure be most pleasurable.

"Uncle Joe," I say, "the crop will soon be laid by and I can fill in for you, and I already know how to drive the White Mule and the Johnny."

"Sonny, that sure would be something 'cause me and Willie ain't never been no farther from home than Dallas."

"Uncle Joe, we can't grind all the time. We got to have some fun besides checkers, dominos, pitchin' hoss shoes, fishing and shooting turtles down on the river. We got extra money in the jar — let's enjoy some of it. Next trip to Schepp's with the milk, take Aunt Willie and buy her a new dress, shoes and such things as women need. Take her to one of them beautiful shops and get her hair fixed and such, not that she needs to be made more beautiful than she already is. Make her feel good. Plan on leaving on the bus for Galveston next week and I'll use the telephone to fix ya'll up in a nice hotel."

After a few moments of solemn thought, Uncle Joe declares, "You've talked me into it, Sonny,"

Aunt Willie is so excited she decides she could do without her appendicitis medicine for two weeks. When they come back from Galveston, Aunt Willie is laughing and singing all the time. She decides to quit taking her appendicitis medicine altogether. Uncle Joe looks kinda peaked, but happy and smiling.

He takes me off to one side and in a loud whisper says, "Sonny, I'm a natural born rabbit man."

In December 1934, we look back over the year and it has been our best year ever. We are doing better and better. One of the New Deal programs is milk coupons so kids have plenty of milk. Most of the farmers are still convinced the only way to make money in our section of the country is cotton. But there is not enough milk production to meet the demand with the milk coupons, and milk is bringing premium prices. We are milking right at 50 head of good Jerseys and have over 1,000 good white leghorn laying hens.

We decide no more cotton. Corn, oats, hay for forage and feed for the cows, chickens and turkeys are where the money is. Uncle Joe buys a second-hand thrashing machine and hammer mill which we power off the John Deere. We buy cottonseed meal and mix most of our feed. We buy some feed in bulk and some good alfalfa hay to make up for any shortage. We are hauling about 400 dozen eggs a week to Dallas at 15 cents a dozen.

The jar is so full that Grandma is now using a five gallon crock. It seems like she spends more time with her ledger than anything else. She always believes in accounting for every bit of money.

"Sonny," she says, "I'm afeared. I ain't never seen such good times, not even in 1917 and '18 during the war. I been giving our tithes and feeding everybody that comes by what looks hungry. I declare, I believe Jehovah has sent an angel to see about us."

"Grandma, it says right in the Bible, the Good Book, that God wants his people to live abundantly. So let's praise Him and give thanks for His blessing and enjoy our abundance."

"You right, Sonny. I ain't gonna fear no more," and she starts singing "Give Me That Ole Time Religion" and smiles and claps. I always did like that tune.

I am past 15 years old now and since I'd skipped the second grade and Texas has that eleven-year school system, I will be finishing high school this coming May, 1935. I'll be 16 in August.

Uncle Joe and I are taking turns every other day on our milk and egg trips to Schepp's and Cabell's Dairies. We make trips every day now and leave at two a.m. Ole White Mule is as faithful and steady as our ole real mules had been. The State of Texas doesn't require driver's licenses I guess 'cause not many folks own cars and trucks.

On one of those trips I try to remember as far back as I can. I am some puzzled about what Grandma had told me about Mama moving to Dallas. I can't recollect anything in particular. I know I had always been sickly and puny and seemed like I always had the whooping cough, flue, colds and chicken pox.

We lived in a one-room apartment where the bed came out of the wall. I went to the City Park Grammar School, which was only a block from where we lived, south of downtown about eight blocks.

We went to the movies and worked jigsaw puzzles and played Scrabble and cards a lot. I didn't recollect ever missing church and Sunday school except when I was sick. We went to the Baptist church on Elm Street, several blocks from where we stayed.

Mama worked in a sewing factory and I learned early on we didn't have much money. I read a lot and stayed in the apartment most of the time.

There was a small two-room shotgun shack behind where we lived and a colored lady named Mammy and her husband Fred lived there. They were kinda old, in their fifties. I would stay with them when I got out of school until Mama come home from work and I stayed with them all day before I started to school. I remember she used to fix chitlins and collard greens, sweet 'taters and such. Real fine eats. They up and moved one night right before I left for the farm and we never saw them again.

Fred was a small man. He told me he had been a flyweight boxing champion but never made any money 'cause people wouldn't pay no cash money to see little ole bitty men box. The bigger you was, the more they paid he said.

"Sonny, you jest like me," he told me. "All my life I been picked on and beat on by bigger and rougher bullies. I'se gonna show you a few tricks to even up the size, 'cause you gonna need to know."

"Mainest thing is to remember you got two feets, and be sho' you use 'em. A good kick in the privates stop most any man. You got a hard head. Remember a good butt in a man's face or belly purt near stop him most times, and remember you can do a man a whole lot of hurt with yo teeth. Remember these: feet, head, teeth," he said as he went through the motions and showed me a few ways to use feet, head and teeth.

I don't like the thought of fighting anyone but there might come a time when I can't run away. I had run away so much from bigger boys at school while living in Dallas that I knew people thought I was afraid — or even worse, a coward.

I am afraid so it makes sense to me to run. I'm five foot six and weigh 110 pounds. I'm hoping I'm going to get my growth in the next three or four years. I don't mind being small. I just get tired of hearing people call me runt, shorty, puny, shrimp, sickly and such names.

I've gone through a change toward girls, but the big fellers seem to do better. I am so shy and bashful I hardly speak or look at any girls. I've read in one of Grandma's Bible books that Paul had been about five foot five and that he was one of the bravest men who ever lived.

When the factory closed down where Mama worked, I tried to find some kind of work to help out while she looked for a job. There just wasn't any job for a sickly twelve-year-old kid. I couldn't even sell newspapers.

When Mama got the job taking care of Miz Adams, one condition was that she had to be single with no live-in children.

It near killed Mama to send me to Grandpa's. She cried for two days. She was in desperate condition and I was scared for her more'n me.

I love my life now, but still feel kinda empty living separated from my mama, she being alone from family like she is. We are prospering and I plan somehow to get her to where I call home now. I think about all of this as I drive to and from Dallas every other day.

I remember Mama had written and told Grandpa what day and what time the bus would get there. We went down to the Continental Bus Station and she cried and said, "I will send for you as soon as I can."

Farming kids out to their grandparents is common in 1932. When I step off the bus, Grandpa says, "Are you Jonathon? I'm your grandpa."

He's slender and about five foot eight. He wears faded blue bib overalls and white hair shows beneath a sweat-stained, wide brimmed hat where blue eyes look out of a red face. I think he's kind and calm looking. I have my few things in a large paper grocery sack.

Grandpa says, "Come on, we'll go over to Levi's store and get us a bite to eat before we start for home."

Grandpa has Mr. Levi cut a chunk of rat cheese and a couple thick slices of bologna. He says, "Just put it on a piece of paper; we gonna eat it here."

He gets a box of saltine crackers and we sit down on a bench in the back. He pulls his pocketknife out and cuts the cheese and bologna into small pieces and tells me to go fetch us a red soda water. This is the best bite to eat I can remember. We top it off with moon pies.

We climb up on a high seat in the wagon. Grandpa fills and lights his pipe and we start to the farm, being pulled along by two big black mules. Their farm is four miles out from town and we arrive shortly after noon. Off the main road, we turn down a lane of pin oaks about 600 feet. Grandpa tells me that the pin oaks had been planted from acorns by his papa 60 years ago.

The house is gray and about 80 feet long with an opening for a porch right in the middle and another long porch the whole length of the house.

Grandpa says Grandma's papa hauled cypress lumber all the way from Louisiana to build it. There are crepe myrtles all around the house, three or four live oaks and some bright green trees called hollies. I can see a long row of red rose bushes in bloom to one side. Grandma's roses are her pride and joy, Grandpa says. A picket fence runs all around the house. I had heard the words "Love at first sight," and now I know what they mean.

We unhitch the mules and give 'em a bite of corn. I get to looking at them mules and I have never seen such kind, loving eyes.

"Grandpa, what are these mules' names?"

"Ruth and Esther, and we got a third mule, Bathsheba."

"They're mare mules, Grandpa?"

"Lady mules sounds better," he laughs. "We call 'em 'The Ladies.'"

In later years, I wonder if Ruth, Esther and Bathsheba would be offended to know that in the far distant future there would be three mules on an East Texas farm named for them. I think they'd be pleased.

Grandpa takes me by the hand up to the house and into a large kitchen with a big wood cook stove, a big brick fireplace at one end, pine walls and a high ceiling.

Uncle Joe gives me a suspicious look and says, "How do, boy."

Aunt Willie gives a big smile and says, "Proud to know you."

Grandma doesn't say a word; she gets up, takes my hand, and leads me into her bedroom where she sits down on a cowhide straight back chair. She stands me right in front of her. I bet she isn't over five feet tall and about 100 pounds. She has auburn hair streaked with a little gray that she wears in a single braid down her back. We look into each other's eyes. Her eyes are so clear blue they look like glass marbles.

"Welcome, Jonathon. I'm going to tell you some rules."

"Yes'm," I say.

"We go to church every Sunday. We pray every day, thanking God for his loving kindness. You must wash your feet every night before bedtime and take a bath every Saturday. You look too puny to do any fieldwork, so you can be my helper with the turkeys, chickens, hogs, garden, washing clothes and such. Any questions?"

"Yes'm. I don't like Jonathon. Will you call me Sonny?"

She smiles and says, "Sonny, I got some kind of special feeling 'bout you."

Where Angels Roost

Recollecting while I make the milk runs, I know I've been special blessed. While making the trips to deliver milk and eggs, I begin to study on how we can make our milk production increase with less labor. Twice a day milking, feeding and cleaning up is taking three men purt near all day, seven days a week. I notice Grandpa rubbing Watkins liniment on his hands three or four times a day. We are wore pretty thin.

I ask Grandma about our cash money then explain this to her.

"Grandma, on my milk run tomorrow, I'm going to the DeLovall Milk Machine people to see if I can get one of them to come down and design us one of the Glazed Block Milking Barns, automatic feeders and milking machines. It will be better than putting more help on the payroll in the long term. I know it's a heap of money, but we all gonna be wore out soon."

"Go on ahead, Sonny. Will ain't gettin' no younger."

In about a month, we have the new barn, feeders and milking machines. Now one man can do what three men were doing. We take turns and have some time off.

Our money crock is about empty but Grandma promises Joe the next thing will be a touring sedan. Ole White Mule is kinda like a plow mule and Uncle Joe wants a nice buggy-type auto to go to town and church. We are moving on.

By February 1935, TJ is one month past two years old. I've been riding him for three or four months. He is about fifteen hands and I worry about his skinny legs being too long. He is sorta narrow in the hips and has a long skinny body. Uncle Joe calls him "broomstick legs."

Grandpa has lots of experience with horses and mules and as he puts it, "I will learn you what I know."

I cut the corn down to near nothing and feed TJ white oats and alfalfa hay with a little dab of molasses. I have salt and mineral blocks set out for him and the Belle.

When I get back from the milk run around eight in the morning, I ride to Field Town about 10 miles every other day. I just about have to learn to ride on my own.

Grandpa knows about plow, wagon and buggy horses, but the kind of horses he rode aren't like TJ. TJ isn't happy unless he's in a long lope just like the Belle; he doesn't care nothin' about walking or trotting. I can't get the little brown stick-legged spoiled thing to slow down to a walk or trot.

By this time, I'm bad wanting to go to Field Town on a Saturday to the brush match races I've been hearing about. I get back off my milk run along the third Saturday in February around eight and light out for Field Town 20 miles away.

Little TJ is long loping in a sorta floating glide and we make it by 10 a.m. I walk him around a while to settle him down some. It is around forty degrees, so he isn't sweating much. A good-sized crowd has collected out at the edge of town and I trot TJ up and down a grass straightaway track 880 yards; there are marker poles to one side every furlong, a furlong being 220 yards. There are men waving greenbacks and hollering and carrying on.

I watch four races and money changing hands and men hollering and challenging somebody to race. There is one foreign looking man in cowboy boots and a big black cowboy hat dressed all in black clothes. He wears a big diamond ring which looks near big as a banty chicken egg.

Two men are following him around, one with a big stack of money writing bets down in a book. The other looks like he is guarding the one who has the money. A third man leads a great big sorrel horse along who must be about 17 hands tall. The big red horse looks kinda bulky and muscled for a racehorse. I say to a man near me, "Is that a race horse?"

"Naw," he says. "He's a quarter horse, about near unbeatable at 440 yards."

The man in black is walking around, acting kinda uppity, and challenging anyone to race.

Finally, two men lead up a nice-looking roan and say they'll maybe race him. "We ain't got but $75.00 if you wanna run for that," they add.

The man in black says, "That's enough. I can make some side bets. Ole Red needs to earn his keep."

I get to looking at that roan hoss, built just like the big red except not near as tall. Little TJ, skinny and long as he is, looks kinda puny upside them horses.

Money changes hands and the man with the book writes bets down and gives out pieces of paper. I guess he is covering all bets. The two horses walk up to the second post — 440 yards — turn and walk up to a line, and a man hollers, "Go!"

I never seen such dirt and grass flying. They come thundering down the track right at us. You can hear them hosses' feet hitting the ground, sounding like thunder. The big red hoss daylights the roan by about 10 yards. It isn't even close.

This is the first race of any kind I've ever seen. It is exciting but I'm kinda fearful. I compare those big powerful horses to my little TJ and I am mighty afraid.

I hear a voice say, "Is that you, Sonny?"

I turn and see Mr. Dillard from the dry goods store with another white-haired man. We shake hands and he introduces me to Mr. Goldman.

"He owns the bank back in town," Mr. Dillard says. "We come purt near every Saturday to these races, one of our mainest pleasures."

"I know Annie and Will Jackson well," Mr. Goldman says. He laughs and adds, "They don't trust me. Never trusted banks to watch out for their money."

"They ain't never had much money for anybody to look out for," I say.

"I've heard they're doing well with their Jerseys and chickens," he continues.

"Tolerable. Mr. Dillard, who is that man all in black with all the money?" I ask.

"His name is Jean Manseur. He's a rich Cajun from over at Shreveport who made his fortune in the oil business. His great pleasures in life are these small town match race gatherings. He loves to have a winning horse. The money is really not important but he'll back his horses to the limit. As far as I know, he's straight and honest. He loves to prance around and show off."

I leave and TJ starts long loping for home. I'm in some kind of fierce turmoil. TJ was bred for running. His ancestors all the way back to Bible times were bred for running. I'm trying to fix my mind to think it is all right to race him. I say the Twenty-third Psalm through my mind and feel more peaceful.

Chapter 6

Every day the next week I have Woody stand to one side of the road going by his house, then I walk TJ up to a line, and Woody hollers, "Go!"

After about 20 times, TJ takes off full running. TJ is smart and eager to please and he learns real quick what "Go!" means.

About mid-week, I ride TJ into town and have the blacksmith put a new set of shoes on him. I want TJ and me to be ready as can be. I count my money Mama has been sending and I have exactly $80.00. I need another $120.00. I ask Grandma if I can borrow it out of the crock and tell her that I will pay it back.

"That's a right smart amount of money. What do you need it for?" she asks.

"I need it for TJ and me, Grandma. That's all I can tell you."

"Sonny, you been working like a full grown man. You been making the milk run every other day and goin' to school all day and we ain't never paid you any money since you been here. You don't need to borrow any money. You can have whatever you want."

I kiss Grandma on the top of her head and say, "I 'preciate that, Grandma." She laughs.

I light out for Field Town Saturday morning. I hold TJ down as much as I can. His trot is so uncomfortable I walk and slow-lope him. We get there about noon and I see right off there is an even bigger crowd than last Saturday. The weather is about 55 degrees and dry.

I look for Mr. Manseur and spot him and his big red hoss walking around the fringe of the crowd.

There is a race going on and some waiting to race. I see horse trailers and horses all over. Must be 50 to 60 horses.

Mr. Dillard and Mr. Goldman see me and walk up and say, "Howdy, Sonny. You thinking about racing?"

"I'm studying on it," I reply.

Mr. Manseur is walking with his two men, loudly challenging anyone to race. He turns some down if the money is too small. As he gets up close to me, I say, "Mr. Manseur? I might race your big red horse."

"That little old skinny looking pony?" he says. "I'm looking to run a horse race, kid."

He reaches and raises TJ's lips and hollers out, "This little ole pony ain't nothing but a two-year old. Come back, son, when you got a shore 'nuff horse."

"This little old pony can out run your big old giant horse," I say.

"Son, you aint' got no money no way. Who are you? Where you from?"

Mr. Dillard speaks up and says, "This is Will and Annie Jackson's grandson. I've known 'em all my life."

"Me too," says Mr. Goldman. "They live about 20 miles west of here in our neck of the woods. Real fine people. They raising Sonny."

"I ain't never heard of 'em," says Mr. Manseur. "How did you get here, boy?"

"I rode TJ," I answer.

"You rode 20 miles?" he asks. "I don't want to take advantage, and I believe I got a big edge."

"You can give odds," I add.

"How much money you got, boy?"

"$200.00." This gets his attention as it's about a year's pay for common working people.

"Well! Well!" he hollers. "This is some different. I'll give five-to-one and go ahead on and take your money. Let me see it."

I get down off TJ, take off my brogan and pull the money out. I hand it to Mr. Goldman and say, "Count it, Mr. Goldman."

He counts it and says, "$200.00 exactly. Boy, is this honest money?"

I tell him grandma gave it to me with no questions asked, sorta back wages. I explain to him that my little ole pony ain't never raced before and he is only two years old and I want ten-to-one 'cause the chances on me winning against the big red horse are purt near nothing.

Mr. Manseur walks around TJ and hollers out, "This is like free money. I'll give you ten-to-one. You got it."

"880 yards," I say.

"Whoa! 440 yards is my hoss's distance."

The man holding the money looks, laughs and says, "This little ole puny looking big Shetland pony don't look like he can run 880 yards. You got it, boy. I don't want to hear no crying when you lose your money."

"I won't be crying," I say. "Let Mr. Goldman here hold the money please."

The man with the money steps up and counts out $2,000.00. Mr. Goldman examines the money as it is counted out.

Mr. Dillard says, "Can I have $100.00 at ten-to-one?"

"No!" Mr. Manseur bellows. "Five-to-one for you."

"I'll take it for Mr. Dillard," says Mr. Goldman. "I'll take the same since Sonny is from where we live."

They saddle the big red horse. I notice it is a cowboy saddle and the man I think is guarding the money puts on a pair of spurs. He looks like he weighs about 150 pounds. I guess that big horse is so stout it doesn't make no difference.

We head up to the starting line 880 yards away. I slow lope TJ toward the line. The big red horse is trotting and throwing his head and dancing sideways. He knows what's coming and he's plenty excited.

My heart is beating fast and I'm so scared I can hardly breathe.

I say a prayer, "Father, your will be done. Bless me and TJ." Then I calm down some.

We turn and walk up to the line. The man standing there hollers, "Go!"

The big red hoss takes off so quick he's shaking the ground and throwing wads of dirt big as dinner plates out behind. TJ takes off, but kinda breaks stride at the dig off of the big red hoss. He gets straightened out but we are a good 20 yards behind.

I lean forward on his neck and start talking to him. "You can do it, TJ. Come on, TJ. Give it all you got, TJ."

I can feel him long striding and I see we're closing some. The man riding the big red hoss is raking him with the spurs and lashing him on the rump with a whip.

We are closing some more and a lot faster. When we go by the 440 pole, I'm about ten yards behind and moving up faster. When we hit the 220 yard pole, I pull up to where TJ's nose is just about to the big red hoss's rump.

His rider is spurring and lashing with his whip and the big red hoss looks like he is laboring some.

TJ surges and his strides are so long I feel like we are floating. With about 100 yards to go, we pull even head to head and I feel Jehovah is with us.

We pull away and win by 20 yards. The big red hoss is throwing foam out of his mouth and sweating heavy. I believe the extra 440 yards have been too much for him. I can see bloody lines along his sides where he's been spurred. I feel bad about that, but I think in my head, *Praise the Lord!*

I ride up to Mr. Goldman and Mr. Dillard and they are hollering and laughing and saying, "Way to go, Sonny! That little ole pony ain't so little now!"

"Suckered!" Mr. Manseur glares at me. "You played me for a sucker. Hornswoggled by a runty little old kid and a puny looking little ole pony."

"I beat you fair and square, Mr. Manseur. If you think you were hornswoggled, or I cheated you in any way, you can have your money back."

He stares right in my face for about two minutes. Then he sticks his hand out and says, "For the first time in my life it is a pleasure to lose. You sumpin else, boy. You shorely are. I'll always remember you and this little ole hoss."

"Thank you," I say, then turn and start for home.

I'm so excited I hum and sing "Ole Time Religion" all the way home. I can't recall ever having such a wonderful feeling before 'cept the morning TJ was foaled. I am happy about the way TJ has raced, how he's proven he is a champion in heart and spirit.

I kinda felt like it was David and Goliath. I know this was only a small-time match race against a big quarter horse stretched out beyond his distance. I have to do some studying about the future for TJ and me. TJ can sense I am glad. I pet him on the neck and praise him going home.

Maybe the blowing in the nostrils deal is true 'cause I feel like we are tight. We get home well before dark. The Belle is excited and nickering at our arrival. TJ is her baby and she loves him about as much as I love him.

I walk him around a while to cool him off. I brush him and wipe him down and check his feet real good. I put out some alfalfa hay and decide to wait a couple hours before I feed him his oats. I want to be sure I don't bloat him. I cover him with a blanket to make sure he doesn't cool down too fast.

I clean out the stall and put fresh sawdust and straw down for him and Belle. They share a big — about 20 by 30 foot — stall. They have 20 acres for grazing but there is hardly any grass this last part of February.

I worry about what I'm going to tell Grandma about the race and the money we have won. I decide the only thing to do is to tell the truth. She comes out on the porch and lets loose one of her turkey-calling screams, "Sonneee!"

"In a few minutes!" I holler back.

I go on and feed TJ a good pail of oats, about three gallons, and start for the house. I am fearful and happy at once.

Grandma looks at me sorta suspicious like and asks, "Where have you been so long? Have you been over to Field Town?"

"Yes'm."

She comes right out with it. "Did you race TJ?"

"Yes'm, Grandma. I wish you could have seen him."

"Did you win?"

I'm excited now. Grandma, Grandpa, Aunt Willie and Uncle Joe sit there looking at me. Tears roll down my cheeks. "Grandma, I wasn't intending to fool you. If we hadn't won, you might have been upset and had a nervous spell."

"TJ was so brave and he run so wonderful. You can be proud of him," I say.

Not a sound for about two minutes.

"Mr. Dillard already called and described everything," Grandma says. "He told me you offered the man his money back and how you acted. He was some impressed. Told me you one of the best young men he ever had the pleasure of knowing."

She starts laughing. "You and TJ flew down that track like you had wings, Mr. Dillard told me. Lordy! I wish I could have seen it."

I pull out the big wad of money and lay it on the table. "Grandma, take out the church tithes and give the rest to Uncle Joe so he can go and buy us the biggest, longest touring sedan in Dallas."

Uncle Joe laughs and shouts, "I'm a natural born Cadillac man!"

He starts in singing "Ole Time Religion" and we all start stomping and clapping and join in. Happy days are here again, as FDR proclaims.

After a few minutes of singing and laughing, Grandma explains, "Land sakes, Sonny! I'm upset cause you and TJ ain't nothing but babies. Rode 20 miles with a two-year old to race for the first time. That took some courage. I'm upset cause you didn't let me know what you was up to. I was some suspicious. My thinking was that when the time came, I'd be with you. We're partners. You, TJ and me."

I'm feeling some better and say, "Grandma, that includes Grandpa, Aunt Willie and Uncle Joe too."

Early the next morning before Uncle Joe gets back from the milk run and we sit at the table drinking our morning coffee. Grandma

Where Angels Roost

says, "I shore hope our friends and neighbors won't think we being uppity buying a Cadillac. Maybe we ought to get a Ford or Chevrolet."

"Grandma," I say, "There's five in the family and we need a big, heavy roomy car to be comfortable and we may be pulling a horse trailer some. I ain't studying on going back to Field Town but we may go some other place some time. Besides, Uncle Joe knows all about such things and he said a Caddy is the best there is."

"Good thinking, Sonny. I hadn't thought about the horse trailer; sets my mind at ease. The Caddy it is."

I check on TJ before Sunday school and church. He is all stretched out and laying down sound asleep. The Belle is standing with her head down over him sleeping and dozing on her feet. I have heard horses sleep standing up; maybe true for some horses, but TJ lays down and stretches out for his sleep.

I've been caring for TJ and the Belle by asking Grandpa and Uncle Joe a lot of questions and using common sense. I plan on either buying a book or checking one out of the library about training thoroughbred racehorses.

Grandma has Dr. Quinn come and check TJ and the Belle every now and then while I'm in school. He gives them vaccination shots and checks for worms and such things. He doubts Belle will ever come into a period to be bred again; something has kind of shriveled up in her. Dr. Quinn says TJ's fit as a fiddle, other than being undersized.

That Monday morning on the way to Dallas with Uncle Joe, I have to tell him over and over how TJ and I beat the big red hoss. I ask him to go by and give Mama $100.00 if there's that much left after the new Cadillac and tell her to buy some new clothes or whatever she needs. Miz Adams, like other people of 1935, only pays four or five dollars a week. I'm too young and have no real idea about money except to know it buys things. It is pleasurable to me to see other people enjoy buying things.

"Sonny," Uncle Joe says, "You come home to us near three years ago. You hit the ground a runnin' as a scrawny little ole kid and you ain't never slowed down. You ain't never played softball, baseball, marbles, tops or any other kid games. You go trotting off to school every morning and come trotting home in the afternoon. You do as much work as a grown man and you don't want nothing for yourself.

"I want you to slow down. You gonna be middle aged 'fore you 18 years old. I'm telling you this cause we all love you and you have put a spirit in the family that we think is a divine miracle."

Such talk embarrasses me. "Thank you, Uncle Joe. I 'preciate that. I'll try and do as you say."

After we unload the milk and eggs, Uncle Joe gets a jitney to take him to the Cadillac store on Ross Avenue and I head out for home.

Later this afternoon, we are all watching and waiting. Sure 'nuff here comes a big black car turning down our lane. Uncle Joe is mashing the horn down trying to play a tune with it.

He pulls up, stops and jumps out and shouts, "I'm a natural born Cadillac man!"

We all crawl in and out and smell and push in the cigar lighter and turn the radio on. We ride up and down Main Street and go out on the highway and are flying along at 60 miles an hour. Grandpa is kinda all swole up cause we didn't get a Henry Ford.

He says, "I ain't never heard of no Mr. Cadillac or Mr. General Motors. Man ought to put his brand on what he makes."

Uncle Joe stops and I drive back. After driving Ole White Mule and Johnny, this is like driving a dream. We all love our new Caddy, thanks to TJ.

Grandma and I start driving over to Field Town every other Saturday to watch the races. She has never seen a horse race before in her life. Grandpa has been to the Philippines, France, New York and all over so he doesn't care about going. The furthest from home Grandma has ever been is Dallas, and not many times there.

I introduce her to Mr. Manseur and he treats her like an elegant lady, calling her madam. We make friends with people and Grandma fits right in. Course, driving our big black Caddy lets people know we're kinda high class.

Coming home, Grandma worries about TJ in comparison to the big horses she has seen. She can't believe we beat the big red hoss.

"Dynamite comes in small packages," she says.

We're both so mixed up about TJ's future we can't figure out where to go. All we can do is pray. Every time I suggest asking Dr. Quinn for advice, she says, "No way. We work it out our ownself."

Aunt Willie is expecting and all pooched out like maybe she is gonna have twins. Uncle Joe is hoping to make up for lost time, which he blames on Aunt Willie's appendicitis medicine. This is about April 1935. Uncle Joe is excited about being a natural born papa man.

We can no way get Grandpa to learn to drive Ole White Mule or the Caddy. He says he's gone all his life without knowing how to drive, has never owned any kind of trucks and cars, and isn't going to start now. He won't even try to drive the Johnny.

Uncle Joe, Woody and I do all the driving and plowing. Woody has bought him and Saree a new Ford. He polishes and rubs on it so much I'm afraid he's gonna rub the fenders clean off.

About the first week in May, I get up and ready for school. I make the Dallas run every other day then get back home in time for school. Uncle Joe is making the run today and it's pouring down rain. Woody is mixing feed so I decide to drive the Caddy to school.

"Makes sense to me," says Grandma.

I drive up and park directly in front of the front door. Some of the kids are teasing me good-naturedly about driving a Cadillac limousine to school.

I have no close friends or enemies that I'm aware of, though Billy Joe Johnson, one of the town boys, has made crude remarks and acted kinda bullish on a few occasions. This morning Billy Joe hollers out, "I don't cotton to no uppity sickly little ole runt what drives a Cadillac to school."

"Billy Joe," I say, "Your papa still working on the WPA?"

He doubles his fists up and makes a motion to swing at me. Billy Joe is 18 years old, six foot two and weighs about 180 pounds. I shore don't want him after me.

"Billy Joe," I say, "I'm sorry. I didn't mean nothin'. You got a good, hard working honest papa. We been blessed special and I shore don't want to be prideful about it."

"You ain't no good and yo mama ain't no good and I is gonna clean yo plow good and proper when school lets out."

Three or four of his friends standing behind him say, "That's telling him, Billy Joe."

I am some worried all day in school. One of my teachers, Mr. Shaw, asks me two or three times if I am upset about anything. Mr. Shaw tells me it looks like I am going to be Valedictorian of my graduating class in three more weeks. He says it has been close between Rachel Ward and me.

Rachel is a good looker, with short curly black hair and big brown eyes. She's five foot five and 115 pounds, maybe six months older than me. I've sneaked a lot of looks at her because I think she's the prettiest girl in school.

We've been running a race for best grades and it looks like maybe I've won. Another thing that I've always wanted to talk to her about — 'cepting I am so shy — is that her papa is Dr. Quinn's partner, trainer and breeder at the Quinn Farm.

I've heard her papa is from Kentucky and he and Dr. Quinn served in France together. I've heard if it hadn't been for Henry Ward, Dr. Quinn wouldn't be alive today. When they came home from France in 1919, Mr. Ward with his French bride joined Dr. Quinn and they started the thoroughbred breeding farm as partners. Rachel's mother died in a flu epidemic and her papa along with her mammy, BB, raised her.

She lives on the adjoining farm but I don't know her 'cept for school. I'm not much to look at and I'm such a loner she probably doesn't even know I live next to their farm.

Ever since I beat the big red hoss at Field Town, Mr. Dillard and Mr. Goldman have told it around and people have asked me about it. She asked me once and I just said, "It wasn't much," and ran.

She was standing by Billy Joe when he promised to clean my plow. Now I'm figuring out how to get to the car and get away from him. I even think about going out the back door and trotting home then having Uncle Joe bring me back for the Caddy later. When the bell rings, I start running for the car as fast as I can.

About the time I start to open the door, Billy Joe grabs me and carries me around behind the school to the softball field. A crowd of kids follow.

Some of the boys are hollering, "Billy Joe's gonna clean his plow good. The smart uppity thing showing off his new Caddy, he got it coming."

I am so humiliated and embarrassed I'm about near fainting. I am plenty scared. Billy Joe is carrying me along like a sack of potatoes. He stops, sets me down and starts in cussin' me.

"Billy Joe," I say, "I ain't never done nothing to you. Why you so mad?"

"I don't like you cause you is uppity and you been making sly eyes at Rachel and you is a teacher's pet and yo family's not good and ever'body know it."

He winds up a big roundhouse right hand. I see it coming but am so petrified I can't move.

WHAM! Upside my head. I see stars and go down.

"Get up!" he bellows.

Like a fool, I get up. It is the first time in my life I've ever been hit by anybody trying to do me bad harm.

WHAM! Upside the head on the other side. I see stars and go down again.

I have the strangest feeling like I'm wanting to hurt a body. I've never thought of doing harm to anyone before. I squat on my feet in a sorta crouch. I can feel and sense Billy Joe bending over me. My legs are plenty strong with all the trotting to and from school and riding TJ. I make my legs like big-coiled springs.

Way back in my memory from our one-room apartment in Dallas I remember Fred telling me to butt, kick and bite. I shoot up off that ground and butt Billy Joe smack in the face. I feel it hit solid. My blood is up now and I don't know what I'm doing. Billy Joe squeals and I see blood flying out of his nose and mouth. He staggers back wiping his sleeve across his face to clear off blood.

I haul off and kick him with my bull hides right in the privates. He squalls so loud you can hear him 'bout four miles around. He falls over on the ground and starts kicking and screaming. He's killed.

I kick him in the side. "Have mercy! You've 'bout killed me," he screams.

Arms are grabbing at me and hollering, "Stop it! Stop!"

One hand's hanging on so tight I look to see who it is. It's Rachel. "Please, Sonny. No more. He's done for. I'm going for some water to clean his face up."

She comes in a few minutes with a bucket of water. I pull my shirt off, dip it in the water and start in cleaning the blood off his face.

I'd cooled down by now and feel plenty ashamed and sorry for what I've done to Billy Joe.

"Billy Joe," I say, "I'm sorry I hurt you. If I hadda known what I was doing, I wouldn't have done it. I don't know what came over me. I never hurt anything before in my life 'cepting snakes and such."

Billy Joe stands up and says, "Sonny, I had it coming. I was jealous of you being the smartest kid in school and driving up in that Caddy set me off. I was just being a big ole bully."

He sticks his hand out and says, "Let's shake and be friends."

We shake hands and I say, "Come on. I'll drive you home."

As we get in the Caddy, Rachel gets in and says, "After you take Billy Joe home, you can drop me off on your way."

When we pull up to Billy Joe's house, his mama comes out on the porch and screams, "Billy Joe, what in tarnation happened to your face?"

He laughs and says, "Mama, I shoulda been listening instead of talking. Sonny here made a new thinking man of me. He ain't no little sissy for sure. We good friends now."

In later years, when we're both in the Thirty-sixth Division in Italy, Billy Joe is my first sergeant and I'm a second lieutenant fresh out of Texas A&M. We become lifelong comrades. But that's another story.

I drive Rachel toward her home. After a few minutes of silence, she says, "You're one strange person. Fierce as fierce can be, then the next minute, gentle and kind as you can be. Can I ride my mare Daisy over Saturday to visit you?"

My heart's beating so loud I'm afraid she can hear it. As I drop her off at her house, I say I'll saddle up TJ and we can ride maybe all the way to Field Town Saturday.

When I walk into the kitchen, Grandma is working on her ledger. She looks up and says, "Lordy mercy! Sonny, where is your shirt? What's happened to your face? Both your eyes are black all the way back to your ears!"

"Willie," she hollers, "Fetch the rosebud. Sonny needs doctoring. I'll brew a batch of sassafras tea, calm you some. 'Pears to me like you been in a fight. You got blood all on your britches."

Grandma and Aunt Willie run around the kitchen hollering at me to calm down. They act like they are having palpitations of the heart.

Grandma's screaming, "Who done it? Who was it?"

I tell her Billy Joe Johnson did it and that I didn't hurt him too awful bad.

She stops running round and says, "Hurt *him?* Why he purt near makes two of you, Sonny. Did you hit him upside the head with a two-by-four?"

"No, Gram. I butted him with my head and kicked him in the privates with my bull hides."

"Then what?"

"Rachel and I cleaned him up and drove him home."

I tell her in complete detail from start to finish what has taken place. Then Grandma and Aunt Willie are calm and still.

"Sonny," says Grandma, "You was being tested. You been tested before and you will be tested all your life. I'm pleased how you handled this test. You my own flesh and blood and I couldn't be more proud of you."

Next morning, I stubbornly, maybe a little too pridefully, insist on trotting to school after my milk run. Billy Joe is waiting for me at the front door with Rachel and some other kids. His nose and lips are swole up and he has two black eyes.

He smiles, grabs and hugs me, and says, "I got some loose teeth but I think they'll be all right and I'm so sore between my legs I can hardly walk. Sonny, what you did was the best thing ever happen to me. You the biggest little feller I know. I shore hope we gonna be friends."

We are lifelong friends. I hear somewhere that you're fortunate in life to have one true friend. Billy Joe is mine, in the not so far future of World War II, as well as in the distant future afterward.

Chapter 7

That Saturday morning I pet and brush TJ and the Belle till they are shining. I'm always afraid Grandma will complain about our brown sugar and dried apple use, but she never does.

The dog we got from Amos starts barking about eight a.m. When I asked him her name, he'd said, "She ain't got no name. We allus just called her Dog."

Rachel comes down the lane on a beautiful gray mare with black mane, tail and stockings. She has on a pair of blue faded bib overalls and a short sleeved blue shirt. She always wears dresses to school. She looks mighty fetching.

When we put the water closet and shower in the house, I got into the habit of taking a good soapy shower every night and sometimes in the morning. I'm real conscious of my hygiene cause most kids and grownups have a little smell about 'em. Some older men put their Unionall long underwear on in October and don't take them off till April.

Lots of folks think too many baths weaken you, causing colds, flu and such. Some kids and grownups wear little sacks of asphittie around their necks to ward off germs. Germs probably can't get past the smell. I always have clean hair and myself scrubbed clean. Rachel has a good clean scrubbed look about her too.

She gets off her mare and says, "This is Daisy. She's a thoroughbred ten years old, 16 hands, and my very own special mare. She's a little fat, but in good sound shape. I've had her all her life and most of mine."

"Come in and we'll have coffee," I say, "Then I'll saddle TJ and we can go for a long ride."

We walk into the kitchen and Grandma says, "Good morning, Rachel, glad to see you. How's your papa Hank?"

"Just fine, Miz Annie."

"Good morning, Rachel," Aunt Willie says. "Set down. I have fresh coffee."

Rachel looks around the kitchen and says, "My what a beautiful kitchen! I was here four years ago but you've completely redone everything."

She flatters Grandma and Aunt Willie, and compliments the new kitchen. Grandma shows her the new water closet, bathroom and the rest of the house. Women like to show off such things.

Rachel makes a fuss over Grandma's long-stemmed roses in a vase on the table. I'm getting bored with such carryings on so I get up and say, "I'm gonna go saddle TJ."

Rachel jumps up and says, "I'll go with you."

On the way to the barn, Uncle Joe comes up and says, "Howdy, Miz Rachel." He turns to me and says, "Sonny, you think it's too late to plant that 20 acres of bottom land in corn? It's almost first of June."

"I think we should go ahead," I say. "We can make a lot of good silage in the dough stage if we need to."

Uncle Joe takes off. "I'm a natural born silage man!"

Grandpa trots up and says, "Morning Miz Rachel." He turns to me. "Sonny, you know that long shed with the gutters to carry off the rain water you was talking about? I think we oughter go ahead. The cows are boggin' up and churning up so much mess, we can feed hay under a dry shed and direct the water off."

"Grandpa, go ahead and phone the lumber yard and order the material. I'll see if I can get Billy Joe and Mr. Johnson to help put it up. Can you figure the material we need, Grandpa?"

"Shore can," he says, taking off for the house.

As I get to TJ's stall, Woody comes up. "Morning, young lady," he says.

"Mista Sonny, what yo think about adding ten or twelve of them big milking Holsteins in with our 50 Jerseys? You said something 'bout we selling most of our production in whole milk. Holsteins got less butterfat but gives twice as much milk and the Jerseys keep the butterfat up."

"Woody," I say, "Let's sell some of our young replacement heifers and add about 15 Holsteins."

"Tha's exactly what I was studying on," he adds.

"We hauling about 2,000 pounds a day now. With 15 Holsteins added in, we can haul 3,000 pounds a day. That's like adding 30 more Jerseys. You can milk 15 better than 30. We'll probably use all Holsteins in time. Plan on taking care of it next week."

"Yes, suh, Mr. Sonny. We getting in high cotton," he laughs.

Then I ask, "Woody, how's little Sonny doing?"

"Jes fine, Mr. Sonny," Woody says as he walks away.

Rachel asks, "Who's little Sonny?"

"Woody's son. He named him same as my name."

"After you?"

"I reckon so."

Rachel looks at me so strangely I think something's wrong. "Sonny, how long you been here?"

"Three years and one month."

"How old are you?"

"I'll be 16 this August. Why?"

"I came over here the last time about three and a half years ago and this ain't the same place. Show me around some please."

I show her the milking parlor, the big new chicken house — we have 1,800 laying white leghorns in a five-acre fenced pen — and a big new turkey house. We have electric incubators and we're hauling about 1,500 turkeys to Dallas a year. We have grain bins, a mixing barn, the cooler house, a silage pit, hay barns, and such things as needed on a good farm.

"I can see most of this has been built and added since you came here," says Rachel. "Did ya'll inherit some money or something?"

"We did everything with hard work, and as Grandma says, Jehova sent an angel to see about us."

She starts laughing, then so do I. I notice she has nice teeth. TJ is stomping and nickering and carrying on. I get him all saddled and we lead him up to where Rachel's mare Daisy is. He snuffles around her and nips her a few times. They make friends and sorta settle down.

We take the road to Field Town, but it has been raining and the sand road is soft. TJ, as usual, wants to move it on out. Rachel and Daisy are staying alongside as we long lope toward Field Town.

"Let him out," says Rachel. "I want to see him run. I've been watching horses all my life and I can tell a good one."

I let TJ go all out for about four furlongs. Rachel is trying to keep up on Daisy but we leave them far behind.

I get TJ slowed down and she comes up beside me and motions to stop. We get stopped and I look at Rachel and her eyes are big. "You got something special in this colt," she says. "I believe he's as good as any colt on our farm. Maybe better. I'd like for Papa to see him. I know all about his mama, the Belle, and his papa, Gallant Hood."

She's laughing and excited and I'm not so shy and bashful as before. "We been special blessed with the Belle and TJ," I say.

"You most certainly have," she laughs. "Let's go all the way to Field Town."

"That's 40 miles round trip. You think Daisy can manage?"

"Sure she can. She needs the work. We can take it easy coming back."

When we get to Field Town, the usual big crowd is gathered at the edge of town for the match races. TJ is acting like he wants to run. We tie TJ and Daisy out at the edge at a hitching rail, then water them from a nearby tank. We don't have any oats with us so we're gonna have two hungry horses when we get back home. Horses have small stomachs for their sizes and get hungry mighty quick.

We are walking amongst the crowd when Mr. Manseur comes running up hollering, "My good friend Sonny Jackson."

I introduce him to Rachel and he towers over her and kisses her hand and exclaims what a pleasure and honor it is to meet such a beautiful young lady. Rachel turns red and says, "Thank you, sir."

"Sonny here is my good friend," he tells Rachel. "I learned a most valuable lesson from him the day he and his little hoss beat my big red. Sometimes the old can learn from the young."

As we walk through the crowd, people stop us to shake hands and I begin to feel embarrassed. Mr. Dillard and Mr. Goldman come up smiling and shaking hands. They both know Rachel, and Mr. Dillard asks if she's my girl. I get so flustered I get tongue tied and say we're just friends.

Mr. Dillard looks at my black and blue face and says, "I heard what happened between you and Billy Joe. You done what was right and good. I'm glad it turned out all right. I understand you're going to be Valedictorian of your graduating class in a couple weeks."

He laughs real big and says, "I remember Miz Annie bringing you in three years ago for your bull hides. Time sure has a way of flying by."

"The best thing I remember is you and little TJ flying down this track three months ago," Mr. Dillard continues. "Put some nice money in mine and Mr. Goldman's pockets. I'll especially remember what you said after Mr. Manseur said he was suckered by a runty little old kid and a puny looking little ole pony. 'I beat you fair and square, Mr. Manseur. If you think you were hornswoggled, or I cheated you in any way, you can have your money back.'"

He laughs and pats me on the shoulder.

I glance at Rachel and she has that strange look on her face again. I suggest we head for home so we can be there before dark. We lope along in silence for four or five miles, then walk a while and come to a country store.

"I'm starving," Rachel says. "Let's stop and get a bite to eat."

Lucky for us I have some money, though I hardly ever carry more than a dollar in my pocket. We stop, go in and I buy two cans of sardines, a big chunk of rat cheese, a box of saltines and two big red soda waters. We come out and sit on a bench in front of the store. We eat in silence and when we're finished, I go back in and get us moon pies.

That soda water has me all bloated up and I turn my head and let out a loud belch. I'm some embarrassed. She starts laughing and says, "I belched while you was in the store getting the moon pies."

We start for home. After a while, Rachel says, "Sonny, what's your real first name?"

"Jonathon."

After about a minute she says, "How strange. That's Dr. Quinn's first name. You know, Papa and I've lived in the same house with Dr. Quinn all my life. He's a wonderful man. I remember when he came home from Boston after Harvard Medical School about seven years ago. He brought his wife from Boston with him. Talk about uppity. She was the uppitiest person I ever seen. Her papa was some kind of senator or mayor or something. She didn't stay long."

"I remember the day she left," Rachel went on. "She marched into the kitchen and hollered out, 'I'm leaving this Godforsaken place. I can't stand it any longer. You need an interpreter to understand the language. Gourmet food is swine intestines called chitlins, collard greens, fried okra, sweet 'taters, clabber and buttermilk, black-eyed peas, rooster chili, sowbelly and such inedible crap. You shop at Levi's General Store and Dillard's Dry Goods. Horse manure smell in the air constantly and the people all stink.

"'The women over 40 all dip snuff, high fashion is a pair of high-top tennis shoes with a big bonnet and a dress that drags the ground. All the conversation is about quilting, setting eggs, killing hogs, soup-making recipes, or all the medicinal uses of coal oil. The big annual event is the East Texas Coon Dog Trials. Entertainment consists of going trot-lining or shooting turtles down at the river.

"'God, we don't even have a radio or a Victrola. A stinking movie theatre that shows nothing but Tom Mix, Hoot Gibson and Buck Jones. I'm outta here. I can't believe I married a Harvard Medical School doctor and we live in such a place as East Texas. Might as well be somewhere in Africa!'"

"After she stormed out the door, demanding to be driven to Dallas to catch the train, we all broke down and laughed and laughed till we nearly was crying. In a few months, Dr. Quinn got the papers, signed 'em and sent 'em back. He said it was all a big mistake. He ain't never looked at another woman. He's kinda like my second papa," she explained.

Rachel starts gazing at me with that strange puzzling look again. We get home a little before dark. Daisy is some wore out. TJ's tired and hungry and Belle is acting up as I start for the barn. Rachel and I stop at the lane coming to the house off the road.

I stick my hand out and she reaches over and shakes it. When she looks me square in the eyes, I see she has long black eye lashes and a few freckles high on her cheeks.

I say how much I enjoyed the ride and her company. I'm so bashful I can't think of anything else to say.

She's silent for about a minute and kinda blurts out, "Sonny, do you think I'm pretty?"

"Yes, Rachel. Prettier than a spotted pup."

She squeals out the loudest laugh then says, "You wanna take me to the graduation dance?"

"I ain't never learned to dance. Wouldn't know how."

"That don't matter. Thing is, we'd be together."

"That shore would be nice," I say. "I'll take you."

"Good," she says and rides off to home.

I have the doggonedest mixed-up feeling like I am riding down in one of them elevators in a tall building again. I take care of TJ while the Belle is fussing and carrying on. I have to start riding her more; she is beginning to feel left out.

On the way to Dallas making the milk and egg deliveries I get to studying about taking Rachel to the graduation dance. We love music in our house. We play the Victrola nearly every day — mostly Al Jolson, gospel music and such.

The main radio music program that everyone tunes into daily is Bob Wills and his Light Crust Doughboys. He always plays and sings "San Antonio Rose," country western swing with W. Lee O'Daniel and other members in the band. We call him the Flour Salesman for Light Crust Flour since he always emcees and exclaims several times each show, "Pass the Biscuits, Pappy!" W. Lee is elected governor, then to the U.S. Senate using the name Pappy Lee O'Daniel. We call his flour "Hillbilly Flour."

I know I need a quick dancing lesson. I don't want to make a fool of myself and embarrass Rachel with my ignorance of dancing and social graces. When I unload the milk and eggs that morning,

Where Angels Roost

I look in the Yellow Pages and find the Dallas Dance Studio and Social Graces classes with an address on North Akard Street.

I call and make arrangements for classes on the next two Saturdays. The next Saturday I make the deliveries and have breakfast. The classes only run for two-hour intervals, so I explain I have only two Saturdays to learn how to dance and ask if I can do three classes in two hours in one day. We make arrangements for this, and one two-hour class on social graces.

Social graces teach you how to hold your fork and cup, keep elbows off the table, open doors, hold chairs — basically how to use good manners. I sure appreciate this as I am drinking coffee out of a saucer with my elbows propped on the table and using eating utensils all wrong.

I do everything like Grandpa and Uncle Joe; just don't know any different. We use biscuits for sopping gravy, syrup, meat grease, or any leftovers on the plate. We sop the plates clean. We sure know how to eat. We just don't do it elegantly or gracefully. We use our fingers a lot and make plenty of noisy slurping, sucking and smacking sounds.

An older lady near 30 teaches the ballroom dance steps. She is some put out with my lack of rhythm. She tells me to concentrate on the fox trot.

She explains, "One, two, bring your heels together, one two," and so on. I finally get it down and I can fox trot to fast or slow music pretty fair to middlin'.

Then we concentrate on doing the waltz. I get this down fair to good. I am kinda cottoning to this here dancing. After two Saturdays of six hours each, I'm about ready for the graduation dance.

Grandma tells me to get what money I need out of the money crock and go to Mr. Dillard's and buy myself a new suit and shoes and such things as I need.

I go into Mr. Dillard's store and he comes running up and shakes hands and puts his arm around my shoulder. He calls me his little race hoss friend. I explain I want a real fine suit, white shirts, ties and a nice pair of dress shoes. As I have never had any such finery, I say I would appreciate his advice on what to select.

Where Angels Roost

Mr. Dillard acts so happy and pleased I'm a little suspicious about what all this is gonna cost. He picks out a wool navy blue suit, measures for alterations, then shirts, ties, even underwear, then the most elegant light-as-a-feather shoes and silk socks. The shoes feel better than anything I have ever had on my feet. I feel like I can sleep in those shoes. They sure aren't for kicking and stomping. He calls 'em slippers.

When we have everything boxed and gathered up, Mr. Dillard invites me into his private office. He opens up a small refrigerator and uncaps me a small green bottle of Coca Cola; I've never had one. I always thought anybody is foolish to buy a little bitty six-ounce bottle of Coke for the same nickel. I take a few big swallows of that Coke then understand why folks buy it. It is tastier than the Big Red ones that I've always bought. I drink lots of Coca Cola after that.

"Sonny," Mr. Dillard says, "I know you are a prideful young man. It would do me great pleasure if you would allow me to do a nice thing for you."

"What's that, sir?"

"Let me buy this suit and shoes and things for you as a graduation present."

I think about the $500.00 he won when TJ beat Mr. Manseur's Big Red and I am some suspicious. I look right into Mr. Dillard's face and say, "I've been special blessed more that I probably deserve and there are other folks not near as blessed. I'll accept your most generous offer if you will give Billy Joe the same as you have offered me."

He looks at me for about a minute, then starts laughing. "Sonny, you sumpin' else. Billy Joe gets the same deal I have just given you."

"Thank you very much. Billy Joe's folks are kinda struggling now, and he would be most appreciative."

As we walk out of his office, he has his arm around my shoulders and Mr. Goldman comes running up to us hollering, "I thought that was your Cadillac out front."

He shakes my hand, calls me his little racehorse man, pulls out a $50.00 bill and hands it to me saying, "For graduation."

"I appreciate this very much, Mr. Goldman, but I can only accept on one condition."

"What is that?"

"The same for Billy Joe," I say. "He could shore use it."

Mr. Goldman frowns and says, "You sure make it hard on a man, Sonny."

I think about the $500.00 he also won when TJ and I beat Big Red. He starts smiling and laughing. Mr. Dillard and I are laughing too. Mr. Goldman yells, "Suckered and hornswaggled by a clever lil ole kid!"

They are still laughing as I go out the door.

The last Saturday at the dance studio I call Mama and she takes a jitney and meets me at the Adolphus Hotel for a nice supper. She explains that Miz Adams has taken a turn for the worse, so she can't make the graduation. She cries and says her loving spirit will be there.

I'd forgotten Miz Adams is a widow with no children; dependent on Mama for everything. I feel sorry for her not only being in a wheelchair, but also not having no close family. Miz Adams has sent a gift of $50.00, and Mama has added $50.00, so I have $100.00 when I start for home.

Money has no real meaning for me at this time of my life even though it seems most people think about money most of the time. $100.00 in 1935 is a right smart amount of money. I'm near about rich and don't even know it.

I am some puzzled why everybody puts so much store in graduation. Seems like a lot of foolishness to me.

Mr. Shaw, my homeroom and English teacher tells me as Valedictorian I will be expected to make some kind of speech, and he will help me write one.

"Thank you," I tell him. "I appreciate that, but I'm not planning on much of a speech at all."

I ask Grandma what I am supposed to day. She says, "Whatever comes to mind will be better than a written memorized talk."

I'm too ignorant to be afraid. The graduation is to start at seven p.m. and the dance with nearly all the mamas and papas present is to start in the gymnasium afterward.

Saturday afternoon we all soap up good with Lifebouy, put on our Sunday clothes — me in my new suit and shoes — load up in the Cadillac and head out for school. Woody, Saree and little Sonny come in their Ford.

There are 34 students in the graduating class. We walk across the stage as our names are called out, and the principal hands out the diplomas. We all wear gowns and caps.

When they read off the names of kids getting scholarships and other honors, I get a full four-year academic scholarship to Texas A&M. Rachel gets a full four-year scholarship to Texas Woman's University. I am disappointed that Billy Joe didn't get one. He and Rachel are about my only friends. I don't socialize hardly at all in school. I feel I'm needed at home and, in 1932 to 1935, there isn't a lot of socializing going on anyhow. Most kids are like me, needed for work.

When the principal asks the Valedictorian to address the audience, I step up behind the podium. As I look out upon the faces, I'm suddenly stricken with fright. I look down at the front row and see Grandma smiling with a prideful look on her face.

I ask my Heavenly Father for help, then say, "I'm nearly about as afraid as I was the time Billy Joe had a holt of me." When mamas and papas laugh, I'm not afraid anymore.

"I don't have any kind of prepared talk in mind," I say, "I'm just going to say what comes to my mind. I want to give thanks to all my teachers for all their patience and tolerance, especially Mr. Shaw, my homeroom and English teacher. I will always remember all of you with love. I want to give thanks to all the hard-working taxpayers in this district cause your hard earned money makes this school possible. I will never forget that."

As I look down on the front row, I see Grandma, Grandpa, Uncle Joe, Aunt Willie, Woody, Saree and little Sonny.

"Thank you for loving me as I surely love you. I give thanks to my mama, who is here with me in her loving spirit. I want to thank Mr. Dillard and Mr. Goldman for being so generous and treating me with such dignity and respect, even if I am a little ole horswaggling kid."

I hear a whoop and look out and see Mr. and Mrs. Dillard and Mr. and Mrs. Goldman laughing, fit to bust, giving me a thumbs up sign.

"If I have left anyone out, it's because my head is sorta spinning around," I continue.

"I save my last thanks for my great loving and merciful Heavenly Father. As I look out upon my neighbors, I see your goodness, your kindness and your love. It makes the second great commandment, Love Thy Neighbor, a wonderful commandment. My cup truly runneth over," I finish.

I walk to my seat and sit down. Grandma starts clapping and the audience joins in. I really feel the things I have said.

We take off our gowns and caps and go into the gymnasium for the dance. I have bought Rachel a nice gardenia corsage and she takes my arm as we walk in. I feel good in my new suit and shoes. Rachel and I start dancing to one of them electric phonographs, a nice slow number. She is amazed at how well I dance.

"Sonny," she says, "Is there anything you can't do?"

She is making me feel some embarrassed.

I dance a number with Grandma and she warns me something fierce about getting my lust up, whatever that means.

After the dance, we all start for our cars. I walk Rachel to her car and open the door for her. We are standing there alone and she asks me if I want to kiss her.

"I ain't never kissed no girl before; I don't know how."

She grabs me behind the head and pulls me to her and kisses me right on the mouth. I'm so flustered I turn and run for our car.

I hear Rachel call, "Sonnneee!"

Rachel grabs my hand and says, "Sonny, you told me you ain't never kissed a girl before. Well, I ain't never kissed a boy before. I ain't never knowed one I wanted to kiss before. Do you think I'm a hussy?"

"No, I'm just sorta mixed up what with being shy and bashful around girls."

She says, "I enjoyed the dance and you dance wonderfully well and I just felt romantic or crazy. I thought kissing you would be nice. Do you feel romantic affection for me?"

"I don't know. I feel something making me afraid. Let's be friends and ride together and study some on our feelings. We shore don't wanna mess up."

We agree to be friends and leave all romantic feelings out of our friendship. Rachel agrees to ride the Belle with me and TJ to Field Town the next Saturday.

I get in the Caddy and Grandma asks, "What was that all about 'tween you and Rachel?" She sounds sorta curious.

"Oh nothing," I say. "We were just saying goodnight and we're going riding Saturday."

"Sonny, you be careful. I need Joe to give you a talkin' 'cept he probably don't know how. You be good, ya hear?"

"Yes'm," I say. I can tell she is some suspicious about something.

Chapter 8

That Saturday morning, Rachel rides over on her mare Daisy for our trip to Field Town. We swap the saddle off Daisy and put it on the Belle. Boy is the Belle ever excited. She knows we are going riding and she is some rarin' to go. We go in the kitchen, have coffee and a fried apple pie.

Aunt Willie is so poohced out she's having a hard time cooking and house cleaning. She's due to foal most anytime.

Uncle Joe is having coffee and pie and laughing as usual. He says, "If this one's a boy, I'm gonna name it after papa Will. If the next one's a boy, I'm naming him after you, Sonny. The next one I'm gonna name after me, Joe."

Aunt Willie screams out, "There ain't gonna be a next one. I'm getting back on my appendicitis medicine."

Uncle Joe laughs and winks at me and says, "We be goin' to Galveston in style next time in a big Cadillac limousine. Willie's going to need a whole new outfit of clothes from Neiman's dry goods."

Aunt Willie starts laughing. "I declare, I wish this baby would come on. Feels like twins."

We all laugh and Rachel says how wonderful it will be if it is twins.

"Where's Miz Annie?" Rachel asks.

"She has a nearly all-day chore with the leghorns and seeing about her turkeys. Feeding, watering, doctoring and crating all the eggs, 30 dozen to the case, and we're getting about four cases a day.

Those leghorns lay a big white egg and they bring premium price – four dollars and fifty cents a case, 15 cents a dozen.

When we leave out for Field Town, the Belle and TJ feel so good that we have to let them long lope for about ten miles. When we pass Bailey's store, I tell Rachel we'll stop here coming back for a bite to eat. When we get to Field Town, we water the Belle and TJ then ride around through the crowd.

"My, what a beautiful pair of matched horses!" people say. I feel like I'm about to bust my buttons with pride.

Mr. Jean Manseur runs up. "My good friend Sonny and Mademoiselle Rachel." He kisses Rachel's hand.

"Do you speak French?" Rachel asks.

"Cajun French," he says.

Rachel jabbers something at him, and he exclaims, "You speak French and much better than me!"

"My mother was born in Paris; that's where Papa met and married her. Mama died in a flu epidemic, but I wanted to speak Mama's tongue in case I ever go to France to see my grandma and grandpa. I've been taking French lessons for a long time," Rachel explains.

Mr. Manseur laughs and yells, "Sonny, you one lucky boy. There is no more loving women in the world than French women."

I can feel my face turning red. I look at Rachel and her face is red but she's laughing.

"Thank you for the nice compliment, Mr. Manseur," she says.

He asks about Madame Annabelle and tells me to give her his best regards. I think him an unusually considerate good friend. We visit around with friends for a while and leave out long loping for home.

When we get to Bailey's Store, we get our usual sardines, rat cheese and box of saltines. Instead of big red sodas, we get Coca Colas. We sit on a bench on the front porch as a wagon pulled by two mules drives up.

There's a man and woman and three kids — look to be about five, eight and maybe ten. The two boys are oldest and the youngest is a small red-head girl with hair the color of a sweet 'tater. The man and woman go into the store while the kids sit in the wagon giving Rachel and me curious, solemn looks.

I speak to the kids. "How ya'll doin'?"

"We doin' jes fine," the eldest says.

I go into the store, get three big red sodas and three moon pies, come out and hand them up into the wagon. The kids look a little skittish.

"It would be more pleasurable for me if you would accept my treats," I say, handing the food to the kids. The oldest one says he reckons it would be all right.

I go back to the bench. Rachel and I eat our sardines, cheese and crackers, and drink our Coca Colas.

"These Cokes are a real high-class drink," I tell Rachel.

The door to the store slams open and the man comes out sorta sideways carrying a big cardboard box of groceries. I run over and say, "Here, let me give you a hand."

"Thank you," he says.

As we set the box of groceries in the wagon, his wife comes out and stands on the porch. He sticks his hand out and says, "I'm Ben Tuttle. This is my wife Nellie. This passel of younguns is our'n."

"My name is Sonny Jackson," I say, "And this is my friend Rachel Ward. Pleased to meet ya'll."

"Man," he says. "Them are some fine lookin' horses. I've heard about you from Mr. Goldman. He tells me I orta look you up, talk to you about your milk and egg operation."

"I know Joe Jackson, Miz Annie and Mr. Will," he continues. "I ain't seen 'em in five or six years. They were in the same fix I'm in. I understand they quit cotton and been making more money than any farmer in the county with milk and eggs."

"We been special blessed," I say. "Could I treat you and Nellie to a Coca Cola?"

"You shore can. I ain't never drank one before, always drank the biggest I could get for a nickel," he says. I go in and get two Coca Colas for Ben and Nellie. They look a little puzzled when they take a couple swallows then start laughing.

"I be doggone if that ain't a plumb fine drink," he declares.

"Sonny, I'm milking twelve Jerseys, but all we selling is the cream we skim off. We feed the clabber to the hogs and chickens. We ain't got but 40 ole' dominecker hens. Don't hardly have any eggs to sell. I doubt we bring in more 'n three or four dollars a week in cash money. I had 20 acres of cotton last year and didn't even make a bale, all that work for nothing. Boll weevils and the land is cottoned to death."

"Any advice you can give me, I shore would appreciate it. Mr. Goldman told me don't pay no attention to how old you are; he thinks you're something special."

"Thank you," I say. "Let's sit down here and study some on this."

"Ben," I say, "Do you have two or three real good friends you could form a sorta co-op with? Someone with 'bout the same number of milking jerseys? Your twelve jerseys are producing about 300 pounds of milk a day. With a little feed boost, some cottonseed cake or meal, you can increase to 400 pounds real quick. Whole milk is bringing a dollar fifty per hundred pounds, $15.00 per 1,000 pounds."

"If you have two co-op friends with about the same as you, you could be hauling 1,200 pounds a day to Dallas; $18.00 a day, seven days a week."

"Sonny," Ben says, "I got two brothers, Tom and Charlie, and we ain't got no money. Cotton farming has 'bout ruined us. We each got 160 acres of land left us by our grandpa."

"Ben, in a co-op partnership, you gotta get along real good; you sure cain't be tolerating no fusses or hard feelings or you can't make it," I say.

"Sonny, we all good Christians and get along real good. We are good, hard-working people; good farmers. Maybe times has gone by us some. We need somebody to steer us in the right direction. We shore ain't making any kind of decent living for our families,"

"Do you and your brothers have any money at all put aside?" I ask.

"I doubt we got $20.00 between us," says Ben.

"The main thing is you got to have a truck to get your milk to Dallas, that's first," I say. "The other things you need will come as you go. The way things are now, $15.00 to $18.00 a day between three families is a heap of money. Seems like a dream. Gas is nine cents a gallon so the expense won't hardly be nothing."

"Ben, if you promise me you and your brothers will work till you think you gonna die, I mean grind, grind and don't give up, I'll see can I get you a truck. You can pay me back as you're able. It'll take me about a week to arrange it. You can make a couple of milk runs with me, and I'll show you how to unload and get paid."

Ben starts to say something but I say, "Wait, Ben. Don't promise me nothing. Promise yourself. I leave Monday at two in the morning. You know where I live; can you be there? We'll be back by eight a.m. It makes for a long day. I been doing it every other day for some time. It don't bother me none; you get used to it."

"I'll be there, Sonny," says Ben. "We need to be moseying on home now. I'll see you Monday morning at two."

As we mount up and start for home, Rachel says, "How's he gonna get there at two in the morning?"

"Probably ride one of his mules, or walk."

"Sonny, I heard all that talk. How you gonna get Ben a truck?"

I shrug. "Something will come in my head."

When Rachel and I get home, we feed the Belle and TJ a nice pail of oats and brush them down real good. I check their feet and clean them with my Barlow knife.

"Sonny," Rachel remarks, "TJ and the Belle are about the smartest horses I've ever seen. They seem so eager to please you. I believe these horses are filled with love."

"Rachel, it's still early. Can you stay for supper?"

"It's our rump roast supper day. We have it every Saturday and Grandpa is the cook. He makes a gravy kinda like redeye, but instead of ham grease, he makes it out of roast drippings. There's mashed potatoes, green beans fresh out of the garden, squash and such. This is our special supper of the week. We'd be pleased to have you eat with us."

"How nice of you. I'll call Mammy BB and tell her I'm having my supper here."

When we go into the kitchen, Aunt Willie and Rachel start in talking. Uncle Joe is listening to some fool radio program and laughing — "Amos and Andy" — I believe it is. Grandpa is cooking supper, bragging about how he learned to cook from a French chef when he was in the war.

I ask Grandma if she can step into the bedroom a minute. She puts her sock darning aside and follows me.

"Grandma, can I see the ledger? I gotta do some figuring on something important. I'll explain it to you after supper."

I look at the balance the ledger shows, and I commence to calculating.

Rachel and Aunt Willie set the table, and Grandpa starts putting the vittles on it. Uncle Joe hollers out, "We eatin' high on the hog!"

Grandpa says the blessing, and the eating begins. My, is it ever good!

"Pa, you the best rump roast cooker there has ever been," Uncle Joe declares.

We all brag on Grandpa till he gets all swole up with his cooking pride. We're near about finished when I offhand remark, "I seen a Ford dealership has reopened for business. It went bust in '32, and has been vacant since."

"I didn't' know Henry Ford built tractors," I say.

Grandpa speaks right up, "I knowed ole Henry built tractors; he was from off a farm. He even builds airplanes. Ole Henry build most anything to help workin' folks." Grandpa's getting excited about ole Henry now.

"Why he pays all his hands five and six dollars wages a day for only ten hours work. He has a rule again' drinking and gambling. Henry Ford is one of the greatest men whatever lived. Why, him and Thomas Edison are best of friends."

"I didn't know all that, Grandpa," I say. "That's a mighty fine reason to like ole Henry. If I had know'd all that, I sure would be wantin' some kinda Ford machinery on the place. We could sure use another tractor, one with a blade and scoop to keep our lots clean of manure and to pull our manure spreader, wagons, and trailers. A smaller tractor, easier to get around with. With the wide front wheels, it sure would be easier to steer around; old Johnny is too big for such work."

"A Ford could help out with all the plowing and planting and other tractor work. We could shore use one of them V8 Ford pickups for all our light hauling chores," I add.

Grandpa says, "A V8 Ford's all ole Bonnie Parker and Clyde Barrow would drive. They even wrote ole Henry a letter thanking him for the V8. When they robbed a bank, couldn't no law catch them in one of 'em."

"Grandpa," I say, "You ain't never learned to drive no machinery. You reckon if we had one of them Fords, you'd take a notion to learn?"

"I shore would iffen it was a Ford," he shouts.

"Monday morning, you and Uncle Joe go to the dealership and check on what they got," I say.

Grandpa is all lit up now. He looks over at Grandma and asks, "How's our money lookin', Annie?"

Grandma is near smiling. "Will, we can manage."

"I believe I can maybe be a natural born Ford machinery man," says Grandpa.

Uncle Joe laughs and hollers, "Two in one family!"

I know I have the first part all settled; now I have to figure out the second problem about replacing Ole White Mule.

Aunt Willie is so big and uncomfortable that Rachel and Grandma clean up the kitchen. "When Miz Willie's time comes, I'll come and do the cooking and cleaning until she's back on her feet," Rachel says.

"Can you cook Rachel?" Grandma asks.

"I was the best cook in my home economics class. I can do canning, sew clothes, make quilts, or anything to do with homemaking."

Grandma says that shore would be good of her 'cause the chickens and turkeys didn't leave her much time for anything else.

"We may have to hire a woman to help out what with the baby coming," she finishes. We will have to see how things go.

Rachel and I walk down to the barn to saddle Daisy for her to ride on home.

"Sonny, I ain't never had no family 'cept Papa and Dr. Quinn, I mean a *real* family like you have."

"You just like me, Rachel. We been special blessed so let's be thankful. You got my family now, and we have each other."

"You mean that, Sonny? About us having one another?"

"I shore do."

"Sonny, this has been a wonderful day. All I got to say is you' something else."

The next day after church, Uncle Joe and Grandpa go back to the church after dinner to play softball. Uncle Joe loves to play softball. He plans on playing Saturday and Sunday afternoons on the church team. Grandpa is the team manager. For the first time in years they are enjoying playing again. We are moving on. That cotton might reach the moon, in time.

Ben is there at one-thirty Monday morning; he walked near about eight miles but said it weren't nothing. We load the milk cans out of the cooler house — 40 ten-gallon cans. It is over 3,200 pounds, 83 pounds of milk per can. We load four cases of eggs, then we have a fast cup of coffee and head out for Dallas. There is hardly anything on the road at this time of morning so we drive a steady 40 miles an hour. When we get to Schepp's milk company and unload, I get a purchase order for $50.84.

Milk has gone up to $1.55 per 100 pounds. I drive down to the market area just south of downtown Dallas and collect $18.00 cash for the eggs. We go into the all-night Market Café and have bacon and eggs.

While we're eating, I say, "Ben, I've just collected $68.84. A lot of smart hard work is involved here. It's simple, but not so simple an idiot can do it."

Ben's eyes are big and he is some excited. "Lawd, Sonny, I've seen it with my own two eyes. I know I can do it."

"Ben, we been near 'bout three years getting here; don't expect it to happen all at once. Remember, keep everything about your milk utensils sterilized and clean. Think about milk production, good feed, planting sudan where you been planting cotton, manure your corn, make silage, make good hay. Think all the time: good feed for my cows."

"Now out of this $68.00, we'll spend about 30 percent for good quality feed for our milkers and chickens. We'll net close to $40.00

Where Angels Roost

a load. Soon as the White truck place opens, we gonna go look at some new trucks."

At the truck place, the man tells me to go home and get my papa; I am too young to be wasting his time. I give him our phone number and tell him to get Annabelle Jackson on the line.

After a while, I can hear Grandma screaming in the phone, "Let me talk to Sonny."

The man hands me the phone. I notice another phone on his desk. I tell him to pick up the phone and listen in.

"Grandma," I say, "everything is fine. I'm over here at the White Truck Company. Ole White Mule is purt near smooth mouth and getting a little gray around the muzzle. I looked at the ledger. We got plenty enough for a new young White mule. It'll make us money and would be a nice surprise for Uncle Joe, sorta a new baby present."

After about a minute, Grandma screams, "We got the money, do what you think best. Don't let that man skin you."

Grandma thinks you have to scream into a phone; she can't believe it doesn't need lotsa voice power.

We hang the phones up. "I don't know if I'm running a truck lot or a mule lot," the man says. "I think I can interpret what was just said."

"I know you understand about the money," I say. "I have $500.00 here in my brogan. You get the balance when I pick the truck up."

I don't have much to pick from; he only has three trucks. I never was much good at tradin' and I don't want to drag it out for half a day, so we settle on a price in less than half an hour. The truck costs $1,275.00 cab and chassis. It even has a radio. That will be nice to listen to on our runs.

We drive down on West Commerce Street to Nabor's Trailers. I buy a sorta covered box to mount on the chassis. I insist on it being well insulated. In the hot summer months we can keep the milk and eggs in top quality condition. A 100 pound block of ice will keep that box cold for a week. The box costs $400.00, so the whole shebang costs $1,675.00.

I make arrangements to pick the truck up ready to go the following Thursday. We start for home and I tell Ben I will sell him Ole White Mule when I pick up the young White Mule.

"We'll talk price and payback arrangements then," I say. "I need to study some on how to work this out. Ben, I didn't intend to keep you away from home this long; it came to me sorta all at once about the truck."

"I ain't never seen the like of it. You movin' too fast for me, Sonny."

We laugh and sing "Ole Time Religion" going home. Ben has a nice bass voice. We harmonize real good.

When we pull down the lane to the house, Grandpa is rubbing wax on a shiny new red Ford three-quarter ton pickup. He's singing "San Antonio Rose" fit to bust. I have never seen him so happy.

"Sonny," he hollers out, "I done been driving the Ford tractor. It weren't hard to learn at all. We in cotton ten feet tall!"

"Grandpa, I knowed you could drive all along. All we needed was some Ford machinery for you. Now you got your own special red Ford tractor and red V8 Ford pickup with a radio to boot."

"Where is everybody," I ask.

"Oh, I forgot. Willie's time come. Joe and Annie has carried her to the hospital," Grandpa says.

I tell Ben to go ahead and drive old White Mule to his home and be back at two a.m. for another run.

Ben is turning around to head on out when we hear this car honking about a mile off. Uncle Joe tears down the lane and jumps out of the Cadillac screaming and hollering, "It's twins! Two boys! We haven' 'em like rabbits!"

He has a box of White Owl cigars and hollers, "I'm passing 'em out two a whack!"

He shoves two in my shirt pocket, hollers at Ben, "You jest in time, Ben."

He shoves six at Ben and says, "Two for you, two for Tom and two for Charlie."

He sticks two in Grandpa's shirt pocket and says, "Papa, you can smoke 'em in your pipe."

"I named them boys Will and Sonny. That don't rhyme, but it don't make no difference. Willie had a pretty hard time but she's fine and sleepy now," says Joe. He looks up at the sky and bellows out, "I love you, Lord Jesus! You answered my prayers!"

Grandpa says, "Amen to that, Joe."

Uncle Joe is laughing and crying. Ben and me are laughing and congratulating Uncle Joe. Uncle Joe yells out, "This is the happiest day of my life!"

Ben drives on down the lane and heads for home.

"First time I seen Ben in four or five years," Uncle Joe says. "A few years ago, him and his brothers was the best softball players in the county. I'm gonna see can I get 'em on our church team."

"Maybe next year," I say.

I go in the house to call Rachel. "If your offer to cook and help out is still good, come on over. Aunt Willie just had twin boys."

"How wonderful!" she squeals out. "I'll be right over."

She's there in about 15 minutes. I show her where everything is, and she gets right to work peeling potatoes and getting supper ready. Grandpa and I drive the new pickup to the hospital to see the babies and Aunt Willie. She's asleep and the babies aren't much to look at — little ole bitty wrinkled-up things. We are all so excited and happy for Uncle Joe and Aunt Willie.

When we sit down to supper, we're surprised at how well Rachel has prepared everything. We have chicken fried steak, mashed potatoes with lots of cream gravy, green beans, squash hot biscuits, iced tea — a real fine table full of eats.

"Rachel," Grandpa declares, "This is plum fine larruping good vittles. You done good."

"I 'preciate that, Grandpa" says Rachel.

I notice she calls him Grandpa instead of Mr. Will. I peep over and see Grandma smiling. I feel real good.

I pick the new young White Mule up that Thursday. I'm having some problems trying to do business on account of my age. "You got to be 21 years old in Texas to do business," the White Truck man explains, "Unless you have your minority liabilities removed."

He tells me to get a lawyer to fix this for me. I intend to ask Mr. Goldman to help.

I drive the new White mule and Ben follows in Ole White mule. I can tell right off this truck is more powerful, real tight and quiet, and handles wonderfully well. *A good investment*, I think.

Uncle Joe would be happy. Uncle Joe is plenty smart, but he doesn't have a good head for money and investments. He leaves all that to Grandma, and now me. Kinda like I'm not very good at machinery, milking, picking cotton and other such farm work. *We make a good team*, I think.

When we get to the house, Ben and I go in and sit down at the table. Rachel pours us a cup of coffee and sets a plate of doughnuts in front of us, then goes back to the sink where she's washing dishes. Grandma comes in, sits in her rocker by the fireplace. Ben's real quiet, acting sorta nervous. I've already figured out how I'm going to handle this.

I pull ten $20.00 bills out of my pocket and lay them on the table in front of Ben.

"Ben, I'm going to sell you the truck for $250.00, add $200.00 extra to get you boosted off. You don't pay back nothing for the first three months. Then pay what you can, as you can. Always keep a little reserve. I can tell from these few days with you that you are plenty smart. I know you'll do well."

Total silence for about a minute.

"Sonny," Ben asks, "How much interest you gonna charge? We gonna sign any papers or anything?"

"No interest, Ben. Why complicate things with paper signing between friends?"

"Sonny, you hardly know me."

"I got a feeling about you, Ben, and that's all that matters."

Ben looks up at the ceiling then looks me right in the eye.

"Why, Sonny? Why do this for me? I need to know."

After about a minute, I say, "I don't know, Ben. It's just some feeling inside me."

Ben gets up from the table, reaches his hand out and we shake. When he starts out the door, I say, "God bless, Ben."

Ten years later, the Tuttle brothers have the biggest dairy in East Texas, milking over 300 Holsteins. That was my feeling.

Rachel comes up behind me and kisses me on the cheek. Grandma stands in front of me smiling and saying, "I know what feeling you got inside you."

CHAPTER 9

In a few days Aunt Willie comes home from the hospital with baby Will and baby Sonny. We all wait on her hand and foot and commence to spoiling and loving them babies something awful. Uncle Joe can't leave 'em alone. He is holding them, singing and laughing all the time. He know'd all the time he was cut out to be a natural born papa man.

Rachel is making a mighty fine hand with her cooking and cleaning. She is there every day from early morning till late at night. I am happy for her being in the house all the time, but kinda uneasy. I'm concerned about her seeing our lack of refinement — the way we talk, our old-fashioned ways.

I mention this to her and she says, "Sonny, I have seen the goodness, honesty, love and humor in this family. Refinement, the way I see it, is in this family. I'll take your family anytime over some ole uppity refinement." I feel good at hearing her say this. We're riding two and three hours purt near every day; we sure have that pleasure in common.

One morning Rachel tells me her papa Hank, partner with Dr. Quinn, has bought the meanest big black stallion up in Kentucky. He wants him for his bloodlines.

They shipped him down from Kentucky, but he is so fiercely mean, they have to keep him chained most of the time. He's already hurt two stable hands and they can hardly handle him. Her papa is fixin' to get rid of him 'cause he thinks the big stallion is mentally deranged. "Crazy, evil, full of Satan," her papa has said.

It's late summer and I've just turned 16. I'm up to five foot eight, but still only weigh about 115 pounds — kinda on the skinny side. I'm hoping for some more growth. I don't much care, 'cepting Rachel is nearly 16 and a half, and she's going to be bigger than me if I don't hurry up.

I'm a little worried 'cause all the boys and men look at her all the time. What with her black wavy hair and big beautiful brown eyes, and the way she's filling out, she is looking more like a woman than a skinny girl. In my eyes, she's a mighty fetching girl-woman. I tell her she is so purty I'm jealous and proud at the same time 'cause of the looks she is getting.

Rachel laughs and tells me she already has her man decided on; she's just waiting for the future. I'm pleased to hear this but concerned about the future. In this day and time, it's common for girls Rachel's age to be marrying up with men 30 to 35 years old. Most all men are some older than the women; we're the exception. That's the way it is in 1935.

The Belle and TJ both love and trust people, especially family. I built a board fence and painted it white like I'd seen in pictures of horse farms in Kentucky. The fence is around about ten acres of good grass directly in front of the house. I like looking out and seeing them and that way they can see all the comings and goings of people at the house. Every time I come out, they let out low knickers — their way of talking to me.

Grandpa's happy with his Ford tractor, but he's always worried about it getting tired. Uncle Joe tells his Papa that a tractor never gets tired; you don't have to stop and let it blow a while. It's not like a team of mules. Grandpa's uncertain about this. He doesn't want his tractor overworked.

We have five mules in retirement: our three and Amos Jones's two. Laudie and Maudie are nearly 20 years old, and our three ladies close behind. They're living a happy life of leisure now.

Time is going by and I've decided to delay my entry into Texas A&M for one year until September 1936. As I'm only 16, there's no problem with this.

I'm positive I want to go to a military school. Anything military holds great appeal for me since Grandpa was in the Spanish American

War, there were Parkers at San Jacinto and we even had one ancestor killed at the Alamo. Military runs in our family heritage.

Rachel decides to delay her enrollment at Texas Woman's University until the fall of 1936, so we will graduate at the same time. I still feel needed at the farm one more year, sorta to get it over the hump. I'm also filled with fear about being away from TJ, the Belle and my family.

About the first part of September on a Sunday after church and dinner, Grandpa, Uncle Joe and Aunt Willie return to church to play in the softball league. It's some kinda hot, nearly 100 degrees. Grandma, Rachel and I are taking an afternoon nap on the sleeping porch.

All of a sudden I hear the most hair-raising horrible scream — an unearthly scream. I think I'm having a nightmare.

When I jump up and look in the direction of the scream, I see a monster black horse chasing TJ and the Belle around the enclosure in front of the house. The big black horse has his mouth wide open showing his teeth. He's chasing TJ, snapping at him, and letting loose with a nightmarish scream. My hair's standing up I'm so shocked.

I slam out the screen door and see a softball bat lying on the porch that Grandpa has been making for his team. I snatch it up and start for the pasture. I leap over the board fence and see TJ and the big black horse standing on their back legs flailing at one another with their front legs. Belle's running in a circle screaming and kicking at the black horse.

The sounds they are making are hideous. I'm about 100 feet from TJ and the black horse when I see that the big black horse is now astride TJ — front legs on one side and back legs on the other side. All that weight has TJ going down, and that black horse is biting and tearing at TJ like a mad wolf.

I run up screaming and swing the softball bat at the black horse's head, but only hit a glancing blow. Then the big Satan-looking monster comes at me with his mouth open. I kinda step to my left and swing as hard as I can, right at his mouth.

The bat hits solid and I see white things fly out with some blood. He screams louder and rears up. The bat is stuck in his mouth as he jerks me down, but it breaks free seconds later.

As I'm rolling around on the ground, he rears up and starts down on me with his front feet. I scramble when he comes down again and he grazes my head. I rise up on my knees, grab the bat and swing as hard as I can at his right front leg.

I feel it hit solid. He screams and rears again. I manage to roll out of his way when he comes down and see his right leg buckle. I swing hard again at the same leg. His scream is even more shrill and piercing. When he hesitates, I can see I've hurt his right front leg bad.

He puts his head down and starts for me. I'm on my feet now but can see blood running out of his mouth and bloodshot eyes. I swing that bat with all I have right above his big flared nostrils. His right front leg is buckled and hanging loose. He stops and I swing right at his eye. His eye pops out then he lets out more of a groan than a scream. I swing again and hit him right between the eyes. He stands there and starts quivering and shaking all over.

When I swing again and hit the left side of his head, he goes down on his side and starts kicking. I throw the bat to one side. This all happens in less than a minute.

I'm conscious of Grandma and Rachel running up to me crying and screaming. Two men are running from the Quinn Farm across the pasture.

TJ's almost up. I run to him and pull on his halter and start talking to him. He's bleeding something fierce around his neck and shoulders. He manages to get up but is shaking. I start guiding him to his stall and tell Rachel to get on the phone for Dr. Quinn. If he doesn't' answer, then she's to get in the pickup and go find him.

I tell Grandma to get some clean towels and a bucket of hot water. The Belle is still screaming, running circles around and kicking at the dying big black stallion.

As TJ limps toward his stall I hear a gunshot, figuring that one of the men from the Quinn Farm has finished off the big black stallion. I get TJ into his stall and turn on the light. He has a dull look in his eyes. He's bleeding from his neck and shoulders where the black horse has chewed on him. Grandma brings the water and towels and I begin washing him off — I can see he is cut up pretty bad.

Rachel rushes in saying the doctor is on his way. In a few minutes, Dr. Quinn arrives with his bag of vet supplies. He takes a big rubber tube out of his bag, then a white pill nearly as big as a banty egg. He sticks the pill in the tube, the tube into TJ's mouth, takes a big breath, and blows into the tube.

He says the pill will sedate TJ some. He tells me to hold his head and talk to him to calm him down. He tells Grandma to see if she can quiet the Belle some. He tells Rachel to drive to his place, get her papa, an IV stand, and two gallons of saline solution. Then he gets a large curved needle out of his bag and what looks to be some silk cord.

"We have to stop the bleeding, keep him from going into shock," he says.

TJ seems fairly calm as I'm stroking and talking to him. Dr. Quinn commences to stitch and close up the cuts. Some of the cuts are small chunks that can't be sewed up, so he puts bandages on these with some kind of salve that smells somethin' terrible.

Rachel and her papa come in and Dr. Quinn sets up an IV on a tall stand, inserts a needle into TJ's neck, and starts the saline solution. Hank, Rachel's papa, says he'd better go get the tractor and drag that killer horse off. "I'll see if I can get a hole dug big enough for him," he says.

TJ seems sorta sleepy. Dr. Quinn says he's lightly sedated and that the IV will take about an hour. He wants a clean blanket to cover him to keep his body temperature from dropping. There's total silence for a few minutes.

"Dr. Quinn," I say, "I'm sorry I had to kill your horse. But I didn't know what else to do. He was tearing like crazy at TJ."

"There's no greater love than a person willing to lay down his life for what he loves," Dr. Quinn says. "This is one of the greatest examples of courage I have ever known. It's a miracle you weren't killed. I can hardly believe a slender boy like you could kill a 1,300 pound horse with a softball bat. A terrible horse trying to kill you."

"In France, during the war, Hank was willing to lay down his life for me. That's why we're closer than brothers, the best of friends, and always will be; we love one another because of that. You and TJ are like that."

"Jehovah was with him," Grandma says. "God is always with those who love him."

Dr. Quinn adds, "Amen to that."

I've been standing in the shadows by TJ's head. Grandma's been holding a powerful battery light while Dr. Quinn is doing his stitching and bandaging. After we cover TJ with the blanket, Dr. Quinn shines a little pencil light into TJ's eyes.

"I'll come every two hours to check on him; I believe he's out of danger of shock."

Grandma turns off the battery light, then Dr. Quinn says, "Son, come here. Let me get a good look at you. Rachel talks about you a lot." I walk over and he puts his arms around me, hugs me and says, "You're one brave young man."

I notice that he has on a pair of those wire-framed glasses and a cap like we all wear. Those caps are so elegant and stylish even girls and women wear them. You only see a few old men and golfers like Ben Hogan wearing them now.

All at once, he takes his glasses off, turns me completely around and stands me directly in front of him. He has a most puzzled look on his face. When he takes his cap off and runs his fingers through his hair, I notice his hair is full and black and sorta curly. His eyes are light blue. His face is very nice. "Sonny, what is your birth date?"

"August seventh, 1919."

"Is your mother in Dallas?"

"Yes, sir."

"How about your father?"

"My papa died in a flu epidemic before I was born."

Dr. Quinn takes Grandma's hand and says, "Miz Annie, I need to talk to you in private. Sonny, you and Rachel stay here with TJ."

He and Grandma start for the house. I watch, and the instant they go into the house, I run for the window and stoop under it to listen to what is said. Being hot, the window is open, so it's like I'm in the room.

Dr. Quinn blurts right out, "Miz Annie, that's my son out there. I'd like an explanation please."

"Jonathan, I've been suspicious for years and I believe you're right. You came home from France in early December 1918. A few days after you went to Harvard in February 1919, Mary left home here and moved to Dallas," she says.

"All of these dates, years and months make things right. This is a very happy day for me — and a very frightful one. I feel like shouting with joy and at the same time I'm more afraid than when I was on the battlefields of France," he said.

Dr. Quinn runs out of the house, gets in his big black Packard, fumbles around, then bends over and starts writing. He runs back into the house and lays some small pieces of paper on the kitchen table. "Miz Annie, this is for starters. I'll be back in two hours to check on TJ. If you'll give me Mary's address and phone number, I'd appreciate it."

He walks back out to his Packard and drives off. I come from the window where I've been listening and peeping, and walk into the kitchen. Grandma's face is white; her eyes are sorta staring into space.

"Grandma, I was listening out the window. I heard everything."

She looks at me calmly and asks, "What are your thoughts?"

"Grandma, I don't know. Since I've never had a papa, I kinda think with Dr. Quinn, it may be nice. I liked him at first sight. But I'll have to study on it some."

I pick up the pieces of paper from the table. They are two checks — one to Mama for $5,000.00, and one to me for $5,000.00.

"Gosh almighty, Grandma! This is a small fortune. He sure means what he says about making things right. Money's not everything, but it's a good generous start. Mama will be pleased," I say as I lay the checks back on the table. "Don't give him Mama's address or phone number. I believe I've figured out what's to be done."

"Grandma, let me get your nerve medicine for you. Take a big dose, then a good dip of snuff to calm you down. I don't believe your nerves can stand any more excitement in one day."

"Good thinking, Sonny."

When I go back to the barn to be with TJ, Rachel is sitting on the stool in the corner. TJ's standing still and quiet. Belle's still acting up some so I pet her and talk to her and she quiets down. Rachel comes over, puts her arms around me, lays her head on my shoulder and starts crying.

"Sonny, I was so afraid I nearly died."

She raises her head up and looks me right in the eyes. My head starts spinning and my heart's beating so hard I think it's gonna bust.

We sit down beside TJ and I say, "Let's just sit here and wait for Dr. Quinn."

A short while later, Dr. Quinn comes in with a stethoscope around his neck. He listens to TJ's heart and lungs, shines a light in his eyes, checks the stitches and bandages, and says he's one lucky little horse. He feels he'll be good as new in a couple weeks.

"Rachel told me this small thoroughbred TJ is a fooler, that he has an extra long stride and can really move. She said you won a match race with him back in February. When he gets better, bring him over to the farm and let Hank check him out."

I walk right up to Dr. Quinn and look him in the eye and say, "I know who you are."

He takes his glasses off and says, "What do you think about it?"

"It'll take some getting used to, but I believe I'm gonna like the idea."

He smiles and says, "I hope so."

Rachel is laughing and hollers, "I've suspected it all along. I'm happy for ya'll."

Dr. Quinn puts his arms around both of us and says, "This is my lucky day."

We walk to the house and go into the kitchen where Grandma's sitting in her rocker with a calm serene look on her face. The nerve tonic and a nice dip of Honest Garret have worked their miracles.

Grandma looks at Dr. Quinn, and says, "Jonathon, I ain't giving you Mary's phone number or address. I got to do some thinking on this." She looks at me and nods.

"Miz Annie, whatever you feel is right. I'm filled with fear that Mary may hate me. I wouldn't blame her."

After a minute, Grandma says, "I don't believe so. There's no hate in Mary — never has been; never will be. Only goodness in that girl. She named Sonny 'Jonathon" same as you. What does that say about how Mary feels? I know in my heart things will be good, 'cause we have an angel amongst us."

Tears are rolling down Dr. Quinn's cheeks. "Thank you, Miz Annie," then he turns to me and says, "Sonny, can you find it in your heart to call me 'Papa'? My emotions are churning me so I can hardly think, but that's in my mind."

"Yes, sir. I feel the same as you. I'll be proud to call you my papa."

When Uncle Joe, Grandpa and Aunt Willie come in from playing softball, they can tell something big has happened.

Uncle Joe in his strong bass voice bellows out, "What's going on?"

Grandma says, "It's a long story, Joe. I'll tell you later. Main thing is Sonny killed Dr. Quinn's big black stallion with Will's softball bat. He was attacking TJ. By a miracle, Sonny wasn't hurt none."

Uncle Joe freezes up. He turns white, then red. "By doggies! Anything happen to Sonny you can start digging my hole." He kinda smiles and continues, "With a softball bat? Boy, you somethin' else!"

I get Papa Quinn by the hand and walk out to his Packard with him.

"Papa," I say, "Don't worry, I'll take care of everything."

He hugs me. "I believe you will."

He starts out of the drive. "God bless," I say.

Chapter 10

Monday morning after breakfast, Grandpa is out at the milking barn. Uncle Joe has not gotten back from the milk run. I tell Grandma I'm going to Dallas to fetch Mama back. I say I might be gone three or four days. I am also going by the bank to open accounts with the checks Papa Quinn has given us.

"Tell Uncle Joe I'll make it up to him on the milk runs. Try to explain the best you can about Mama, Papa Quinn and me. Grandma, don't worry. I'll take care of Mama. Take your tonic if you feel a spell coming on," I add.

I put a change of underwear and socks in a sack, load up the Caddy, and head out for the bank. I go into the bank lobby and look around for Mr. Goldman, then ask the teller to fetch him for me and tell him it is Sonny — he'll know.

In a few minutes Mr. Goldman comes out of his private office smiling and hollers, "My good friend Sonny; what a nice pleasure! How can I help you?"

"Mr. Goldman, I need to open an account here at your bank."

"Wonderful. Come back here to my office and I'll handle this personally."

He sure knows how to make you feel important. "How do you want the account set up?"

I tell him I don't know anything about bank accounts as I ain't never had one. I want the account in Mama's name, Mary Jackson, and in my name, Jonathon Jackson.

"Fine, fine," he says. "A joint account." He asks a few questions, address, phone number and such. "How much do you want to open with?"

I hand him the two checks and say, "Ten thousand dollars less one thousand I need to take with me." He looks at the checks a long time.

"Something wrong?" I ask.

"No, the checks are as good as the many more I've seen from Dr. Quinn. This is such an enormous amount of money."

He looks at me with a kindly look on his face and says, "I've known Jonathon Quinn since he was born. I consider his father Doc Quinn my best friend. I knew your mother well too and I've known Will and Annie Jackson all our lives. Sonny, I look at these checks and I look at you sitting here. I think I know what's happened. I knew the first time when I seen you at the races at Field Town. All I can say is you are one fortunate young man."

"Thank you, sir."

I leave the bank and head for Dallas. On the way, I study and decide on what I'm planning to do with Mama. I pull up in front of the Swiss Avenue mansion, walk up the long walk and ring the doorbell. After about a minute, Mama opens the door. She has the most puzzled frightened look on her face and says, "Sonny, is anything wrong?"

"No, everything's fine. We need to tell Miz Adams you're leaving, coming home."

"My, I don't understand! Miz Adams will need a few days to replace me and I'm not sure I want to go home."

"Mama, I know everything. If you love me, you'll do as I'm asking you to do."

"Oh Sonny!" she starts crying. "The shame, the disgrace, I don't think I can stand to go home. I don't believe I can ever live it down."

"Mama, believe me, please, everybody knows it. There's no shame, no disgrace, nothing but love for you. Papa Quinn is waiting for you."

"Papa Quinn!" she cries out.

"Come, let's tell Miz Adams you're leaving. She can call a job agency to send someone out. You can help her with your replacement," I say. "Doggone I wish I hadda brought Grandma's nerve tonic! You could shore use it."

She smiles and asks, "Mama still taking her nerve tonic? How 'bout the Honest Garret?"

"When she feels the need. Come on, Mama! Where's that Parker-Jackson courage? Take a deep breath. Suck in a big breath of pride. You have nothing to be ashamed for," I say.

"You're right, Sonny. I have you to be proud of."

"No, you have *you* to be prideful for. Come, let's talk to Miz Adams."

We arrange for the job agency to send someone out. Mama agrees to help with the job qualifications and to explain what duties will be required.

Miz Adams is some upset but I explain to her that Mama is needed at home. I thank her for being good to Mama and tell her we will visit often. She settles down some and we tell her we are in no hurry to leave, however long it takes to find her a replacement.

I load Mama in the Caddy for a trip to Neiman Marcus dry goods in downtown Dallas. We go in and I get directions for ladies apparel. I tell the saleswoman to outfit Mama in all the latest women's finery; several of each, money is no matter. Mama has a shocked, surprised look on her face.

"Mama, you a rich woman, thanks to Papa Quinn. You got $10,000.00 and we gonna make up for being without."

After about four hours of shopping, we walk down two blocks to the Adolphus, have a good dinner, then have all the finery from Neiman's delivered out to Miz Adams's.

I ask around about one of them beauty shops where they do things to women's hair and such. We find one nearby. I go in and tell the lady Mama wants her hair fixed beautiful, manicure, the whole shebang.

"The whole shebang?" the lady asks. "A pedicure too?"

"What's that?" I say.

"We do the feet."

"I ain't never heard of no such thing."

She says rich people have their feet manicured.

"Well, Mama's plenty rich, she just ain't used to it yet. She ain't gonna be going barefoot, but go ahead on."

"Do you want the eyebrows plucked?"

"No, don't mess with the eyebrows; we aint' uppity rich," I say.

The lady starts laughing, then asks, "Ya'll from East Texas?"

"Yessum. Where you from?"

She laughs again. "I'm from down near Tyler. Don't concern yourself about your mama. She don't need much to make her more beautiful than she already is."

The lady tells me I might as well go see a movie or something; Mama will be there for two or three hours. I walk up to the Majestic and see "Mutiny on the Bounty." After the movie, I go back to pick Mama up.

When I walk in, Mama stands right in front of me. "Well, what do you think?"

"Mama, I don't know. You have always been the most beautiful woman in the world to me. I don't think a son can be the judge of his mama's beauty."

I pull out a big roll of money and asked the lady from Tyler how much we owe.

"Six dollars plus tip," she says.

"Plus tip? What's that?"

She explains that for people in her line of work, if you are pleased with their service, you give a little extra.

"How much would a reasonable tip be?"

"Twenty-five cents, or a more generous amount would be fifty cents."

"I'm happy you explained this to me. We ain't used to havin' money. Now I know how to tip. Who else do you tip?"

"Waitresses, cab drivers, bell boys, anyone who provides personal service," she says.

I give her a dollar extry and always remember what I learned from this East Texas lady about being generous.

The next morning we talk to two people who have been sent out from the job agency. Mama and Miz Adams settle on a nice looking young lady so we can head out for home tomorrow. This afternoon, Mama goes to the medical arts building to have her teeth cleaned and polished. We are ready for the big reunion. I hope Grandma has prepared Grandpa Will and Uncle Joe for our arrival.

The next morning we carefully pack all the finery from Neiman Marcus into the trunk and back seat of the Cadillac. We have nearly a full load. An abundance of nice clothes seems to make most women happy and put 'em in good spirits. Mama is no exception.

She has on a purty black dress with black high-heeled shoes, so with her black hair and white complexion, it makes her light blue eyes stand out. She has on the gold locket I have given her last Christmas. Her hands look nice what with the manicure. Sure doesn't look like she's been washing many dishes at Miz Adams's.

I figure Papa Quinn is gonna have one of them heart palpitation surprises since he hasn't seen her in nearly 16 years. She isn't too old, only 34, and has a high-class, dignified look about her. I calculate Papa Quinn to be about 39. To a 16 year old like me, that's getting borderline old.

As we drive for home, I'm puzzling on how I'm gonna manage this reunion with Papa Quinn and the rest of the family. When we reach the lane to the Quinn Farm, it comes to me all at once.

I drive up to Papa Quinn's big, beautiful two-story red brick house with white columns in the front. First time I've been here. A big imposing Southern mansion kind of place. I pull around a circular drive, stop directly in front, and start blowing the horn. I look over at Mama. She's some upset.

"Sonny, what has come over you?" she cries out.

A colored lady comes out the front door, looks at us, then goes back inside. After about two minutes, here comes Papa Quinn. He walks sorta quick, stiff like, with a curious look on his face. I get out of the car as he comes near.

He comes up, hugs me and says, "Where have you been? I've been over several times to see about TJ. Miz Annie won't tell me diddly squat."

"I got Mama here."

I go around the car, open the door, and say, "Mama, come here."

I take her hand, lead her around to stand in front of Papa Quinn. He doesn't have his cap on but he runs his fingers through his hair.

They stand and look at one another for what seems a long time. Mama sticks her hand out. He takes it, but instead of a shake, he holds on to it.

"I see you still run your fingers through your hair when you're nervous," Mama says. That kinda breaks the ice.

"A lifelong thing I can't help," Papa says. "Mary, you look more beautiful than I can remember; I'm practically speechless. Right now, I just want to look at you. The last time I seen you — you looked like a cute girl. Now, I don't know."

"No talk of the past," I say. "Only the here and now, maybe the future."

I take Mama's hand, lead her back around the car, open the door, and sit her down. Then I open the driver's side, and tell Papa Quinn, "Get in. The car's full of gas, go driving. Drive a long time. That way you can talk in private and get reacquainted. I'll wait here for you."

"Fine with me. How 'bout you, Mary?"

"A wonderful suggestion."

They both smile. I'm beginning to feel some good about this predicament. Papa Quinn calls out, "Go on in the house. Mammy BB will fix you a snack," and they drive off. As I go up the walk to the front door, Mammy BB comes out to welcome me. She's all smiles and looks most happy. Hard to tell her age, anywhere between 40 and 60.

"Come right on in, Mista Sonny. We headin' for the kitchen. See can I find you somethin' special. I know you ain't never seen me just like I ain't never seen you, but I know you right off. I go to the same Baptist church with Woody and Saree. We sing in the choir together. Woody done told me all about you. He think you special.

"Miz Rachel, she just like my baby. I be managing this house 'for she born. I came here when Mr. Jonathon was a little boy. I know Miz Rachel got a good feeling about you. I ain't never see Mr. Jonathon as excited as he is right now. He might be trying to hoss doctor some poor human while he's so fuzzleheaded."

As we go into the house, I see a big formal looking parlor on one side of a winding staircase, a huge formal dining room on the other side. It is much larger and more elegant than the Swiss Avenue mansion of Miz Adams. I'm pleased at the idea of a papa who lives in such elegance.

Mammy BB leads me into a big kitchen near twice the size of ours. Another colored lady is fussin' around the stove.

Mammy BB explains, "I have two other girls I oversee. This a big house. Takes lots of help." She speaks to the girl, "Come here, Ruth. Meet Mr. Sonny."

Ruth smiles real big and says, "Welcome, Mr. Sonny."

"Thank you, Ruth. I sure never knew Rachel lived in such elegance. She shore don't act in the least bit uppity."

"Praise the Lord she don't," Mammy BB cries out. "Sonny, sit right here at the table. Let me fetch you a bowl of peach cobbler with some ice cream. I got fresh coffee made."

I take a bite of the cobbler and ice cream, then take a swallow of the coffee. "This is good rooster coffee," I say.

"Rooster coffee? What kind of coffee that be?"

"Mammy BB, you know early in the morning, near 'bout sun up, we got a big ole dominecker rooster what rares his head back and lets out a piercing crow. Sounds like a bugle blowing reveille. It wakes you up sudden like. Well, this good strong arbuckel coffee jolts you awake right brightly so we call it rooster coffee."

Mammy BB and Ruth start laughing. "Rooster coffee, I say."

After my cobbler, ice cream and coffee, Mammy BB says, "Come with me. I want you to see the library. You being a young man, you really 'preciate this."

We go into a huge, high-ceilinged room, all paneled with beautiful light wood, floor to ceiling windows with a French door and balcony overlooking a large rose garden and other kinds of landscaping. The room has two walls of bookshelves. Must be 1,000 books or more. Leather sofas and chairs are arranged in front of a huge marble fireplace.

Two extra large wall paintings of horses catch my eye. I move up close and look at one. A small copper plate identifies a rather large black thoroughbred as Sir Barton. The other one is a large red thoroughbred identified as Gallant Fox, with Earl Sandee, his jockey.

Mammy BB says, "Mr. Jonathon and his papa Mr. Doc both love horses. Like Miz Rachel's papa, Mr. Hank."

I tell Mammy BB how much I appreciate her goodness toward me.

"Sakes alive, Mr. Sonny! I knows a young gentleman when I sees one. It's my pleasure to be doing nice things for such as you."

I smile and say, "Mammy BB, you just like Woody. One of the nicest people ever was. Do you live in this house?"

"No. I got my own special quarters over the carriage house. Motorcar house now. Real fine quarters. Water closet, bathing room, even my own small kitchen with stove and electric icebox. I even got an electric Victrola with lots of gospel records.

"I has a big Emerson radio. I got a right smart amount of money in the bank. I ain't never found me no man what wasn't no count. I is still looking. I ain't too old yet. If you meet up with a good one, put in a good word for me," she says.

"I surely will."

"Miz Rachel won't be home 'fore dark. She runs for your house early every morning. Say she needed to help till Miz Willie back on her feet. She sure feeling important. I think it's good for her. Mr. Hank left yesterday for the racetrack, the fair grounds, down to New Orleans, with eight horses for the race season. He be gone 'bout three weeks, then he start getting ready for Hot Springs — the big race, the Arkansas Derby."

At this information, my heart starts fluttering all at once. I'm stricken with a desire to see about TJ. I have to learn patience. I have to concentrate on Mama and Papa's predicament. I have to figure out how I can help settle this problem.

I know I have my very own special papa and I am beside myself with joy. A special kind of papa: a war hero, a hoss doctor, a human doctor at the hospital in town. I know in my own heart he is a good man. I believe Grandma is right; there really is an angel looking out for us.

Mama is perfectly special too. I know two such special loved ones have to be brought together. I have been saying my prayers at bedtime with more feeling than just flying through my "lay me down to sleeps." I have been giving out with lots of gratitude for my blessings — possibly begging some.

Mammy BB tells me to go into the library, lay down on one of the sofas, and take a nap. She'll call me when Mama and Papa return. It has already been nearly two hours. I think the longer the better. I go into the library and lay down. I must be all tuckered out 'cause I go right off to sleep.

Voices wake me up. I can tell by the light through the French doors it is late afternoon. We arrived about ten that morning. I figure they've been driving nigh on to six hours. I rouse myself up and go into the kitchen where Mama and Papa Quinn are eating sandwiches.

They're smiling, laughing, seem like old friends.

Mammy BB cries out, "Rooster coffee! Cobbler with ice cream comin' up. Heh,heh. Rooster coffee."

"What kind of coffee is rooster coffee?" Papa Quinn asks.

Mama laughs and says, "I'll tell you about it later. My Papa Will started that years ago."

Mammy BB says, "Miz Mary, you shore did turn out to be one handsome woman. I remember you coming here years ago. You shore look different now. Most handsome."

"Thank you for the nice compliment, BB."

Papa's eyes are kinda bright. I can tell he's all nervous, excited like.

"Papa," I say, "Day after tomorrow, Saturday, would you like for just us two to ride over to Field Town? You need to be in pretty good shape; it's 40 miles round trip. You can ride the Belle. I don't know if TJ can manage so soon. If not, I'll ride Rachel's mare Daisy. We could get better acquainted, and you could have supper with us."

He kinda hesitates a bit, then says, "Splendid! Splendid idea."

"We'll leave out about eight," I say. "Mama, we need to get moving on. We got big doings facing us."

A sad look comes over Mama's face, a fearful look. "Don't be afraid, Mama. We about got this whipped."

Papa walks us down to the car and says, "I'll be over to see about TJ tomorrow. I'll be ready for our ride Saturday."

We start for home, five minutes away, and I'm barely creeping along. "Mama, tell me what happened."

In a real quiet voice Mama says, "Sonny, he asked me to marry him. He actually proposed. I've had this dream for years. I think I must be dreaming now. How can this be? Dreams never come true."

"Mama, dreams do come true. What did you tell Papa?"

"I told him to give me some time. We need to consider the sacredness of our commitment. He told me to take my time. He's hoping by Christmas. I told him by then I'd know positively."

"I hope maybe sooner."

"I've always loved Jonathon. I've never once thought of any other man," then she pauses. "A mother shouldn't talk to her son like this. I hope you understand."

"I do."

We pull down the lane to the house. Dog is barking, so I know everyone has been warned of our arrival. I open the car door, take Mama's hand, walk through the gate, open the door to the kitchen, and we go inside.

Grandma, Grandpa, Uncle Joe and Aunt Willie are all standing in a row. Rachel's off to one side. She has never seen Mama.

Grandpa comes and hugs Mama, kisses her on the cheek, and says, "Welcome home, my baby girl!"

He takes his bandanna out of his overall pocket and commences to blowing his nose. He's smiling.

Grandma hugs and kisses Mama, and says, "Good to have you back home."

Aunt Willie kisses Mama and says, "Mary, I got twin boys since I seen you. Sonny was Papa Will's only grandson, now he has three."

Uncle Joe looks at Mama, smiles, and bellows out, "Hallelujah! Sister Mary, you jest like the prodigal son coming home 'ceptin' you a girl, and you ain't been doing no debauchery or squandering no inheritance or wallering in no hog pen. I ain't got no rang for your finger; don't look like you need any robes. We ain't gonna kill no fatted calf but come Saturday, we gonna eat a big rump off of one."

At Uncle Joe's fine welcome, we start laughing. We laugh till tears are coming out. I love my Uncle Joe. He comes through when he's needed. A good laugh works its miracles.

Laughing, Rachel walks up to be introduced. "Mama, this is Rachel Ward, a very special friend."

Where Angels Roost

Mama stops laughing, looks at Rachel, then looks at me, then Rachel again. She puts her arms around Rachel, kisses her on the forehead, and says, "Me too." Whatever that means.

Uncle Joe puts a record on the Victrola, "Ole Time Religion," our favorite. We are singing and stomping so loud, I bet we can be heard near 'bout three miles. I am so happy, I'm near swooning.

Grandma shows Mama her bedroom. She is some impressed with all the improvements to the house since she has lived here.

"Hurry," I tell her. "Get your stuff unloaded. Change clothes."

I want her to see the Belle and TJ.

I get some brown sugar and dried apples. I want Mama to give them their treats so they'll be friends. We run to the barn, and TJ and the Belle are some excited. They are nickering, snuffling, looking for their treats. TJ's stitches look like zippers where Papa has stitched around on his neck and shoulders. He looks like he is good as before, but I'm not sure about riding him to Field Town in two days.

I'm already studying on how I can work him somehow into entering the Arkansas Derby. I know nothing about what is required. I'm hoping Papa and Mr. Hank Ward can figure this out for me. We have about four or five months to work on this problem.

Mama doesn't know much about horses but I can tell she wants to learn. She gives them their treats, pets them, talks to them, and promises to learn how to ride, so we can ride some together.

I show Mama the milking parlor, as we call it, the chicken and turkey houses, and the hatchery and brooder houses. I call and whistle until Ruth, Esther and Bathsheba come trotting up. Mama gives them the rest of the treats. I proudly show Mama all that has changed since she lived here.

Woody comes toward us. "Woody," I say, "I want to introduce my mama, Mary."

Woody takes his hat off. "Miz Mary, a mighty fine pleasure to meet up with Mr. Sonny's mama. Miz Mary, we shore been lookin' forward to your coming home. Sonny been frettin' about it a long time."

"Thank you, Woody. I'm glad to be home."

I hear Grandma call from the house, "Suppertime!"

We have a nice supper — fried chicken, mashed potatoes, gravy and all the trimmings. We talk, laugh a lot, and I finally say, "I need to go to bed. I got the milk run to make in the morning." Uncle Joe says he'll make it but I firmly insist.

What with the babies being fed and all the noises babies make in the night, I know Uncle Joe is tuckered out. Rachel says her big house is too lonely and she wants to spend the night, so Grandma fixes her a pallet on the sleeping porch.

The next morning I load up and head out for Dallas. I always do my thinking and planning on these trips. I get so far into the future about the Arkansas Derby I have to say "Whoa!"

I know the Good Book says to live the best you can one day at a time. That is good peace-of-mind instructions, but is it ever hard! I don't know that that also means dreaming. I am always a big dreamer. I believe dreams do come true. I'm not sure if this is right or wrong, I just know how I feel.

As I'm unloading, Ben Tuttle backs up to the dock whistling a happy tune. He sees me, smiles real big, and yells, "Sonny, soon as I unload, we'll go to the Market Café for breakfast. I'm buying."

"Sounds good, Ben."

Ben laughs. He tells me they are near 'bout to get over the hump. He asks me if I will hatch him off some white leghorn chicks. I tell Ben I can hatch off 500 at a whack, about 50-50 roosters and pullets. He can eat and sell the young roosters for fryers and keep the pullets for his egg production.

The first batch will be 21 days, the second 21 days later. That will give him about 500 laying hens in about five months.

Ben is so happy he shouts at me, "Sonny, we 'bout getting into some high cotton! Me and Charlie and Tom moving on."

He says Mr. Goldman told him to come by the bank if they need some capital.

"Iffin I do," Ben says, "It won't be much. I afeared of being in debt. Owing you money, Sonny, is different than owing a bank. We soon gonna start paying you back."

"No problem, Ben. Do it as you are able."

Ben laughs and says, "Sonny, you shore wouldn't make no banker."

I tell Ben about Mama coming home and suddenly I have a sinking feeling about Papa Quinn. I know I'm going to have an uncomfortable period about this situation. I think time will take care of that.

Ben says, "Adios, Sonny. Hope we can do this again soon. Maybe regular like."

"I hope so, Ben. I'll let you know about your chicks. Give me about 30 days for the first batch," I say.

Going home, I'm some concerned on how I'm going to handle this discovery about Papa Quinn being my papa. I know the Quinn family has been in a well-respected position for generations. The Jackson side has always been highly regarded farmers — good, honest, hard-working people. I sure am some worried about any shame being placed on anybody. Some folks like this so they can do some narrow-minded gossiping.

I know on Mama's side of the family, our love will overcome, but I don't know if there are any more Quinns besides Papa. I have never heard mention of any. Maybe I will be the last to continue the line. I'm some confused. I hope we can sort things out.

What difference does it make? I think. *Let the good people rejoice and the bad ones do their gossiping.* In my heart, I know things will be good for all.

When I pull in at home, I see Papa's Packard between the house and TJ's stall. I run to the barn. TJ and the Belle nicker and snuffle at me some; I pet them, brush them, then check TJ's stitches.

They've been removed. Some narrow, pink-looking little lines look closed up. Fresh pads are on the gouges. Looks good to me. He is nervously stamping around. I know he wants to go for a ride — a good sign.

I walk into the kitchen where Uncle Joe and Papa are having coffee. They're smoking one of Uncle Joe's baby cigars, the White Owls.

Uncle Joe blows out a puff of smoke and solemnly declares, "You know, Doc Quinn, this is one mighty fine cigar. I've smoked a lot of cigars, and this is the best was ever made. Course they outta be; they cost a whole nickel a piece."

"Indeed they are, Joe. I've never smoked better."

I can see the plates where they've eaten breakfast. Papa says, "Come sit down, son. You too young for one of these White Owls, but join in."

Rachel is fooling around at the sink. She comes to me with a cup of coffee and asks if I want breakfast. I tell her I've eaten breakfast with Ben Tuttle, that he is happy, doing real fine and needing some leghorn chicks.

When Grandpa comes in and sits down, Rachel pours him some coffee.

"Doc," he says, "'member in September 1918, when we was moving up in the Argonne forest? We was really doing some bodacious artillery work."

Papa joins in and tells a story about him and Rachel's papa. They are laughing and having a good time. First I've ever heard Grandpa say anything about the war. I suppose the only people you can talk to about such things are the ones who were there. Surprising how many funny things they remember.

I'm sure feeling good about this situation. Papa talks fluent East Texas with just a touch of refinement, not hardly so you will notice.

Mama and Grandma come in from tending the chickens and turkeys. Mama has on a pair of her old overalls Grandma has packed away. They are both laughing, talking about some fool thing that happened years ago.

Papa's eyes light up. He jumps up, pulls out a chair for Mama, then for Grandma. Rachel comes laughing with the coffee and a plate of doughnuts.

Mama and Grandma both say at once, "Thank you, Jonathon."

"My pleasure," he says.

Boy, hidey! Things keep getting better, I think.

Papa looks at his watch and says, "I'm due at the hospital in ten minutes. Joe, I enjoyed your White Owls and our conversation. Mr. Will, a pleasure to be in your home. You are most gracious." He starts for his Packard.

Mama jumps up and says, "I'll walk to your car with you. Thank you for doctoring TJ."

I peep out the door. Papa reaches for Mama's hand and kinda swings her arm a little. They are both laughing. Seems to be a whole lot of laughing going on around here lately.

Very good indeed, I think. I go back into the kitchen where Grandpa is kinda all swole up prideful looking with importance.

"That young Doc Quinn is mighty comfortable to be around," he says. "Has a way about him. Puts you at ease." His voice rises a little. "He asked me for my permission to court Mary. Shows good breeding, good rearing. Most unusual in this day and time."

"What'd you tell him?" Rachel asks.

"I told him permission granted, with my blessing."

"You know I was a top kick sergeant in the army. Doc Quinn was a little ole whippersnapper of a first looey — on 'count of his education. I believe I could have served with him easy. In a nice quiet way, he seems to be a natural born leader of men. I like him real fine," Grandpa continues.

Rachel lets out a squeal, hugs Grandpa from behind, kisses him on the cheek, and says, "Grandpa, you're the most wonderful grandpa there ever was."

Grandpa shouts out, "Shore! I'm getting to be a grandpa man; got gran'chillun all about me. Got me to driving a Ford iron mule tractor, a V8 Ford pickemup. Managing a softball team. Swapping war stories. I orta be about near ready for my rocking chair. The way things has been goin' these last three some odd years, I ain't gonna be needin' no rocker till I'm purt near a hunerd."

"Will," Grandma says, "I don't know what's come over you but I'm liking it right smart." She says this with a bright glint in her eye, then jumps up, runs and gets Grandpa a piece of pie and refills his coffee cup. Kinda squeezes him on the neck.

"Papa," Uncle Joe says, "I'm gonna add somethin' to your gran'chillun, iffen I can."

"Not if I can help it," Aunt Willie says.

No way can you ever be sad or unhappy with this family, I think.

As our President FDR is having sing-a-longs, "Happy Days Are Here Again," we are living the song. Years later when people talk of the terrible Great Depression of the 1930s, they are right. But in our family, we think them the best of our times. Grandma never lets us forget for one minute to be grateful for our blessings.

Chapter 11

When finishing the milk run the next morning, I rush a little bit and arrive back by seven. Papa is already there. He rode Daisy to our house and is standing out by the barn. I run for the barn.

"Let's examine TJ," he says.

He carefully goes over the scars, checks the gouged places, and says, "I believe with some cotton padding over these gouges, it will be right safe to ride TJ."

"Will you ride the Belle?" I ask. "She loves to be ridden. She has a nice easy ride."

"With pleasure," he says, then he hands me a box he has under his arm.

"I went by Mr. Dillard's; he knows your sizes. I got you a present of a cap and shirt."

I pull the cap out. It is one of the stylish kind — a medium blue. The shirt is a shade darker blue. They are just like what he has on. He has khaki pants and brightly polished cavalry boots on. His pants legs come over the boots, not tucked in. He sure looks a high-class gentleman.

"Thank you, Papa. This is one of the nicest gifts I can remember. Change the saddle from Daisy to Belle and saddle TJ while I run change clothes."

I run into the kitchen. "Grandma, I need my khaki britches that I wear to town. I can't be going with Papa in these overalls."

Everybody laughs as I run into the bathroom to change.

When I come out in my new shirt, new cap and starched pressed khakis, Mama, Rachel and Grandma exclaim, "You look just positively marvelous."

"You be needin' some nice ridin' boots," Grandma says. "See can I get you a pair. You getting too old for bull hides anymore."

Papa leads the Belle and TJ up to the gate. I go out and we mount up. We sit there side by side for a couple minutes and I hear Rachel cry out, "I sure wish I had my Kodak!"

Papa is a medium-sized man, about five foot nine, 140 pounds. I think he is just right.

As we trot up the lane for the road to Field Town, I tell Papa that we will have to let them long lope for four or five miles as they are so full of energy, then we can slow 'em down some. Then I suddenly realize that Papa is an expert horseman.

He laughs real big and says, "Let 'em run. These kind of horses are most happy when they're moving on."

We long lope about five or six miles. The Belle gets her run out and is ready to slow down, but I believe TJ can go four or five more. Amazing how much ground you can cover long striding — about ten miles an hour, I guess. Papa wants to walk a while, so we walk along leading the Belle and TJ.

Papa says, "Son, I don't have any experience being a father. If I make mistakes, it'll be due to my ignorance. I don't know if I should be authoritative, a teacher, a counselor or just a good friend. Any suggestions I make to you, my one thought will be what is good and right for my son."

This kind of talk makes me some confused. I'd never done a father and son talk before either so I change the subject.

"Papa, when you speak of a horse's breeding, what does all that mean?"

"Centuries ago," he replies, "When early man discovered animal husbandry, he learned by selective breeding process that he could produce not only horses, but cattle, sheep, goats, dogs or other animals for special purposes. We have horse breeds like Percheron, Clydesdale, quarter horses, trotters, pacers — for different kinds of things. A thoroughbred is good for fast transportation, moving about, speed and endurance. Then, mainly for sport contests. Racing is known as the sport of kings."

"Some years ago, man began keeping records, or pedigrees. We can trace the Belle's and TJ's ancestry back a long way."

"Why don't mules have babies?"

"Mules are a hybrid animal, a donkey-horse cross, bred for strength, stamina and intelligence. An animal modified by man," he says.

"Papa, how 'bout humans?"

"Of all the billions of humans that have lived and died, no two have been alike, not even identical twins. There's not one person exactly like you, never has been, never will be. You are you. I'll say this to you, son. Life's maybe like a horse race. If you have love inside you, you'll be a winner."

"Thank you, Papa, for telling me this. I believe I have it inside me."

"I believe so too, son. You'll cross the finish line a winner. I don't want to make you uncomfortable. Later we'll talk more, perhaps in front of a big fire in the library at the house. Right now, let's ride."

When we arrive at Field Town, we water the Belle and TJ. I don't want to tie them and leave them away from us, so we walk and lead them along behind. These people are all horse people, so this is common.

Field Town has become like a second home to me on account of all the horse lovers. Racing might be the sport of kings, but lots of common ordinary people love racing too. I'd told Papa about Mr. Jean Manseur, and sure enough, here he comes.

He is acting some flamboyant. He cries out, "My good friend, little young man Sonny!" He greets me in the French Cajun fashion, hugs and kisses me on the cheek.

"Mr. Manseur," I say, "Let me introduce you to Doc Quinn."

"Doc?" he asks. "Is that a nickname, or are you a doctor?"

"He's a well known physician from where we live, I say. "People call him Doc."

Papa sticks out his hand, "With much anticipation and pleasure, I've wanted to meet you, Mr. Manseur. Please call me Doc. Sonny speaks of you as a special friend."

"You two like peas in a pod," Mr. Manseur says. "Are you papa and son? I am thinking Sonny's name is Jackson."

"Sonny Jackson Quinn," I say.

"Aha. No difference. Maybe something mysterious. You both my good friends."

"Papa is also a veterinarian, mainly a horse doctor."

"Aha. I ride my horse into the hospital, we both get doctored at the same time. Hope you not get us mixed up," he says.

We both start laughing at this. Papa says, "On one of my bad days, it could happen."

Mr. Manseur asks about Madame Annabelle, then says, "Be sure and give Mam'selle Rachel, the beautiful dark French girl, my regards."

"With mucho gusto," I say.

"Bah! You never learn French," and he walks off laughing.

Papa laughs and says, "Sonny, I'm enjoying your friends."

I amble along speaking and shaking hands. People are asking about TJ and if I intend to race him here again. I tell one group I am studying on the Arkansas Derby. Dead silence. I feel embarrassed, and laugh and say, "Only fooling. Acting a fool."

Papa gives me a funny look. I believe he knows I am seriously set on it.

"Heh, Doc Quinn!" Mr. Dillard and Mr. Goldman come hurrying up. They stop in front of us, pause a minute, and Mr. Goldman says, "A remarkable resemblance."

They are smiling big, and vigorously start shaking our hands. Mr. Dillard says, "Words cannot express my pleasure of seeing you together. I can't think of any two people I admire more."

"Thank you both," Papa says. "You make us very happy."

We mount up. When we clear town and the crowd, I say, "Papa, I'd like to open TJ up some. Not all out on account of his sore neck, but out some. Would you look closely at his stride, the way he moves and all, and give me your honest opinion? Don't try to make me feel good. I'll respect your judgment. I could be fooling myself, Papa, but I have this dream about TJ and me."

"Sonny, TJ is a small thoroughbred. Most champion racehorses, with few exceptions, are much larger than TJ. I know disappointment is difficult to contend with. Let's see. Gradually work up to near full out. I'll watch his stride and the way he moves. He seems to be extremely athletic. Let's go."

We are slow loping, then move up to long loping, then move up a notch to running. TJ has his ears back. His head bobs backwards and forwards. He begins really digging out. I can hardly hold him down. He really has his blood up. I can feel he has plenty left. I can tell he is happy and wants to go. We have gotten some ahead of the Belle.

I start pulling him down, talking, "Whoa! Hold up. Settle down. Whoa." I get TJ to settle down some. We lope on in silence for four or five miles. Both horses are sweating now. Finally we get them slowed down to a fast walk. They are good easy rides.

"Whew!" Papa says. His eyes are big and bright. He has a pleased look on his face.

"Sonny, I believe we could have a winner here. Great possibilities."

I feel my heart fluttering like it is in my stomach. "Oh, Papa! Can we see about the Arkansas Derby?"

"Don't set your sights too high; that would be in competition with some very fine horses."

"That's my dream, Papa. If I don't win, that's all right. My dream is to give TJ his chance."

"You love TJ very much."

"Yes, Papa. A special feeling, different from our love, is the love between TJ and me."

"I understand. As soon as Hank returns from the fairgrounds at New Orleans, we'll get our heads together. You'll have to apply for an apprentice jockey's permit. We may have to pay an entry fee or possibly see about entering in a two-horse, perhaps three-horse entry."

"Hank'll have to work with TJ and you as jockey. Let me study on this. Don't ask a lot of questions now. Hank and I will explain the details as we progress."

"Thank you, Papa. I'll do exactly as you say." My heart is jumping so fast I can hardly breathe.

Papa says, "Let's head out for home and Mr. Will's rump roast. I believe we can really do it justice."

We ride home, unsaddle, and lead TJ and the Belle around a while. Then we brush 'em down good. Papa examines TJ's sore neck, puts some smelly ointment on the gouged places, then says, "Nice, very nice. He's gonna heal fine. Hardly any scar tissue at all."

We give 'em an extra ration of oats, give Daisy a ration and head for the house. As we enter the kitchen, Grandma yells out, "Take your caps off!" She doesn't allow caps or hats to be worn in the house.

Papa says, "Yessum, Miz Annie. Thank you for reminding me."

Grandpa has on an apron. He is singing some fool song about women with bells jingling on their toes. He is jigging and jumping about, and yells out, "Doc, you and Sonny have a nice ride? I hope you didn't stop off at Bailey's Store and fill upon moon pies and sody water, ruin you appetite."

"No, Mr. Will, we've not eaten anything since early this morning."

"Very good indeedy."

Mama and Rachel are helping with supper, but it is plain to see Grandpa is doing the directing. We all sit down for our Saturday special supper.

Grandpa asks Papa if he will say the blessing. Papa does, then pauses, adding, "I give special thanks for this wonderful family that has welcomed me into their lives. Amen."

We all mumble amen and Grandma says, "Joe, you watch your manners, we got company."

"Don't mind me." Papa says. "Eat the way you enjoy eating."

Course we all brag about the rump roast. That is the best part of our Saturday supper, pleasing Grandpa.

Papa says, "I declare, Mr. Will. However do you do it? I believe you could open a restaurant, call it the Rump Roast, and do a stand-in-line business."

This sets Grandpa off — a little dab of this, a little dab of that, a sprinkle of this, a sprinkle of that. Of course, you start with a well-marbled, aged piece of meat.

"I like to never figured out how to use this infernal contraption cooking machine (butane stove)," Grandpa says. "Got funny knobs, buttons, heat measuring lines. Once't I figured ever'thing out, I like it better than the wood stove. Some modern things, I must admit, are better than the old."

I notice Mama looking so happy and excited she kinda glows with radiance. Sure looks better than I can remember. Not the slightest trace of sadness.

Papa says, "Son, would you go to the barn and look on a shelf to your right as you go through the door? There's a box there for Joe. I left it there this morning."

I get up and start for the barn.

"I'll walk with you," Rachel says.

When we go through the door, she says, "We can never be alone anymore. There's always someone around."

"Let me take this box back," I say. "Then we'll go for a walk."

I carry the box back to Papa and he unwraps the paper. It is a box of White Owls and he gives them to Uncle Joe.

Uncle Joe says, "Come on, Doc. Let's us men go out on the porch and have an after dinner cigar."

I go back to the barn and take Rachel by the hand. We start across the pasture.

"Rachel, you've been so good helping with everything. You've been a blessing for the family. I don't believe we could've managed without you. Without your support, I don't think I could've gotten through this past month. Thank you very much for your sweet loving ways."

"Sonny, I 'preciate that. I like being needed. Let's just hold hands and walk awhile in silence."

We walk about an hour without saying one word. How nice it is. When we arrive back at the house, Papa has saddled Daisy to return to his house. Rachel decides to spend the night and sleeps in Mama's room.

I talk Uncle Joe into letting me make the milk and egg runs daily to Dallas. I like it cause I can do a lot of thinking that way — go back over our milk and egg production, study on ways to improve, make plans and just think about things in general.

I anxiously await Mr. Hank's return from New Orleans. I feel Mama and Papa's situation will take care of itself. It is plain to see it is only a matter of time; looks to me like a short time.

Monday morning after arriving back from the milk run, Grandma insists on going to Mr. Dillard's for a pair of riding boots.

I agree to this suggestion. When we walk into Mr. Dillard's dry goods store, he comes at a trot, greeting us with pleasure.

"Sonny be needin' a nice fancy pair of ridin' boots," Grandma tells him.

"Miz Annie, I don't keep nothin' like that in my inventory. I order from a boot maker out in El Paso, Tony Lama Boot Company. He tailor makes 'em to order. Let me fetch the catalogue. Pick out the style you want and I'll measure Sonny's feet for exact fit. I'll send the order off, takes about two weeks for delivery."

"Now we want extry fine boots," Grandma says. "The best a body can buy."

"Miz Annie, they don't come no finer than these Tony Lamas."

We look at some pictures and decide on a pair of boots that come up to about half way between ankle and knee with a slightly pointed toe.

Mr. Dillard carefully measures both feet, writes the numbers down and suggests we order two pair: one brown and one black.

"Good thinking, Mr. Dillard," Grandma says. "Order two pair and call us when they come in."

Two weeks later, Mr. Dillard calls, sounding excited. "Your boots has come in!" he hollers.

We go to town in the Cadillac. We have to park down from the store in front of the Chili Bowl Café. When we walk into the store, Mr. Dillard smiles and says, "Come back here in the shoe section and have a seat."

In a few minutes, he comes back with two boxes, opens one, and hands me one of the most beautiful boots I have ever seen.

"Try it on," he says.

I tear my bull hides off, put my feet into them there boots, stand up and walk around some. Them boots feel so good, I never wear another pair of bull hides. Years later, Tony Lama boots are still my choice of footwear.

While we are sitting there, kinda behind a low partition, a man charges into the store and yells at Mr. Dillard, "I just tore the blasted seat out of my overalls. Got caught in a bobwire fence. Got 'em pinned up in back. Crying shame a man so poor who's only got one pair of overalls. I seen the Jackson's Cadillac parked down the block; them's the luckiest people there ever was."

"Four years ago they was comin' to town driving mules, wagons and carts. Delivering butter and eggs, sellin' fryers. Now they got a big hauling truck, going to Dallas ever'day. Tractors, V8 pick-emups. Their house is better than city folks' houses. Why even their hired hand has a new Ford and a good house," he says.

"We been in a three-month dry spell. It don't even bother them. They drilled a deep well into the Wilcox sand 'bout three years ago. Got a heap of water. I never seen the like. Most folks barely getting by; some on relief, workin' on the WPA."

"You shore are right, Clyde," says Mr. Dillard. "Course every member of that family is working twelve hours a day or more, six days a week, and some on Sunday. They also working smart; 2,000 laying hens, 2,000 turkeys, 70 head of milking cows takes a heap of water. That well was planning ahead. Seems the harder and smarter you work, the luckier you get."

Clyde walks on out of the store mumbling 'bout luck.

Mr. Dillard comes back to where we are sitting and says, "Don't pay no never mind to what some folks who's full of envy say."

"I shoulda told that man Clyde we been special blessed," Grandma says, "Instead of just being lucky."

"Amen to that," says Mr. Dillard. He can see I am some uneasy at what Clyde has said.

"Don't fret none 'bout it, Sonny," he says. "It's only human nature to feel envious."

I think maybe we should've gotten a Ford instead of a Cadillac.

"Is Emma here?" Grandma asks. "I need a few things I don't want no man to see." Emma is Mr. Dillard's wife.

"She's in the office doing some paperwork. I'll get her."

Emma comes out to help Grandma and Mr. Dillard takes me into his office, saying, "Miz Annie buying some unmentionables."

Mr. Dillard opens us each one of them Coca Colas, packs and lights his pipe, looks at me kinda serious, and asks, "Somethin' bothering you, Sonny?"

"Yes sir. Billy Joe is having a hard time finding any kind of steady work. He's been painting houses, doing some carpenter work, odd jobs. Ain't nobody seems like has any steady type work. I could give him some work, but Billy Joe's a town boy. He tries, but he don't cotton much to farm work. I thought with you adding refrigerators, stoves, washing machines, radios, furniture, and such, you could use some help."

"If you would train him, teach him, be patient — Billy Joe ain't too quick — once he learns, he would make you a good hand. 'Bout three months training would probably do. I got it figured, $15.00 a week, $60.00 a month, $180.00 for a training period. I got $180.00 in my pocket here. If he don't work out, you ain't lost nothing."

I pull the money out and lay it on his desk. He sits there and puffs on his pipe, and doesn't say one word for about three minutes. He stares me right in the face.

"Whatever gave you the notion I was planning on this here big expansion?"

"I thought you said something about it at one time. You got plenty space, that big back storage room is empty, all upstairs above is empty. Mr. Goldman at the bank is willing to furnish capital. He offered the Tuttle brothers capital, and they doin' good now. They be wanting things for their houses. We got electricity out in the country. I thought you said somethin' about it."

He doesn't say a word for another three minutes, takes the $180.00, folds it up, and puts it in his pocket. "I'm taking you up on your offer," he says. "If things work out, I'll return this money. I'll go by Billy Joe's house and offer him a job."

"Thank you, Mr. Dillard. That relieves my mind some."

"Sonny, I ain't got no boys. I got three girls: one in Dallas, one in Houston, and one finishing up school down in Austin. If I had a son, I'd be happy if he was like you. You're not an ordinary young man."

Talk like this embarrasses me. I get up, stick my hand out, and we shake. "I'll keep you informed," he says.

Grandma gets her unmentionables. I gather my bull hides and extra pair of boots. I wear the brown ones and we go into the Chili Bowl Café. It is only ten o'clock in the morning, but we decide that a big bowl of chili sounds mighty fine since we left home before breakfast.

Chapter 12

The long awaited day arrives — Mr. Hank gets home from New Orleans. Papa calls late at night when I'm already in bed and asks me to be there the next morning for breakfast at eight o'clock. I make my Dallas run in a fearful turmoil. I have no idea what to expect about TJ and me.

I get home about seven a.m., go to TJ and the Belle's stall, brush 'em good, and give them their treats. I saddle TJ, then unsaddle him. I think maybe I should wait to see what Mr. Hank wants to do first. I run to Papa's house and go to the back door.

When I knock, Mammy BB cries out, "Mr. Sonny, get your self right in here. Git to the table. Ham and eggs comin' right up."

Papa and Mr. Hank are sitting at the table having breakfast. I've only seen Mr. Hank one time and hadn't gotten a very good look then, 'cause of TJ being hurt and all. He stands up and says, "Morning, Sonny," as we shake hands.

He is a tall man, nearly six foot. Slender. I guess 160 pounds. Full head of black hair and brown eyes, sorta deep set. About 40 years old with a friendly open face.

I ask him if he had a good trip down to the fairgrounds. He says tolerable. Being from Kentucky and living in East Texas a good many years, he has a nice, soft southern East Texas voice.

"The purses are so small now," he says. "It's hard to break even, much less make any money. Pari-mutuel wagering has fell off 'cause of the Depression; ain't nobody got money to wager on no hoss race.

The State of Texas has already banned pari-mutuel tracks. You can still race, but who's gonna race for nothing?"

This is not a good time for horse racing, except the big races. Mr. Hank says him being a registered, certified trainer and breeder, he can fill out the required forms for my apprentice jockey permit.

"We'll have to get you up on some horses so you can get the feel for how different horses ride; no two are alike," he says.

"Some you have to lay on the whip, some you talk to, some you talk to with your hands through the reins, some your knees, and so on. You'll learn. I have a good assistant, a retired older jockey who can train you," he explains.

"Mr. Hank, thank you very much 'cepting there's only one horse I'm ever gonna ride — my own horse, TJ. I don't plan on ever being a jockey to ride any other horse. You see, I have this dream about TJ and me, and it don't have any other rider for him, or any other horse for me. Besides, I hope to grow some in the next year or so, and I'll be too big."

"I weigh about 118 now, and at this weight, I can only ride maybe six more months. By then, TJ and I will have lived our dream anyway. I know I sound foolish, maybe tetched. I promised TJ we would try for one big race, maybe two, if the first one was promising."

Total silence for about two minutes. Rachel comes in and quietly sits down.

"I remember when TJ's mama was born," Mr. Hank says. "The odds on her living were very long. She made it. She foaled this colt TJ. Your odds are long, long, long on TJ winning anything. Be prepared for heart break."

"Mr. Hank, I'm prepared. I've been preparing a long time. If we run dead last, we will have lived our dream and my promise."

"Well, all I can say is I'll do everything I know how to get you ready."

Papa and Rachel start smiling, and Rachel says, "Thank you, Papa."

Mammy BB cries out, "Mr. Sonny, get after them eggs and ham 'fore they get cold. Roosta coffee coming up. Roosta coffee, heh, heh."

After breakfast, Papa leaves for the hospital in town; Rachel leaves for our house to help Aunt Willie. As she leaves, she calls out, "I'll see you at dinnertime!"

"Come on," says Mr. Hank. "I'll walk you around the stable and paddocks, and introduce you to Asa and the boys.

We go through the stables. Seems to be about 40 stalls all told, many empty. Barrels of water and buckets every 20 feet, and fire extinguishers hanging every few feet. Through the stable runs a 20 foot wide passageway lined with concrete blocks. "Any kind of fire is a catastrophe around horses," says Mr. Hank.

"No Smoking" signs are posted everywhere. I look at the horses in the stalls and can't help but compare them to TJ. All are some bigger, but none as handsome as TJ. We go into an office at the end of the stable where a small older man sits at a desk. Seems his head is a little large for his body. Mr. Hank introduces him as Asa. "Naturally, with a name like that, we call him Ace," Mr. Hank adds.

I shake hands with Asa. "You have a nice name. Asa was a great king of Judah. A good king for about sixty years."

Asa looks at me with some puzzlement. "You're the only person I've ever met who knew what my name meant. How did you know that?"

I say I learned it in Sunday school.

"You and me gonna be good buddies," Asa says. "Anybody what knows about my name is ace high with me."

"Amazing," Mr. Hank says. "This littly cranky cantankerous sawed-off short man don't like nobody." We all laugh. Off to a good start, I hope. Mr. Hank tells me the boys (three of them) are curious and are going to ask me a lot of questions. "Be prepared," he warns.

Sure enough, as soon as Mr. Hank leaves for the main residence, they start asking questions. The big curiousity: Tell us how you killed the black stallion. I tell them it was over and done with so quick, I can hardly remember. It was sorta in a bad nightmare. I just did it without thinking.

"Warn't you afraid?" they ask.

"Mainly for my horse, TJ."

I sense they look at me with some respect. Then they want the details of the match race at Field Town with Big Red. I tell them it was all TJ, I just rode him. They know about the $2,000.00 I'd won. They really show some respect now.

"How did you and Doc Quinn get lost from one another, and find each other, after all these years?"

"I don't know," I say. "I'm just happy we did. I don't know the details or how it happened."

Asa speaks up, "You're a little ace high man with all of us. It's none of our business. We're mainly gonna get you and TJ ready for come what may. I personally have a strange hunch you gonna fool some folks."

The boys, as they are always called, have a nice spacious bunkhouse. Have their own kitchen, bathroom, a big room consisting of parlor/kitchen/dining combination, two bedrooms, two to a room. Asa is the oldest; he is Mr. Hank's straw boss, second in command.

At dinnertime, our noon meal, I cut across the pasture and climb over the five foot tall board fence. Asa has told me the black stallion sailed over that fence with room to spare. He's the one who shot the black stallion to put him out of his suffering, a .45 revolver, he tells me.

I become concerned about my weight and barely eat. Rachel, Grandma and Uncle Joe begin to act worried.

At dinner I tell Uncle Joe I'll make the Dallas run every morning, but I won't be able to do much else.

"You go on and work with Mr. Hank and TJ," he says. "We got all this machinery now. Pa is really turning out a heap of work now that he's got that Ford and Son tractor all figured out."

"Mary is helping Ma with the eggs and turkeys. Woody and me can handle the milking. Rachel and Willie is doing the housework and cooking. We got it covered."

Back at the Quinn Farm after dinner, Mr. Hank wants me to get familiar with everything before bringing TJ over; he figures two or three days. The farm has only one stallion standing at stud: Gallant Hood. He is nice and gentle for a stallion, an eleven-year-old bay, about 16 hands. TJ looks some like his sire, 'cept Gallant Hood has a white spot between his eyes.

There are 15 brood mares with three or four mares being boarded to be bred. Six geldings make up what they are actually racing as well as six yearlings, six months to a year old. I am surprised the race stock is geldings.

"Keeps their minds on their business," says Mr. Hank. "Makes 'em more manageable. Sometimes we geld one we wish we hadn't, but it works out best for us in the long run. That's the way we do it; not all stables operate the same. We've been taking most of our colts to the sales. We've barely broke even these last six years. Not many small thoroughbred farms are making money this day and time."

Hoss racing is known as the sport of kings and it just about takes a king to keep a stable of horses.

When I ride TJ over for his first day of training, he nickers and talks to the other horses as we ride down the lane behind the big house. Horses like to talk to each other and I like the sound.

Asa and the boys come up to look TJ over. He has filled out some, not near as puny looking as before. They agree, except for being undersized, he is a right smart looking little hoss. Asa checks my saddle. He wants to know where I bought it. I tell him it had been a Christmas present in 1932. I believe it had been ordered from Sears and Roebuck.

He tells me it's a good saddle, but not a racing saddle. There are several saddles in the tack room. Asa gets one out, takes TJ's saddle off, and puts the racing saddle on. The stirrups are so short I have to bend my knees, sorta like squatting in the seat. This saddle is so light I bet it doesn't weigh more than a pound, and it has no skirt, just a small seat.

Mr. Hank climbs up on a tower, about twelve feet off the ground; he has his binoculars. He tells me to slow lope TJ around some to loosen him up, then to take a turn around the mile track. He tells me not to go all out and to raise my hand when I'm ready.

As we slow lope around the track, I can feel TJ quivering some, he seems a little nervous. I can tell he is raring to go and I feel uncomfortable with my knees drawn up in those short stirrups.

Asa and the boys are at the rail by the tower. As I come up to the line at the tower, I raise my hand. I let TJ know to move on out. He surges, grunts a time or two, then he digs off. He hits his floating stride and I just hold him there all the way around one mile. When we go by the boys, they let out a cheer.

I feel goose bumps at this show of approval. I turn and come back to the line. The boys are out on the track. Asa tells one of them to walk TJ around. They are petting and talking to TJ. He loves people and is some happy.

"Doggone it!" says Mr. Hank. "I didn't have my stopwatch but I can see right now, TJ is something. We gonna fool some folks. I got to get right on entering him into the Arkansas Derby."

At this news, I nearly fall over in a swoon.

"Sonny, you alright?" asks Mr. Hank. "You sure look mighty pale. I don't want to get you up too high; the fall coming down could be mighty painful. TJ looks promising. I can tell more after we train and let him race with some of our horses. TJ seems to be fit as a fiddle. Have you been riding him often?"

"Yes, sir," I say. "I've been riding him just about every day. I usually ride to Bailey's Store and back. Almost every Saturday, we go to Field Town."

Mr. Hank stares at me and kinda roars out, "Bailey's Store is 20 miles round trip! Field Town is 40 miles there and back! That's way too much distance. Wonder he ain't wore down to a nub."

I say I didn't know no different. It doesn't seem to tire him.

"Don't change now," Mr. Hank says. "No wonder he's in such top condition. Don't do nothin' different. Don't change feed; don't add anything to his feed. Do exactly as you have been doing. I don't even want to know what, or how much, you been feeding. Changing anything now would do more harm than good."

I get plenty excited about the way Mr. Hank, Asa and the boys are acting about TJ. I have a hard time staying calm on the outside, and on the inside, my nerves churn something fierce.

The next day we start on TJ's gate manners. Some horses never learn gate manners. Sometimes, when they're nervous, they refuse to go into the starting gate.

TJ balks some at first. After nearly all day going in and out of the starting gate, over and over and over, he decides it is nothing to be afraid of. He calms down about the close confinement in the gate.

He walks right in and quickly learns the bell means "Go!" He never is much at getting off to a quick fast start though.

After three days of gate work, Mr. Hank puts one of his horses in the gate. When the bell clangs, the other horse shoots out of the gate ahead of TJ. He doesn't get far ahead before TJ hits his stride and commences closing and passing.

Then we put two other horses in the gate with TJ. He still can't seem to get out as fast as the other horses. Mr. Hank decides he's just a slow starter.

"Not so much how you start as how you finish," he says.

I've always used a hackamore bridle, but Mr. Hank switches me to a bridle with a bit in the mouth for TJ. He says it will give me a lot more control.

It's plain to see any horse out in front of TJ sets him off. He gets so fired up if he's behind I can hardly manage him. Mr. Hank says it's his hot racing blood. He isn't too hard to teach. He learns when to hold, when to move up. The more he learns, the more he seems to enjoy the training.

Mr. Hank says he is young, but full of win. TJ understands he wants to beat any competition.

After a period of about three weeks, Mr. Hank brings out the top horse of the stables: a colt, not a gelding. AP Hill, a coming three-year-old in January with lots of promise. He's entered in the Arkansas and Kentucky Derbies. Being entered doesn't mean he'll run. It means if he stays healthy and shows he has a chance, he is eligible.

AP Hill, two other horses, and TJ walk to the starting gate. AP Hill is a tall bay, over 16 hands tall with a white streak down the length of his face — a big, beautiful horse. TJ's some smaller, only about 15 hands.

When the bell clangs, AP Hill leaves the gate like he's been fired from a cannon. Even so, the other two horses get off ahead of TJ. I have a hard time holding TJ. He acts like he's some mad about being behind. I ease up a little and he begins digging out.

We catch and pass the other two horses but AP Hill is some 20 lengths ahead. He looks to be running very smoothly, no strain at all.

Asa rides him. I can feel the fire in TJ; he's in his nice long floating stride now. We begin to make up some of the gap.

At the half-mile post, we close to about ten lengths. TJ is really moving now. At the three-quarter post, we are only five lengths behind. I can tell TJ still isn't going all out. At the one-eighth pole, before the finish of the mile, we close to where TJ's head is at AP Hill's right hip.

I lean forward, work my knees a little, slacken the reins, and holler, "Let's go!"

TJ grunts, surges a little, and we fly right by AP Hill. We cross the finish about five lengths ahead. By the time I get TJ settled down, we are more than half way around the track. I ride on around to where Asa, Mr. Hank and the boys are standing at the finish line.

I don't know if Asa has held AP Hill up some, or if TJ really beat him on the square. I'm hoping we'd won fair and square. I'm nervous and shaking as I ride up to where everybody stands. It doesn't seem like there is any excitement, just real quiet.

Mr. Hank and Asa come over and start petting TJ and talking to him.

Asa looks up at me and says, "This little hoss is gonna make a whole lot of folks mighty happy. Maybe put some money in their pockets."

I get off TJ, look at Mr. Hank and Asa, and ask, "Did you hold AP Hill up?"

"I rode him like I was trying to win a race," he says. "Your little hoss just plain run us down."

Mr. Hank adds, "Sonny, every once in a while, not often, there comes along a horse so competitive, he won't be beat. I think we have one here in TJ. His papa, Gallant Hood, has some of that in him. He injured his leg before he could race anymore, so we retired him to stud. TJ's mama, the Belle, is a fighter too. Else she wouldn't be here now. In about a week, we're going to do this again, with AP Hill and the other colts starting out 50 yards ahead."

No matter how far we start the other horses ahead of TJ, he won't allow any horse to stay ahead. I don't really have to do anything: just ride and hold him in place till I give him the word, "Go!"

We're working mostly a mile and a quarter now, the distance of the Arkansas Derby. The distance has no effect on TJ. It seems the last quarter mile, he's as full of go as at any distance — more so, perhaps. TJ seems to be in his element. He acts most happy to get in the gate. He knows he's gonna do what he loves best: Run!

It's near the first of December and Mama and Papa have been going out two and three times a week. They go to Dallas or Tyler for supper and a picture show. Rachel and I go along some Saturdays. I'm making the milk and egg deliveries every morning, so I don't go to bed when we get home, usually after midnight.

Grandma and Uncle Joe fret about me getting enough rest but I'm so full of excitement about TJ's training, and Mama and Papa, I never feel tired or sleepy.

At our special Saturday supper, Papa and Mama announce that they are getting married the following Saturday, the tenth of December, at Papa's house. The parlor is going to be used for the ceremony and the big dining room for the reception and buffet dinner. The wedding will be at noon and then they will catch a six p.m. train for New York and be back in time for Christmas. They plan on some Broadway shows, museums, shopping and such things.

They have reservations at the Waldorf Hotel. Papa says their plan is for all of us to go to Europe the summer of 1937, after Rachel and I finish our first year of college. We will visit her grandma and grandpa in Paris and among other things, tour World War I cemeteries and battlegrounds. Rachel is delighted at this announcement. I'm just happy about everything.

Grandpa's excited about giving Mama away. Mr. Hank will be Papa's best man. Grandma's happy about Papa being a Baptist since Mama has always been a Baptist. Papa explains they will belong to the Baptist Church and tells Grandma that the preacher will perform the ceremony. Mama and Papa send out invitations to their friends, emphasizing *positively no gifts*.

I drive Mama, Aunt Willie, Grandma and Rachel into Dallas so they can buy themselves new dresses, shoes and other such things.

They go to all the beautiful shops and carry on so foolishly it is downright pitiful silly. Such things as make women happy is always mysterious to me. I can never figure it out. We visit Miz Adams, and she tells Mama, "I am so delighted for you." After a day of this, I want to get home pronto quick.

The next week our usual work routine gets all out of whack since everybody is preparing for the long awaited big event. Mr. Hank suspends TJ's training for a week; says we can all take a week off. Says sometimes you can over-train. Some horses will lose interest but not TJ. He is always ready.

I help with the last of the turkeys to be hauled to Dallas for the Christmas market. This will lighten Grandma's work some to be shed of the turkeys. I plan on hauling the last load the Monday after the wedding. Turkeys are up some in price, about 18 cents a pound.

Our crop of turkeys — 2,000 — look like, after feed costs, will make us near about $5,000.00. That is a heap of money. Our milk production runs over 4,000 pounds a day, at $16.00 per thousand pounds, and egg production up to five crates a day at four dollars and fifty cents a crate. Our angel is still looking after us.

Grandma's opened an account at Mr. Goldman's bank, but she still pores over her ledger every day. Our prosperity has come gradually so we don't feel sudden rich; we know where it comes from. I feel that cotton reaches half way to the moon.

Grandma warns us every day not to get uppity. Be sure and give our thanks to the one who deserves all the credit. I feel so blessed I give thanks sometimes all the way to Dallas and back.

I go into town Thursday for a haircut. Grandma has been cutting my hair since I've been here so this will be my first barbershop haircut.

I stop in at Mr. Dillard's and see refrigerators, washing machines, stoves, furniture and such, all toward the back. He has knocked out a wall and everything sells now in one big store. He sees me and comes running, smiling and laughing. "Sonny," he says, "I had my biggest profit for November in all my business life. I believe this month I'll do even better."

"That's wonderful, Mr. Dillard. How's Billy Joe doing?"

"Just fine. To tell the truth, better than I'd hoped. I gave him a raise to $20.00 a week. Come on back to my office. I want to return your $180.00."

"Mr. Dillard, put $20.00 with it and give Billy Joe a Christmas bonus."

He looks confused. "That's a right smart sum of money, Sonny."

"It will get him and his mama and papa over the hump. Besides that, it will make you money. Helping others always makes you more prosperous."

Mr. Dillard starts laughing and says, "Come on, Sonny. Let me buy you a bowl of chili."

As we're eating our chili, he says he looks forward to Mama and Papa's wedding. He'll sure be there even if he has to close the store. "Sonny," he says, "I'm sure eating high on the hog now."

I go into the barbershop to get my hair cut. The barber's name is Zeke. "Boy," he says, "Who's been cutting yo hair?"

I tell him my grandma. He says it's way too long, calls it a chili bowl haircut. He comments about how clean my hair is. Says most men have so much grease in their hair, it makes it hard to cut. I tell him just to trim it; I'm used to the way it is. I didn't know it then, but in the near future, at Texas A&M, I would lose it all.

The Saturday of the big event — December 10, 1935 — I have breakfast at the Market Café in Dallas with Ben Tuttle. He's paid his truck loan down to a $100.00 balance. Ben, Charlie and Tom and their families are all invited to the wedding. Woody and Saree are invited too. About 30 or 40 people will be in attendance, two of Papa's physician partners, two judges, lawyers, professors and prominent businessmen. A sorta mixed bag of people from the top to the bottom of the social classes.

I feel generally comfortable with any class, but I really like people considered common folks. There is just not enough room to accommodate everyone. I sure hope no one feels left out. Being a doctor, Papa has hundreds of friends.

When I get back to the house from Dallas, about eight a.m., there are women shrieking and hollering and carrying on so. I go out to the barn, saddle TJ and lope off toward Bailey's store. I get back about ten o'clock, then brush TJ and the Belle.

I hear Grandma holler. "Sonneee!"

"Be there directly!"

I scrub real good and put on my graduation clothes. We commence loading up — Uncle Joe, Aunt Willie, Mama in the front seat of the Caddy; Grandma and me in the back seat.

Grandpa insists on driving his Ford pickemup.

When we get to the big house, as we call it, there are cars everywhere. We pull around back and go in the kitchen door where Mammy BB barks orders to three or four girls. I notice Asa and the boys are helping out.

Mammy BB is all dressed up. Has on a black dress trimmed in red with a big, funny-looking hat, red high-heeled shoes, looking very elegant. She has the happiest smile on her face.

"Mista Sonny, I be sitting right on the front row."

"How 'bout sitting by me?"

"I'd be honored," she replies.

Mama, Grandma, Uncle Joe and Aunt Willie go on through the kitchen. I tell them I'll be there directly. I wait for Mammy BB. When it comes time to go in, I put my arm out for Mammy BB. She looks surprised, but takes my arm, and we parade through the dining room into the parlor.

There are several rows of chairs with an aisle through the middle. We head right down to the front row and sit down with Grandma, Uncle Joe, Aunt Willie and Rachel. I notice Woody and Saree on the back row. A big grand piano sits in the front of the parlor and a lady very softly plays a medley of tunes.

The preacher is standing directly in front holding a Bible. I hear a murmur and glance back over my shoulder. Here comes Mama and Grandpa, him all puffed up looking proud as a peacock. Mama has on a regular white dress, not a wedding-type dress. She looks so beautiful she shines.

Then here comes Papa and Mr. Hank. They are dressed in black suits, very calm looking, not the least bit stiff or nervous. The preacher asks for God's blessing on this man and this woman, and says the Lord's Prayer. He follows with the sacred marriage vows.

It is over. Grandma, Aunt Willie, Rachel and Mammy BB cry and laugh at the same time. I feel like doing the same, but men don't cry.

Where Angels Roost

The lady at the piano calls out, "Attention please!" We quiet down.

She says, "I have the honor to present Mrs. Saree Wood, who has graciously consented to sing for this glorious occasion." This surprises me.

Saree steps up and smiles really big. The lady starts playing and Saree, in the most beautiful clear voice imaginable, sings "America the Beautiful." We all love our country even though we are in the midst of the terrible Depression. I have the best thrilling feeling as that song lifts all our spirits. I hug and kiss Mama on the cheek. I shake hands with Papa.

"Sonny," he says, "We need to be at the Union Station in Dallas at four o'clock. Will you and Rachel drive us?"

"With pleasure, Papa."

After all the hugging, hand shaking, and congratulations, Mammy BB announces in a loud voice that the buffet and tables are set up in the dining room. Champagne is iced in buckets along with small delicate looking glasses for those that want it. Tastes like Dr. Pepper to me. Seems as if people have kinda grouped off. Nobody seems to be having a happy time. Stiff like.

All of a sudden, Uncle Joe's roaring voice calls out, "I ain't believing my own two eyes, they's a whole big mess of oysters on the half shell here with a bucket of that there red hossradish sauce. Willie," he calls out, "Come a running. You know what these here oysters do to us. I'm a natural born oyster man."

Everybody starts laughing, then gets more friendly. From that time on, the reception becomes a lot more fun. Laughter brings people together.

Along about two-thirty p.m., Papa asks me to bring the Packard up near the back kitchen door. He and Mama want to sorta slip out and leave quietly. I get Rachel and drive up to the back door. Papa comes out carrying two big bags, turns, goes back in and comes out with two more big bags.

I pick one up; it feels heavy. The others are empty. "Papa," I say, "Why the empty bags?"

"We're going to bring them back full," he says. "We're going to go shopping at places like Saks Fifth Avenue and other fine stores."

"Is Saks some kind of special dry goods store? Like Mr. Dillard's, only more fancy?"

Papa laughs. "Something like that."

He has changed into a white turtleneck sweater and a three-quarter length navy blue coat. The weather is dry, cold and windy. Mama has on gray slacks with a white turtleneck sweater and a navy blue three-quarter coat as well. They have matching blue caps on. I am proud to have such a classy elegant Mama and Papa.

We manage to slip away, Papa and me in the front, Mama and Rachel in the back. I drive. We arrive in Dallas at the Union Station near four p.m., plenty of time to check the bags, confirm Pullman berths, and have a quick cup of coffee.

As we walk out on the platform and prepare to board, Papa asks, "You want me to bring you anything from New York?"

"Nothing for me, Papa, but if you would, bring Grandma and Grandpa sweaters just like you and Mama have on."

"I'll surely do that."

As we stand there waiting for Mama and Papa to board, I say, "Papa, be sure you count your blessings every day. Remember your sacred vows, especially the part about love and cherish."

Papa looks me right in the eye and sticks his hand out. We shake, and Papa says, "I will, Son."

I turn to Mama and say, "Mama, you take good care of Papa and remember to count your blessings and remember your sacred vows, especially the part about love, cherish, and maybe obey."

Mama stands on her tiptoes and kisses me on the cheek. "Sonny," she says, "You were right — dreams do come true."

When the train pulls out, Rachel and I stand and wave till it moves out of sight. We are so happy we laugh and sing silly songs all the way home.

Chapter 13

The next week proves to be a busy hectic time. After the milk and egg deliveries, I haul the rest of the turkeys in for the Christmas market. We have about 1,000 turkeys left and I haul 250 a day all that week. Then we clean out and sterilize all the roosting quarters and are through with this year's crop. This cuts a little slack in the workload. We have another prosperous year and have put up plenty of corn, oats, hay silage and other feed for the winter months.

Our prosperity results from more of a daily thing with the milk and eggs. Except for the turkeys, most farmers' money comes when cotton is gathered late in the fall. There isn't much prosperity among the cotton farmers. Seems we are in a sea of cotton farmers and they are all drowning.

Grandma declares our good fortune as a miracle blessing from above. We refuse to be embarrassed or feel guilty about our prosperity.

On December 24th, Christmas Eve, Rachel and I go into Dallas to meet the train and pick up Mama and Papa. Mama gets off the train wearing a full-length mink coat and a saucy looking little mink cap. The bags are all heavy as they've really done some high-powered shopping. Mama and Papa can't stop laughing.

"Drive to the Adolphus Hotel and we'll have a nice supper before heading out for home," Papa says.

This is about eight o'clock at night. After all this constant laughing, I finally ask, "How come you two laughing so much?"

"Sonny, I can't stop," Mama says. "I suppose it's because we're so crazy happy."

At this reply, Rachel and I join in. We are laughing so much I fear we're making a spectacle of ourselves.

Mama describes all the shows, sights and unusual things about New York. She thinks the people of New York are the nicest people. She loves their way of talking and they love hers. Everything about their two weeks in New York has been just about perfect.

The next day, we have Christmas dinner at Grandma's. A big, corn-fed turkey is the centerpiece of dinner. Papa gives Grandma and Grandpa their turtleneck sweaters. He gives Uncle Joe a box of imported Cuban cigars. We frown on extravagant gifts at Christmas. All the gifts exchanged are useful and reasonable. We know the reason why Christmas causes us to celebrate. We take great pleasure in our family being well and able to share our love. We know the meaning of "Good will toward everyone."

After January first, 1936, TJ is nigh full three years old. He begins to look more like a genuine thoroughbred, though he is still smaller than the average racehorse. The month of January is a cold, icy month. We cut training time back some because of the sloppy training track. On some of the milk and egg deliveries, I have to use mud chains on young White Mule for traction.

The Arkansas Derby time draws near. The season opens at Hot Springs in mid-February, and the Derby proves the climactic finish of the season, the second Saturday in March, 1936. That will be the tenth day of March.

The last week in January, I go up to the big house for coffee with Mr. Hank. I don't eat breakfast, only have coffee and toast. I really have to watch my weight. All the horses in the Derby are carrying 126 pounds. We are allowed five pounds for being an apprentice jockey. We are going to be carrying 121 pounds.

Mr. Hank says, "Sonny, we've been notified we have to put up a $1,500.00 entry fee. TJ is a maiden, never raced before, with an apprentice jockey. They can't have the track cluttered up with unknown quality horses. If we weren't a well-known reputable stable, I don't believe they would have accepted TJ at all.

Where Angels Roost

The Arkansas Derby is one of the top events of the racing season before the really big races: Kentucky Derby, Preakness and Belmont, all three-year-old horse events. A lot of disappointment and heartbreak happens in these races, but also a lot of joy and great expectations; $1,500.00 is an enormous amount of money to risk.

"Mr. Hank," I say, "I'll have the money here for you to send off as quick as I can get to the bank and back."

Mr. Hank acts surprised. "You have this kind of money in the bank? *Your money?* How did you, in this day and time, ever accumulate so much?"

In 1936, it is practically unheard of for a 16 year old kid or any workingman to have that much. I tell Mr. Hank about Papa giving Mama $5,000.00 and me $5,000.00. I tell him I have used $1,000.00, and deposited $9,000.00 dollars for Mama and me.

Mr. Hank looks at me for a minute or so, then smiles real big, lets out a laugh, and says, "Let's do it! I've gotten caught up in your dream. I have this feeling about you and your little brown horse."

At the bank, I ask for Mr. Goldman; he is such a fine gentleman. He walks me into his office, has coffee brought in, and asks, "Sonny, how may I help you?"

"I need a $1,500.00 certified check made out to the Arkansas Racing Commission for TJ's entry fee."

Mr. Goldman loves horseracing and gets plumb excited at this news, wanting to know all about TJ's training. He says he and Mr. Dillard might come to the race. He wonders what the odds on TJ will be. Probably real long odds, maybe even as high as 100 to one.

"I remember very well your race at Field Town." After having the check prepared and giving it to me, he walks me out to the car, puts his arm around me, and says, "You just might do it."

Mama and I still have $7,500.00 left in the bank. Papa's gift of money becomes more than just money; it provides the ticket to my dreams.

Mr. Hank starts preparing the horse trailers. TJ will ride in a one-horse trailer that has a rubber floor, rubber padding around the sides, a water tank, and a small hay rack. We check the tires, lights and brakes. TJ balks at first, but when he gets the idea of what we want him to do, he walks right into the trailer, and backs right out.

Our plans are for Asa and me to go together, pulling TJ's trailer with Grandpa's pickup. Mr. Hank and the boys will pull the big trailer with four horses behind a big bobtail truck. None of the four horses are entered in the Derby; they are running in lower class races.

Grandma, Grandpa, and Uncle Joe will drive up in the Cadillac Friday before the race, which starts at four o'clock on Saturday. Rachel, Mama and Papa are driving up in Papa's Packard Thursday. We have rooms reserved at the Majestic Hotel. Aunt Willie wants to stay home to look after the twins.

Before I leave, I walk down to Woody's house to see if he needs extra help with the deliveries and milking and eggs and such. He insists he can handle everything.

"Mr. Sonny," he says, "Don't you fret about nothin'. Ole Woody here can take care of everything. Me and Saree be prayin' for you an' little TJ. Don't you be worrying yo head about nothin' but runnin' yo race."

Mr. Hank and the boys leave out with the big trailer and four horses on the fifth of February. Asa and I will follow with TJ on the last of February, giving TJ plenty of time to get used to the track and being away from home. Hot Springs is a twelve- to fourteen-hour trip, depending on weather and road conditions.

On Febuary 28, Asa and I pull out for Hot Springs. We leave at five in the morning. TJ has his blanket cover on in the trailer and some alfalfa in his rack. He has a nosebag for oats. We have a thermos of rooster coffee and some sandwiches. When we get to Texarkana, I back TJ out of the trailer and lead him around some while we gas up the truck.

The weather is cold but dry. We turn at Arkadelphia and wind around through the foothills of the Quochita Mountains. About six p.m., we top a rise and look down into the beautiful town of Hot Springs.

We can see the track only a short distance from the downtown area which has mostly large hotels. People come to Hot Springs from all over for the curative hot mineral baths. Many of these bathhouses sit on a long street called Bathhouse Row. Hot Springs is known as a fun town. The race season attracts people for the baths, fine eating, shows, and the big events — the races.

We drive the truck down a side street off the main entrance and through a gate with a security guard. We park the truck and trailer. I lead TJ around some and we go to the stall area. We find our four other horses and TJ's stall next to them. All the stalls have numbers; we have five stalls total. Mr. Hank and the boys are happy to see us.

I put TJ in his nice, roomy stall, put some hay in the rack, and give him a pail of oats. He seems calm and satisfied. I've been planning to sleep in the stall with TJ, but Mr. Hank convinces me it isn't necessary. We leave the stables at eight p.m., then check in to the Majestic Hotel. The bellboy carries our bags to our separate rooms.

I give the bellboy a generous tip. He acts kinda surprised and most appreciative. I think if you're gonna travel first class, tip first class. Word gets out and the service is more than excellent.

That night Mr. Hank, Asa and the boys scarf down barbeque ribs with all the trimmings while I eat a tuna sandwich. The waitress remarks, "I can tell you're a jockey; you poor boys never eat any real food."

At five the next morning, we go to the stalls. I pet and talk to TJ some, then saddle him and walk onto the track for some exercise runs. We long lope around the one-mile track three times, and I let him out a little more twice more around. We walk around about near an hour, then I feed him his oats. After that I just explore the stables for a long while lookin' at the other horses.

I say, "Good morning, how ya'll doin'?" to several trainers and jockeys; a most satisfying morning.

The day's races begin at one o'clock. We have a horse in the fifth race, a small purse race. I know the horse well, and TJ beat him easy during our training at the Quinn Farm. Surprisingly, he is short odds, four to one, and even more surprisingly, he wins the race. He will race again next week.

I never tire of watching the races. They run from one till five p.m. I never place a bet on any of these races; I just like the racing competition and beautiful horses.

I walk around with a heap of money in my boots. I have withdrawn $3,000.00 out of Mama's and my account at the bank. I plan on betting it all on TJ. I haven't told anybody yet. At this time in my life, money is mostly numbers. I always feel the less thinking about money, the better. Work and do what's right. The money will take care of itself.

I feel strangely calm about everything, even comfortable. I read Psalms and Proverbs in bed every night, usually an hour or so, before falling off to sleep.

Two days before the Derby, I am walking TJ when I lay eyes on the most handsome, magnificent looking horse I've ever seen: a big 17 hand tall gray colt with black mane, tail and stockings. He has big pink nostrils and some pink on his lips. Mr. Hank and I just stand and stare at this amazing horse.

"That's Warsaw," says Mr. Hank, "The big odds-on favorite for the Derby. He's a late entry. You can bet there's no entry fee for him. He's actually coming down in class. He's unbeaten in eight starts. This race is merely a good warm-up for the Kentucky Derby the first week in May."

"Warsaw's a funny name for a horse," I say. "That's the capital of Poland."

"His owners immigrated to this country several years ago. Warsaw was their home, and they named this beautiful horse for their home city. Some people think Thomas Jackson may be a strange name for a horse."

Horses have the most unusual names and there are usually reasons. As I look at Warsaw, I feel fear creeping into my head. How can TJ possibly beat this outstanding, perfect-looking racehorse?

Mr. Hank says, "One thing about Warsaw being in the race. There have been some scratches, and that narrows the field down to six or seven horses. If I had known Warsaw had entered, I would have considered talking you out of paying the $1,500.00 entry fee. Some plenty smart hoss people think he could be one of the greatest of them all. The odds will be so short, he'll probably only return the minimum ten percent. A two dollar ticket will return two dollars and twenty cents."

"Mr. Hank, what's your prediction on TJ's odds?"

"Oh, somewhere in the range of 80 or 90 to one," he says. "Don't fret none about it, Sonny. It's only a horserace, not the end of things. You and TJ do the best you can. There's always a miracle chance."

I am most happy to see Mama, Papa and Rachel when they arrive that evening. A week without them seems a long while. I perk up a little, but again feel some fearful thoughts after seeing Warsaw and hearing about how great he is.

Grandma, Grandpa and Uncle Joe arrive Friday evening the day before the race. They can tell I am acting some upset. Uncle Joe tries to cheer me some, but I can't shake off the dreadful feelings.

The big day, the one I've dreamed of, finally dawns. This is the one. I don't even go to the track until one o'clock. At two, I lead TJ around, pet and talk to him.

He can sense we are preparing for a race. He has no idea how big a race. I see Warsaw being led around in the distance. I sink fast. I go into TJ's stall with him, shut the half door, then get on my knees and pray to Jehovah, asking for his merciful blessing. I begin to feel much calmer.

Mr. Hank opens the door and says, "Sonny, this is it. Lead TJ out. Bring your saddle, we'll go get on the scales for the weight check."

I wear a costume riding suit. Our colors are blue and gray. I feel like a silly looking clown. I notice the other jockeys all seem to have large noses. The smallness of these men — men much older than I — seems most peculiar.

I meet Eddie Palomo, Warsaw's jockey. He is in his 30s and calls me "kid." He has a strange accent and says he comes from New Jersey. "I know you're nervous this being your first race," he says. "Try to relax and let the horse do the work. I notice you're listed as one of the owners, very unusual."

"Good luck, kid," he says as we leave the jockeys' room to go mount up.

Mr. Hank holds TJ as I walk up and mount. He says, "Sonny, the only advice I can think of is don't let Warsaw get too far ahead. This is not like at home. If he gets very far ahead, it's all over. You can't overcome a big lead with this horse. Watch him, and stay close, even if you have to let TJ go all out. It's your only chance."

There are seven horses entered. I draw number seven, so I'll be on the outside. Warsaw draws number one, next to the railing. As we walk by the finish line heading for the starting gate a quarter mile away, I see Grandma, Grandpa, Rachel, Mama and Papa standing right behind the rail. Behind them stand Mr. Dillard and Mr. Goldman.

I am the last horse in line. TJ looks over and sees our family, sticks his neck toward them, and lets out a nicker. Everybody laughs. All I can see is a lot of white teeth.

I got Uncle Joe off from everybody that morning and carefully explained how to bet the $3,000.00: 15 minutes before race time bet $1,000.00; five minutes before race time bet another $1,000.00; one minute before time bet the last $1,000.00. Uncle Joe quickly understood this. Keeps a lot of money from coming in and keeps the odds up.

As we go by the tote board, I can see number seven is 80 to one. The total win money bet on number seven is a little over $3,000.00. The last $1,000.00 Uncle Joe bets will probably drop it down to about 70 to one.

"Don't say nothin' to nobody," I tell Uncle Joe. "No sense upsetting them."

Bless my Uncle Joe; he keeps our secret. "Sonny, you callin' the shots," he said.

TJ and I slow lope on beyond the starting gate. He feels fine as frog hair. I've let up some on his training just before the race. He is some excited and knows what we're fixin' to do.

TJ walks right in to the starting gate. Two of the horses are actin' a little cantankerous and have to be helped. I notice Warsaw seems calm in number one. I plan to do like Mr. Hank says: pretend he is the only one I have to stay with.

The bell clangs and we're off. TJ, much to my delight, gets off to a little better than the usual start. We go by the grandstand and finish line in a pretty good bunch. A mile to go, Warsaw begins to pull ahead. I push TJ right on up. Warsaw really moves down the backstretch. I hold about five lengths behind him. I suddenly notice that Warsaw and TJ are pulling away from the other five horses.

TJ runs in his long stride float. So does Warsaw. As we make the last turn for home, I realize it is a two horse race. I have to decide: now or later. We have nearly a quarter mile to go.

I holler, "TJ, let's go!"

I can feel and sense the fire in TJ. We pull up head to head. Warsaw goes a neck ahead, then TJ goes a neck ahead. We are flying toward the finish line.

I can hear a hysterical scream in my ears, "Go, TJ! Go, TJ! Please help us, Father! Please help us!"

Eddie changes hands with his whip, slashing one side, then the other. The finish comes in a rush. I see the gray head come back to about my knee, then the roaring crowd screams as we flash over the line. I hear a loud piercing sound that every razorback hog within five miles hears. I know it's Grandma.

I'm crying so bad I know I have to get hold of myself. I don't know why I'm sobbing; I should be laughing. That will come later.

I look up and say, "Thank you. I love you."

When I get TJ under control, we turn and start back for the finish line and the trophy presentation. The entire stadium crowd stands and applauds and cheers. Now I begin to laugh.

Eddie comes by on Warsaw. "Great ride, kid. Great horse."

I holler back, "Thank you, Mr. Eddie. Lots of good luck."

When we get to the finish line, Asa comes running to meet us. He starts kissing TJ all over his face, screaming, "You sweet little darlin'! I love you! You've made old Asa and the boys plenty happy."

The photographers take some pictures. Then I get off of TJ and Asa leads him off to the stall rows. I look at the tote board, and it shows TJ, number seven, has paid $142.00 — 70 to one.

Grandma smiles and runs to me, stands on her toes, kisses me on the cheek, then whispers in my ear, "Did you give thanks?"

"Yes'm," I say.

Rachel comes flying up and hugs me and kisses me on the lips. I can see she's been crying. Mr. Hank, Mama, Papa and Uncle Joe are smiling and laughing.

I say, "Thank you, Mr. Hank, for your advice."

Uncle Joe acts quiet, for him. "I got all the money down," he says. "I guess I'm really a big natural born crybaby, I can't help it."

Here comes Mr. Goldman and Mr. Dillard running and laughing. All at once we hear this huge caterwauling scream. Sounds like Tarzan calling his apes. A loud gurgling noise, then a yippee rebel yell sounded.

Someone says, "There's some old man over there having some kind of fit."

Grandma looks at me and goes over to a crowd of people and sees it's Grandpa. He screams out, "My little ole TJ got a heart bigger than a three-gallon syrup bucket, and so's my grandson!" He sees me and Grandma and waves a handful of tickets in our faces.

"Lookie there!" he screams. "I got me 50 of them there two-dollar bill tickets. I'm gonna need a new bailing machine to bale my money up."

I turn to Grandma and say, "You got your tonic in your bag?"

"I shore do," and she pulls out a pint bottle, unscrews the cap, hands it to Grandpa, and says, "Will, get you a good snort of this here tonic. Settle your nerves down some."

Grandpa's hand shakes so he could hardly get it to his mouth. He drinks about a third of it, makes a face, stomps the ground, and manages to say, "Annie, if we had any sheep, this shore would make some powerful sheep dip."

Grandma takes the bottle, turns it up and drinks the rest, looks at me and says, "I got another bottle in the Caddy."

"Grandma," I ask, "You don't happen to have a sack in that bag by chance?"

"Just so happens I do," and she pulls a clean flour sack right out of her bag.

We get Grandpa by the hand, and I run for Uncle Joe, saying, "Uncle Joe, you and Grandpa and Grandma cash in the tickets and get an escort to the Cadillac. Head for home fast but careful. Don't stop for nothing but gas. I'm coming right behind soon as I can get TJ loaded and the trailer hitched up."

I run and get Rachel and tell her to ride with me. Mr. Hank says, "I'm sending Asa along in case you have trouble."

I tell Papa, "Check us out of the hotel. You and Mama will probably catch up to me by the time we get to Arkadelphia. Just follow along behind."

Papa and Mama hurry off. I change out of my riding costume and run for the stalls. Asa has walked and rubbed TJ down. He has his blanket cover on and a nosebag with oats. Asa is going to ride in the trailer with TJ. We get all loaded up and head out for our East Texas homes.

We drive in silence to Arkadelphia. I drive extra careful on the narrow and winding roads. After we clear Arkadelphia, it smooths out. Good thing, it is getting dark. We're more relaxed now.

Rachel says, "Sonny, you never cease to amaze me. You are giving orders to everyone, even my own daddy, and no one in the least seems surprised. They just jump around and carry 'em out. You know you're only 16."

I think about this and begin to get embarrassed. "Rachel, I hope no one takes offense. It just comes over me sometimes. I don't know why I do this."

She laughs and says, "It's just your nature. No one seems the least bit offended. Quite the opposite."

"Sonny," she continues, "I can't explain the feeling I had when you and TJ were flying down the track looking so small beside Warsaw. You passed right by me, and I could hear you crying out, 'Help us please!' When I seen you barely won, I started crying with joy and relief. You and TJ wanted to win so bad. Your dream came true. TJ is not a fine specimen of a racehorse, and you shore would not be considered tall, dark and handsome — but in my eyes, you and TJ are the most handsome and beautiful things in the world." She leans over and kisses me on the cheek.

After a while, I say, "Thank you, Rachel. I will always cherish this day and your feelings about TJ and me." Such talk gets me all flustered and tongue-tied.

"Rachel, up ahead of us heading for home, Grandma has a flour sack full of money, plus the purse money of $20,000.00. I bet $3,000.00 on TJ to win at 70 to one."

"Sonneee!" Rachel cries out. "That staggers my imagination. There's not that much money in all of East Texas. Do you feel rich? Do you feel any different?"

"I don't know."

"Where did the $3,000.00 come from?"

"Papa gave it to me. No one knows about it besides you and Uncle Joe. Somehow, between here and home, I have to figure on how to divide this money."

We stop in Texarkana to gas the truck. Asa declares he and TJ are fine as silk. Asa walks TJ around about 15 minutes. Mama and Papa pull in while we are gassing up the truck.

"Let's stay together," I tell Papa. "We still have about six more hours of steady driving."

It is nearly midnight and I hope to be home by daylight. When we pull down the lane to the house, the Belle stands at the board fence in the pasture in front of the house. She lets out a piercing nicker and TJ answers with one. Belle is tearing out for their stall. She is so excited when we lead TJ in that she is nickering and snuffling all over him. He is her baby. If she knew what he had just done, she would be some busting with pride mama. She loves her baby, and he loves his mama.

Papa pulls in right behind me. Asa takes care of TJ and says he will cut across the pasture to his house. He is practically asleep on his feet. Twelve hours in a horse trailer gets you ready for bed.

I begin to feel extra special good all over, foolishly happy.

Rachel, Mama, Papa and I walk into the kitchen where Grandma, Aunt Willie and Uncle Joe are at the table. The full flour sack sits on the floor next to it.

Grandma sets out cups, and says, "I got a fresh pot of rooster coffee."

The coffee tastes good and strong and we begin to wake up just like the roosters.

I ask, "Where's Grandpa?"

"He took another good snort of tonic as we were leaving Hot Springs," Grandma says. "Slept all the way home. He won't be up for another eight hours."

"That must be some kind of powerful tonic," I say.

"He ain't used to it like me," says Grandma. "It just calms me down. Puts Will to sleep."

I reach down and pick the flour sack up saying, "Clean the table. I got a most pleasurable chore to perform."

I turn the sack upside down and dump bundles and bundles of money right on the table. The only sound is Uncle Joe breathing. I count out twelve bundles of $5,000.00 each — $100.00 bills with brown paper wrappers — and push it over in front of Grandma.

I then count out twelve more piles and push them over in front of Uncle Joe.

I count out twelve more and pull them in front of me.

"Grandma," I say, "The purse check is $20,000.00. Give that to Grandpa to give the church. Ask Grandpa to request a new organ and a new softball diamond with some spectator benches, maybe some lights. The rest goes to the general offering."

"This other $30,000.00 I would appreciate if you agree, $15,000.00 for Woody and Saree, $10,000.00 as a bonus for Mr. Hank to divide as he sees fit for him and the boys for the extra special work with TJ and me, the other $5,000.00 for Mammy BB and her girls for the extra special good job for Mama and Papa's reception," I list aloud.

"And maybe, if Papa will let us use his house for a celebration, we can share our blessing with our friends."

Papa speaks right up, "Not my house, Sonny. Your home. Mary's home. Our home together. Superb, splendid idea! Magnificent idea indeed."

"Papa, don't forget, we talk East Texas," then I ask everyone, "Is this division agreeable?"

Uncle Joe gets up, comes around and puts his arms around me and hugs me so hard I can't breathe.

"Sonny!" he roars out. "I'm a natural born speechless man."

Aunt Willie squeals out, "Joe, now I can have my own house."

"What's wrong with this one?"

"A woman needs her very own house."

Grandma speaks up, "She's right, Joe. Plan on you and Willie a nice big house. You gonna need it. She's expectin' again."

Aunt Willie screams out, "I ain't never eatin' another oyster long as I live. I'm studying on getting fixed after this one."

We all laugh till tears come partly 'cause the tension is relieved.

The phone rings, two shorts and a long. I say, "Rachel, grab that."

She picks the receiver up, and holds it about a foot from her ear. I can hear a loud jumble of funny sounding words all the way across the room.

"Sonny, it's for you. Mr. Jean Manseur."

"Hello," I say.

A big blast comes out. "Sonny, I bust out every bookmaker in the whole state of Louisiana. I see in the paper where you and your little TJ is running in the Derby. I have this special feeling for you and your little brown hoss. I see the odds, and I think 'Whoooee. I bust 'em all!'" Mr. Manseur yells.

"I want to send you and Mam'selle Rachel a little something for when you maybe be married in a few years."

"Uno momento!" I say. "Here's Rachel."

I put the earpiece in Rachel's hand, and put my ear close. He shouts so loud I can hear him easily. He starts using a lot of Cajun French and Rachel and I can't understand much of it.

Rachel says, "Merci beaucoup, Monsieur Manseur. About four years from now. Mr. Goldman at the bank. Au revoir."

She hands me the earpiece. "Au revior, Sonny, till we meet again," he closes.

I say, "Auf Wiedersehen," and hear a loud "Bah!" and a hang-up click.

Mama says, "What was that all about?"

"I don't know for sure. I couldn't understand most of it. Please explain, Rachel."

She laughs, but I notice she also blushes and acts bashful. She reports, "Mr. Manseur is sending Mr. Goldman a check to be held in trust for Sonny and me, and given to us the day we are married."

I laugh and say, "I won't be 17 until August. We'll graduate in May of 1940, that's four years off."

"That's what I told him," Rachel says. "He said let it accumulate interest until then. He didn't say how much. He says his attorney will handle the details. I suppose Mr. Goldman will be the trust officer."

Rachel looks me in the eyes and squeals out, "If I'm dreaming, please don't ever wake me."

I yawn, and Grandma says, "Bedtime! Sleep time! Ever'body get to their beds!"

I wake up after I don't know how long to a faint sound of singing and clattering noise coming from the milk parlor. I dress and look at my watch. It is midnight. I realize I've slept for nearly 15 hours. I really make up for lost sleep. I hardly slept the last three days at Hot Springs. Guess I just collapsed.

I walk out to the milk parlor. There shines a dim light and I can hear Woody singing sumpin' 'bout riding "The Glory Train" as he loads up the milk cans for delivery.

Woody sees me, does a little pigeon dance, and shouts out, "Mr. Sonny, I is the choicest, primest, center-cut happiest man in all East Texas."

He laughs and grabs me, hugs me, and says, "Mr. Will done tole me all about how you and little TJ beat the big great gray hoss Warsaw."

He, busting with pride, adds, "I had one of them there heart palpitating attacks and ever'thing turned red, then green, heh heh. Green, the color of money."

He explains that Miz Annie's sheep dip tonic saved him. Woody screams out again, "Mr. Sonny, I had me ten of them two-dollar bill tickets on you and TJ. Mr. Will got 'em for me. He done counted me out $1,420.00. I is one of the richest colored men in East Texas."

He sobers a minute then says, "That ain't right. Having Saree, my baby and you and Mr. Joe and all this family makes me richer than any money could."

"I been blessed with both. Now I can buy Saree a good second-hand piano. That girl love her music. She been wanting one, she already taking lessons. The rest I can add to my little nest egg."

Woody's happiness becomes contagious. I am laughing. I know right off Uncle Joe hasn't given Woody the $15,000.00 yet. "Woody, what if you suddenly received ten times that $1,420.00?"

"Laud, Mr. Sonny. I recon me and that ole temptation would have us one terrible fight."

"Woody, get ready. I'm in the same fix. Let's join in this fight together. Remember, lead us not into temptation. Woody, if you feel a weakness coming over you, or if I feel one, 'cause of sudden large money, let's holler for help."

"Mr. Sonny, I don't understand."

"You will," I say. "Soon as Uncle Joe surprises you with your love and affection money."

We finish loading the milk cans and I insist on making the run to Dallas. I tell Woody he has been going about 20 hours a day for the last three days. He needs to take off a day. We will be back in our normal work routine for a while. The Kentucky Derby is two months off.

I have to get my head set to do the best I can one day at a time. I begin having spells thinking about Churchill Downs and the first week in May.

When I get to the Schepp's Dairy in Dallas, I meet Ben Tuttle and we go to the Market Café for breakfast. Ben pays the last money he owes on the truck and he wants another batch of 500 white leghorn chicks. Ben is laughing and giggling so I think something is wrong.

"Sonny, me, Tom and Charlie sent $30.00 by Mr. Goldman to bet on you and your beautiful little ole hoss. He calls me in the middle of the night screaming and hollering about how you won the big race at Oak Lawn Park in Hot Springs. He brought the money out to the house at four o'clock in the morning — $2,130.00. We're buying a good used John Deere Iron Mule, hay baling machine, pickemup, adding some Holsteins, heifers."

Looking suddenly solemn, he declares, "Sonny, we getting in some mighty tall cotton."

I feel some goose bumps at this kind of talk. I get so happy I start laughing and giggling with Ben. I sing all the way back home. My voice is not completely through changing so I'm sure if anyone could have heard me, they'd think I have some voice defect. Sounds like a frog croaking one minute, and a chicken squawking the next.

When I get home, I brush TJ and the Belle, clean out their stall, and put fresh sawdust in. TJ is full of pep and feeling good like he's raring to go. I trot up to Papa's big house and go to the back kitchen door and knock.

Mammy BB opens the door and squalls out, "Mr. Sonneee!"

She grabs me and starts in hugging me, calling me her young fine gentleman. Then Ruth grabs me and does the same. I am most surprised at this display of affection. I can see Papa, Mama, Rachel and Mr. Hank at the table having breakfast.

Papa says, "I gave Mammy BB the money for you."

"Not for me, Papa, for all of us."

Mama and Papa's eyes are shining with happiness. The look on Rachel's face makes me feel like I am dropping down one of them elevators in a tall building again.

Mr. Hank speaks up, "Sonny, we're right in the busiest time of breeding season. Runs from mid-February to mid-April. I booked 20 more mares for Gallant Hood. Our win at Hot Springs set the phone to ringing. I'm going to be busy for a while."

"You just keep TJ well exercised. Bring him up about once a week for some gate work and running against some competition. I'm sure we'll have a very profitable year. The yearlings will bring more money and our breeding fees will about double. Amazing how winning one big race generates so much attention. I love it. Mr. Gallant Hood is gonna be one busy hoss the next two months."

I turn to Rachel and ask if she would ride with me to Bailey's Store. I say she can ride the Belle.

She lets out a little whoop. "I'm ready when you are." We will be constant companions for the next five months till college time.

I ask Papa if we can postpone any celebration for a while; I just don't feel like celebrating yet. Things are moving a little too fast and I don't want any unnecessary distractions. Papa agrees and asks if I will come to the hospital for a luncheon to meet some of his staff. He says I'd be the guest of honor. How can I refuse?

"With pleasure, Papa. I'll bring Rachel." Papa seems most pleased.

Chapter 14

Rachel and I run back to the house and saddle TJ and the Belle. They are so excited I have to scold them some to get 'em settled down. It is cold for this time of year and the cold weather makes them extra anxious to be moving on out. We long lope nearly all the way to Bailey's Store. TJ has power to spare. He grows better all along.

When I go to pay Mr. Bailey for our snack of sardines, cheese, crackers, and Coca Colas, he says, "What do you mean? You won the big race. This is a small token of honor for me." I can see to refuse would cause him discomfort, so I thank him.

As we are riding back, I tell Rachel I am some upset about not paying for our snacks. Rachel tells me I am a good giver but not a good receiver; that I need to be more gracious about receiving. "It makes people happy to give. Add to their pleasure by being graciously enthused," she instructs.

I think about this for a moment. "You're right. Thank you for telling me this. I don't have any experience at receiving things of this kind."

"Better get used to it. You have some fame and fortune now and I don't believe it'll be fleeting. You can buy anything you want but just be on guard against getting all puffed up with pride." I think about this as we ride for home.

After a while I say, "Rachel, I can't think of one single thing I could buy that I don't already have. If you catch me acting uppity or the prideful fool, would you be so kind as to please tell me?"

"Sonny, I'll be the first to notice and I'll tell you pronto with mucho gusto!" We laugh.

Rachel says, "I'm counting on you being able to handle fame and fortune. In some ways, I am much more mature than you. In your innocent way, you have some very mysterious power. Grandma Annie says you have an angel on your shoulder. I'll be with you as much as possible these next few months."

I become dumbstruck at this talk, then start laughing. "Let's move on out for home." We make the same trip the next two days.

As we come by Woody's lane to his house, I hear the faint sounds of a piano. I pull TJ up and Rachel pulls the Belle up. We sit and listen for a few minutes. "Let's visit Saree and Woody," I say, and we ride down the lane to their house.

Woody comes to the door and roars out, "Mr. Sonny, Miz Rachel, come right in! Saree, bring yourself in here!"

Saree comes in from the other room, all smiles and pretty white teeth. She gives me a big hug, kisses me on the cheek, hugs Rachel and says, "Sit right down and let me get us some refreshments." Little Sonny walks now. He comes over and climbs in my lap.

Woody says, "Mr. Sonny, you know what we talked about, the temptation and all? Well, when Mr. Joe come down here and give me all that money, I purt near had one of Mr. Will's heart palpitation attacks. I thought on some of Miz Annie's sheep tonic."

"I got holt of my fool self and commenced to thinking 'bout a big red Caddylack with a long coon tail on the radio antenna, spoke wheels, white walls and such. A diamond ring big as a pigeon egg. Some yellar shoes, purple shirts, fancy hat. Dat ole temptation had done grabbed me. Saree got me to my senses. She start crying and worrying over me.

"I got to studyin' 'bout it. I got Saree and my baby counting on me. I got you, Mr. Will, Mr. Joe, Miz Annie and Miz Willie counting on me. I remember the first time I ever saw you. You asked me if I would make you a good hand. I had a few pitiful rags and a few sticks of furniture less than four years ago.

"Mr. Sonny, I bought my church a new piano and Saree got a good secondhand one. I give thanks for all my blessings. I put the rest of the money in the bank and shut the door on my mind 'bout it.

I won that fight with Mr. Temptation. They won't be no foolin' me. I ain't wanting nothing I ain't already got."

Rachel looks at me. We start clapping and laughing. Saree, laughing, sets a piece of coconut cream pie in front of us and pours some coffee. I feel so good I'm dizzy. Woody says, "Sonny, you better put Little Sonny down, he subject to pee on you."

I laugh and say, "He already has."

While we are brushing TJ and the Belle, Rachel says, "Sonny, being with you is never dull. Some strange way you keep the pot boiling. I love it this way."

"Your confidence is most pleasing," I say.

Rachel proves true to her word. She rises early and makes the ride with me to Dallas every morning. Early means leaving at two a.m. We usually arrive back by seven or eight a.m. We enjoy our constant companionship. We talk of school coming in the near future, some about our future together, sing songs, and enjoy lots of laughter and humor.

The big topic is the upcoming Kentucky Derby. We will both get so anxious thinking about it we decide not to discuss it for our own peace of mind. Fear of the unknown has a way of creeping in.

A few days later, we arrive back home from the milk run and Grandma tells us Mr. Goldman has called all excited and wants Rachel and me to come to the bank after toast and coffee. I've gone back to watching my weight.

We go to the Cadillac to drive to the bank when I realize I still have not deposited my money from Hot Springs. It's in a shoebox under my bed and I've forgotten about it. I run back in to get the money, tie a string around the box, and head out with Rachel to the bank.

When we walk in, Mr. Goldman comes a running. He acts some excited. You can hear him all over the bank.

"I have papers, documents, everything from Jean Manseur. Come here into my office. Let me explain."

"He called me. I had a difficult time understanding him over the telephone. He mumbled something sounded like rabbit's foot, four leaf clover, a dead cat, gibberish about Mam'selle, Sonny, little hoss, Big Red, love, bust 'em all out, some in Arkansas," he reports.

"Howsomever, I have a $25,000.00 check with some exceptions for you and Rachel. I'm the trust officer. This money will be deposited to draw interest until the day you and Rachel are legally pronounced man and wife. If not within five years, the money will be divided between you. I have some papers for you to sign."

For some strange reason, I become uneasy at this exception about being presented on our wedding day. Seems to me we are taking a lot for granted. I've never talked of any such thing. How could we know? I am three months shy of 17. Rachel seems some puzzled also, but we sign all the papers. Why worry about such a magnificent generous gift? How can anything about it not be good?

"Sonny, Rachel," says Mr. Goldman, "This is one of the most stupendous acts of generosity I have ever known."

Rachel says, "We'll write a long letter expressing our gratitude."

We shake hands and start to leave. Mr. Goldman hollers at us as we near the door. "You forgot your shoebox!"

"Oh, I forgot! I need to deposit it into my account."

We go back into his office. I untie the string and stack all the money on his desk. His eyes seem extra big and shiny. "My! Oh my, my!"

"Has Uncle Joe and Grandma been in yet? They have the same amount."

He commences laughing till tears come.

"Sonny," he croaks out, "this little ole East Texas community has brought a truck load of Arkansas money home. I thought Dillard and me done some damage, but nothing like this. My deposits have jumped more this week than any week since 1929.

"My number one absolute obligation is to protect my depositors' money, then serve my community with capital. I'm beginning to love my job again, starting to see a little daylight," he says. He stares me in the face for what seems a long time.

Rachel speaks up quietly, "Me too, Mr. Goldman."

Whatever *that* means. I get ready to leave.

We shake hands and Rachel and I walk out. I ask Rachel if she minds waiting while I have my hair trimmed. She says that'd be fine. "I can read the Farmer Stockman Magazine while I wait."

Where Angels Roost

When we go into the barbershop, Zeke smiles real big and says, "Come right in, Sonny. Welcome. Be with you in a minute."

As he starts trimming my hair, he congratulates me for winning the Arkansas Derby and asks about the Kentucky Derby — much more friendly than the last time I sat here. No hair tonic; I don't cotton much to the smell. He brushes the hair off extra good with his little brush broom.

He proclaimes, "No charge, Sonny. My pleasure." I look over at Rachel who winks and smiles.

I remember. "Hey! That's great, Zeke. I appreciate it. Very nice of you." Rachel is right, makes him most pleased.

By this time, I am so hungry I decide I just have to indulge in one of the Chili Bowl's all-the-way big hamburgers. When Rachel and I walk in, Red, the owner, hollers out, "Heh! My good buddy Sonny, winner of the big race up in Arkansas."

Some other folks chime in, "Hey Sonny! How ya'll doing?"

I smile and reply, "Thank you! I've never been better."

Rachel smiles. "You're learning," she says.

I know what's coming so I leave a five-dollar bill under my plate for the waitress. Sure nuff, my money is no good. I thank Red with enthusiasm. We are walking toward the bank for the car when we hear a shout. "Hey, Sonny! Wait!"

It is the waitress. "Sonny, you must have made a mistake." She has the five-dollar bill in her hand.

"No mistake," I say. "I want to make up for some of the times when I didn't leave much of anything, or nothing at all." She hugs my neck, turns and runs back to the Chili Bowl.

We start laughing and Rachel says, "Boy hidey, are you ever learning." In 1936, five dollars is a heap of money.

We stop off at the big house going home. I still haven't gotten used to the idea that it is my home. I think, *Shucks, not many kids got two fine homes at the same time. I can live in both of them.*

Mama and Papa are having a sandwich in the kitchen. Mammy BB is doing something in another part of the house. Papa runs his eyes up and down me and says, "How much you weigh?"

"I'm holding, but barely, at 118. If I can hang on at this weight for seven more weeks, I'll be okay."

Papa frowns a little. "Don't forget tomorrow, Saturday at noon, we're having a luncheon in the board room. You and Rachel come an hour early and I'll show you around. No need to dress up — just wear your khakis and maybe your light blue shirt. Matches your eyes."

I try not to show that I don't much go for this formality. "Thank you, Papa. I'm looking forward to it," I say. I want to please my mama and papa.

When Rachel and I get home on Saturday morning, we saddle TJ and the Belle and ride to Bailey's Store. We slow lope about five miles. TJ is so fired up to run that I have to scold him and hold him back. Going home, I let him run about two miles. Not a hard run, a light run.

We ride back to the big house so Rachel can get ready for our trip to Papa's hospital. I lead TJ and the Belle back to their stall, brush 'em good, and put out oats and fresh hay. Then I go to the house and scrub up real good with Lifebouy, wash my hair and commence getting ready.

Grandma has my khakis starched and ironed and my black boots shined real bright. I stand in front of Grandma and she looks me up and down all over. Looks at the shirt, looks into my eyes, and says, "Good match. You cleaned up real good now. Mary and Jonathon will be proud."

I drive the Cadillac up to the big house and go in. Mammy BB exclaims, "Sonny! You da spitting image of you pappy when he you age. Mmmm, 1912 that would be."

"Mammy BB, how long you been here?"

"Less see. I come here in 1894 when I be 18 years old. Uh oh, you done figured me out. I is 60. I tell you this, Sonny. You papa and you grampa is gentlemen of the highest order. You jes like 'em."

"I appreciate that, Mammy BB. I'd like to talk with you some more about this some time."

"Anytime, Mr. Sonny."

Rachel walks in; I nearly fall over in a swoon. "Lawd!" Mammy BB shouts. "Look at my baby all dressed up like a little princess!"

Even though Papa says there is no reason to dress up, Rachel has on black high heel shoes, silk stockings, a low-cut black dress, a single-strand pearl necklace and matching ear bobs. This is the first time I've ever seen her with make up on, even lipstick.

I stare at her so long she finally says, "What do you think?"

"Good thing I can't get my hands on Grandma's tonic. I need somethin' to calm my nerves. I ain't never seen you dressed up like this before. Not even at graduation."

She laughs real big. "Thank you very much for your compliment. I feel like I want to look like a woman. I sure hope I'm not making a fool of myself; no one has seen me like this before."

I feel a sudden state of anxiety. "You sure gonna be turning some heads."

"There's only one head I'm interested in turning." I feel a slight quiver at the thrill of this reply.

"Remember our promise," she says, suddenly serious. "To remain pure and virtuous until we take the sacred vows of marriage. It's so important, Sonny."

"I know and I will."

When we arrive at Papa's hospital, he stands out front dressed exactly like me — khakis, blue shirt, black riding boots. Mama waits inside while visiting one of her friends.

The building is two-story red brick, much bigger than I realized, with beautiful landscaped grounds. Everything smells clean and appears fresh looking. Papa leads us into a spacious foyer and directly to a large brass plaque which reads: "This Place of Healing built and endowed by James and Martha Bradford Quinn, 1910."

Right below this it reads: "James Quinn February 1864 – April 1912. Martha Bradford Quinn, August 1870 – April 1912."

"Papa," I say, "was this my grandpa and grandma?"

"Yes, son, my parents. Many times I sense their spirits in this building. They died in each other's arms when I was 16."

"Please explain, Papa."

"My parents made a trip to Edinburgh, Scotland, a famous medical city, for a six-month advanced seminar on internal medicine. On their return voyage, they sailed on a big, newly built great steamship. They were nearly home to New York when it struck an iceberg and sank. Many lost their lives, but their spirits live on in this hospital that Papa built."

I become speechless for a moment, questions and thoughts whirling in my head. "What does the word endowment mean?" I ask.

"Perpetual funds for the operation of this hospital," Papa answers. "Father made an investment in an oil company shortly before the Spindle Top field came in. Fortunes were made; this hospital and our farm are some of the results. There are more. My grandfather, your great-grandfather Joseph Quinn, was lost at Little Round Top with Hood's Texas Brigade, seven months before my father's birth. That's one reason our horses have names like Gallant Hood, AP Hill, Longstreet, Pickett's Charge — in honor of their memory."

I become overwhelmed in a dizzy state. Papa looks at his watch and says, "Let's hurry through the building; it's nearly time for our luncheon. Some of Mammy BB's friends are catering it for us."

We rush through the hospital. "Calm down," Papa says. "I shouldn't have laid so much on you at one time."

Rachel takes my hand, squeezes and says, "I'm here beside you."

We enter a large beautiful room with paneled walls, chandeliers, a long, large elegant table with plushy chairs. "This is our staff and board meeting room. Probably some on the extravagant side, but Dad wanted it this way. Top class," Papa says.

People start coming in, about 25 all told. I am surprised to see Mr. and Mrs. Goldman. I later learn he is on the board mainly for financial purposes. It is a happy lunch with lots of pleasant talk. You can see the friendship. The table has name cards and everyone finds their seats. Papa sits at one end of the long table. I sit at his right, Mama across the table at his left, and Rachel next to me.

When Papa stands up, everybody gets quiet. In a nice calm voice, Papa says, "As you all know, this is not a board and staff meeting. This gathering, my dear friends, is to introduce and honor my son Jonathon, better known as Sonny. A week ago this day, Sonny and his exceptionally fine horse, Thomas Jackson, won the Arkansas Derby, which has brought recognition and pride to our community.

"I'm proud to say TJ was produced at the Quinn Farm, although I unfortunately had no hand in raising him. Miz Annie Jackson, my mother-in-law, and Sonny get all the credit.

"I fear I've been stricken with a common affliction known as parental pride. I will simply say his mother Mary and I are very proud of our son. Thank you for coming to share our pleasure and happiness."

Papa sits down, then says, "Sonny, stand up." Rachel squeezes my hand.

I stand up. "I hope I'm not expected to say anything." I can see the smiles. They sense my distress. I remember what Grandma has told me: say what comes to mind. I calm some.

I say, "The one who should be honored and recognized is not here. She's home tending her turkeys and seeing about her chickens. Most all of you know her as Miz Annie. To me, she's Grandma.

"The parental affliction Papa spoke of also strikes the children. I give thanks every day for my mama and papa. I love them very much. One of the great commandments I pray I will never violate is "Honor thy mother and father."

I look at Mama; her cheeks are wet. Papa becomes quiet with a sort of sad, serious expression on his face. Rachel smiles and gives me a wink. It is very quiet. I say in a loud voice, "Papa, can we eat now?"

Papa hollers out, "Yes! Yes! Let the eating begin." Everybody commences laughing and talking.

The gathering of friends, the eating and the visiting are over about four p.m., and Rachel and I start for home. I drop her off at the big house to change clothes. She will come to Grandma's to spend the night. We are pretty tuckered out and go right to bed. Sleep time.

We awake about midnight to load up the milk cans for the trip to Dallas. For some reason, seems like toting the milk cans is getting heavier. To keep my weight down, I barely eat. If I can somehow get through these next six weeks before the Kentucky Derby, I feel everything after this is no matter. I know it will be my last race. I am growing too fast.

We load up and head out for Schepp's Dairy Company. We are up to right at 8,000 pounds of milk a day now, about 100 ten-gallon cans. We laugh and sing, "When the Roll is Called Up Yonder."

Rachel says, "Sonny, you were the center of attention yesterday at the hospital. I watched you closely and you handled yourself very well. I'm proud of you."

"It was Papa Quinn and Mama Mary that were acting so foolishly prideful. I heard one of the men say what a remarkable resemblance you and Papa Quinn had. Papa Quinn immediately went into the miracles of reproductive genes and the internal as well as external similarities. He lost me with all that genetic doctor talk. I tell you, he's some proud papa. He gives the impression that this is his greatest achievement in his entire life. Nothing else is close."

I think about this. I feel good that Papa feels this about me. I feel the same about him. Papa is a courageous war hero, decorated and honored for his bravery in battle. He had the determination to finish college, went off to war, came home, then went to a far distant place for his medical training. All of this after his mama and papa died. I knew in my own heart that my papa was a special wonderful man.

Mama is a very courageous woman too. Life had not exactly been handed to her on a platter. I think about the struggles she's endured with a sickly kid, me. At this time I am really glad I have some of those reproductive genes.

As we get closer to Dallas, about ten miles off, we can see the big red flying horse on top of the Magnolia Building which lights up at night. On a clear night, you can see it from way off, ten miles or so.

When we back up to the unloading dock at Schepp's, I ask Henry, the man I've been checking my load in with for a long time, if I can make a run through the plant. He says, "Sure 'nuff, Sonny, go right on."

We go into the bottling section where the milk is being automatically bottled — amazing, all the complicated-looking machinery. We go into another section where butter is being made in big revolving churns. This is in the days when artificial butter, margarine, is not well accepted. We go into another section where ice cream is made, then the cheese section, and so on. They even have their own ice plant.

When we come back out to the truck, I ask Henry how many people work in the plant. He tells me right at 100 people. We talk a while about the delivery system. Seems a lot of the trucks are owned and operated by independent owners. This tour reveals really more than I can understand. I have an idea in the back of my mind, a kinda naggin' thought I've been having for some time.

On the way back home, Rachel says, "Your mind is working on something. I can tell. I know you too well."

"I'm studying on something. I need to get it all sorted out."

When we get home, we unload the empty cans for steaming out and then go into the kitchen where Uncle Joe and Aunt Willie are having breakfast. Grandma is working with her chickens; Grandpa is helping Woody finish up.

Uncle Joe declares, "Sonny, we is got so rich, we eating store-bought toasted light bread three mornings a week now. Talk about high class. Willie don't even make my buttermilk biscuits but four days a week now."

Aunt Willie laughs. "It sure is nice having store-bought things. I used to do without."

Uncle Joe has about 160 acres across from Woody and they are commencing to make serious plans for their new house. Aunt Willie is beginning to show. Uncle Joe teases her about swollering a watermelon seed or maybe one of them oysters making a big pearl.

There stands land for sale all around. Seems most of the farmers are going bust, selling out, moving off. Hard to believe that good farms are selling for $10.00 and $15.00 an acre. A big, nice, fancy brick house can be built for $5,000.00 or so.

I ask Uncle Joe if he will consider giving Woody and Saree a deed to the old Jones farm so's they can build them a new house. "I done been studyin' on that very thing," he says. "I shore would hate to think 'bout him and Saree ever leaving. They just like family. I like my family to be around me. I'm a natural born family man!" he shouts.

We laugh and shout, "Amen!" to that. My Uncle Joe fills to the brim with goodness.

When Grandma comes in, Rachel gets up and pours her a cup of coffee. She reminds us we need to start getting ready for Sunday school and church. I have lost track of time and don't even realize it's Sunday.

After church and Sunday dinner, Rachel and I ride TJ and the Belle on our usual route until late afternoon. I've not been going to the training track at all. It is right in the rush of breeding season, which seems to make TJ nervous and a little hard to manage. Mr. Hank explains he can smell the mares. I check the fences closely everyday, anxious for breeding season to end.

The next two days after unloading the milk, I go through the milk plant again. Many independent operators are unloading their trucks at four a.m. I ask a lot of questions. Some are making deliveries as far off as 80 or 90 miles; some are doing home deliveries. There is a big home delivery dairy company called Metzger's that has over 1,000 single horse-driven delivery wagons.

Wednesday morning, when Rachel and I get back from our trip, instead of going home, I say, "Let's go to the Chili Bowl for breakfast," which for me is toast and coffee.

We park the truck and go in. The clock reads seven-thirty. I look around and sure 'nuff there sits Mr. Goldman, Mr. Dillard and Billy Joe.

They immediately holler out, "Sonny, you and Rachel come join us."

We sit down and say our good mornings. Mr. Dillard asks, "Just getting back from your milk delivery?"

"Yes, sir," I say, and add, "It sure would be nice to have a small, for starters, bottling plant and butter making plant right here in town.

"If you stuck a pin in the center of town, and drew a circle of about 100 miles, you would have Dallas, Fort Worth, Tyler, plus all the other good-sized towns – close to a third of the population of the whole state of Texas. We got good roads for truck deliveries.

"Maybe get cotton farmers to thinking dairy cows. Good grass, hay, forage and such. In no time, maybe two or three years, we'd be the perfect spot to become the dairy center of Texas which I believe would make a whole bunch of folks a lot more prosperous than they are now."

I say all this as nonchalantly as I can like just making conversation. I really want to plant a seed in the minds of two of our community's most respected businessmen.

We have a few laughs, then tease Billy Joe some about wearing a white shirt and tie now that he is a businessman. Talk about the Texas Centennial coming up this year, celebrating Texas's 100th anniversary of independence from Mexico. Talk of the upcoming Kentucky Derby.

During all of this conversation, I can see I have planted the seed I set out to sow.

Chapter 15

We stop off at the big house to ask Mr. Hank for any advice about TJ's training. He tells us in two more weeks he will be finished with the breeding for the season except for a few stragglers. Seems to be a steady stream of trucks and trailers coming and going. Mr. Gallant Hood is real popular.

Mr. Hank advises, "Just keep on like you been doing."

He mentions something about the farrier coming out with his portable hoss-shoeing equipment in two or three weeks.

We go into the kitchen of the big house where Mama and Papa are eating breakfast.

Mammy BB looks at me, frowns, and says, "Mister Sonny, you ain't much bigger than a broomstick. I be glad when you big race is over, then I be putting some meat on them bones."

Rachel and I sit down. She has a good appetite but feels if I can't eat much, she won't either. So we just have more coffee. Papa tells me to slow down to no more than three cups a day. Tells me to eat more fruit — apples, oranges, one banana a day. He believes I will always be some on the slender side.

While we are sitting at the table, I say, "Papa, I'm embarrassed to ask you a very personal question and if you tell me 'none of your business', I'll understand."

He looks at me for a minute or so then says, "Ask away."

"Papa, do you have extra money for an investment opportunity should one come up?"

"Why do you ask, Sonny?"

"I have a feeling Mr. Goldman and Mr. Dillard will maybe approach you in the near future."

"How much money are you talking about?"

"As near as I can guess, about $50,000.00 for you, the same for me. Mr. Goldman knows how much I deposited from my Arkansas money."

Papa starts laughing and says, "Pardon me, Sonny, I can't help it. I thought you had some fool nonsense in your head. I should have known better. Yes, I easily have this much money."

He smiles and says, "I shouldn't tell you this but I bet $500.00 on you and TJ. I feared it would set a bad example for you to know your papa gambled on a race. I usually don't, not even on my own horses, but I made an exception in your and TJ's race. I felt I had an obligation. So the investment you speak vaguely of is the result of you and TJ. I have also heard that Mr. Goldman and Mr. Dillard did quite well."

I start laughing. "If this works out like I think it will, we oughta name our milk plant TJ Dairy Company."

A week later, after Rachel and I get back home and unload the milk cans, Grandma says Papa wants me to call him at the hospital.

I call and Papa says, "Mr. Goldman has invited us to his house for supper tonight. Says to bring Rachel. Come to the big house and we'll go together — your mama, Rachel, you and me."

I change the oil in the truck, grease and service it out complete. Then Rachel and I saddle TJ and the Belle for our morning ride. When I tell Rachel we are going to Mr. Goldman's for supper, she doesn't say one word, just smiles. After a light noon meal, I drive Rachel to the big house and return for a few hours sleep. I tell her I'll be ready and back at six p.m.

Grandma wakes me at five o'clock and I commence scrubbing and shampooing and getting ready. I dress in my khakis. I don't know if I should dress up in my Sunday clothes or what. As well as I know Mr. Goldman and his wife Miz Clara, I feel no need to dress up and feel some better.

Rachel leads me into the kitchen, stands and looks me up and down and says, "You'll do."

Where Angels Roost

Mammy BB says, "Mr. Sonny, you come from some mighty fine champeen gentlemen, but you could maybe be the blue ribbon one. My baby Rachel here sticking to you so close she almost like you rib. I ain't even worrying mysef 'bout how you gonna act."

Sometimes I have no idea what Mammy BB tries to say but I feel it to be something good.

Rachel starts laughing, hugs Mammy BB, kisses her on the cheek and says, "You're so right."

Mama, Papa, Rachel and I load up in Papa's Packard and start out for Mr. Goldman's. He has a nice spread with a one-story red brick house out at the edge of town — a nice, comfortable-looking home, not overly fancy, modestly impressive.

As he later explains to me, "The town banker has to be careful — reasonable, modest home, no fancy cars, give the appearance of being frugal and conservative. By nature, people are suspicious of money lenders."

We walk into a friendly warm welcome. Miz Clara is a very gracious likeable-at-once sort of person. Miz Emma and Mr. Dillard are all smiles. I'm sure everyone feels they are in the company of best of friends. Mr. Goldman and Mr. Dillard have known Papa's papa, my grandpa, very well. I guess them to be in their early 60's. They address Papa as Doc, and Mama as Mary.

We exchange greetings and go right into the dining room where a colored lady sets food on the table.

She looks at me. "You be the Mista Sonny Mammy BB, Ruth, Woody and Saree done tole me 'bout. We all in the church choir. I fixed you somethin' special on count of you keeping you weight down. You can call me Lou."

I shake her hand. "Pleasure to meet you, Lou."

She smiles and goes off to the kitchen.

We sit down and Mr. Goldman says the blessing. We start passing plates of food and Lou comes out of the kitchen with a plate for me. Steamed squash, steamed carrots, English peas, a thin slice of roast beef and sliced tomatoes.

She says, "Mista Sonny, this all fresh out of the garden and greenhouse."

"Thank you very much. I appreciate your thoughts of me. It won't be long till I'm gonna eat cobblers, cake, ice cream and lots of it. I might even have to go to Mr. Dillard's for bigger-sized clothes." I notice at this Papa quits frowning and starts laughing.

After our most wonderful supper, Mr. Goldman says, "Let's us men go into the den for a cigar and coffee."

As we start into the den, I take Rachel's hand. "Can Rachel join us?" Rachel has been my constant companion long enough for me to feel she is somehow a source of confidence for me.

Mr. Goldman says, "Certainly, come right in and join us tobacco-stinking old men." Rachel quietly sits in a corner away from the center of the room. Mr. Goldman stands in front of the fireplace. It is cool for late March, and there is a small fire going, a most comfortable relaxing room.

"Doc, Sonny," Mr. Goldman says, "Dillard and I have a proposition for you. We are in full agreement as to the merits of our proposal but we need two more very special partners.

"We propose to build a dairy plant for our town and community. Start moderate, then build up to a larger plant in two or three years. We need that much time to persuade the cotton farmers to convert to dairy. Our milk supply will be fairly limited to begin with. I'm sincerely excited about our unlimited future being the dairy center of Texas. I can visualize a community of prosperous dairymen," he continues.

"Cotton in our section of the country is dying fast. We can change our economy for this section of Texas. We'll have a nice payroll and I'm sure we can get a five-year tax abatement. The possibilities are unlimited. Of course, this takes money and lots of it.

"What I propose is incorporating for 200,000 shares at a dollar a share: 50,000 shares for each of us; $50,000.00. I've made inquiries and consulted with engineers, architects, accountants and such. With this amount of capital, we can build the most modern plant and be doing business within six months. The first two years we'll plow the profits back into the company. I believe we can realize a return of ten percent on our investment. Mind you, there is a risk involved but I think a very small one. I think this plant will impact several hundred families in our area for the better."

Dead silence for about two minutes. Papa speaks up, "Sounds good to me. More than good. A very splendid idea. I'd like to be a part of it." At this, Mr. Goldman and Mr. Dillard start smiling and shaking Papa's hand and patting him on the back.

Mr. Goldman looks at me and says, "Sonny, is something wrong? I know you're a young man and this may not sound very exciting to you but it will be a good safe long-range investment for you. What do you think?"

"Mr. Goldman, you're right. I'm a young man and ignorant of business. If I was a partner in this enterprise, would I have a say in the decisions of the plant operation? Or would I be ignored as a kid who don't know nothing?"

"Papa is a physician, he's not a businessman. One of us would need to be involved some since $100,000.00 between us is an enormous sum of money. Papa will need to sign the papers to have my minority liabilities removed. I understand that allows me to do business as an adult." I stand up. "Let Papa and me study on this for a few days before we give our commitment."

At this, Mr. Goldman frowns slightly. "I hoped for an answer tonight."

"I'm sorry, Mr. Goldman, Mr. Dillard. I can't think of any two gentlemen I'd rather be in business with. If we should accept this proposal, there's something I would like to add," hoping this delay will convince them to agree on what I propose next.

"My and most of Papa's portion of the investment come as a result of TJ winning the Arkansas Derby. My thoughts are to name the plant TJ Dairy Company. Since my grandma is responsible for TJ being here, and I'm half owner, handed to me as a loving free gift, I propose that she get four percent of the profits as partner and royalties forever. What do you think about this, Mr. Goldman, Mr. Dillard?"

They both look at me for what seems a long time, then Mr. Goldman comes over, puts his arms around me, and just hugs. Mr. Dillard says, "Me next," and does the same.

I say, "I assume then that this is agreeable. If so, we have a wonderful future partnership."

Mr. Goldman laughs really big. "We agree this night to create a winning partnership!" All the tension disappears. We are all laughing and talking at once. As we leave, I tell Mr. Goldman that Papa and I will be at the bank to escrow our money and to get the paper flying.

Going home, Papa says, "Son, you're right. I'm a physician, but I've been blessed with a loving wife and son to look out for me."

I laugh. "Papa, if it wasn't for you and Mama, I wouldn't be here to look out for anybody. Thank you for having me."

He lets out a whoop and hollers, "My pleasure!" We are all so happy it is downright pitiful.

We have only four more weeks before the Kentucky Derby. Breeding has finished for this year; few thoroughbred race stables ever breed after April, although a small number of stables that don't race will breed for a short while yet.

All race stock has their birthdays — regardless of their actual birth dates — on January 1. Most, if not all, want the foals born during January, February, no later than March. The gestation period of horses is eleven months so we are winding down for this season. Mr. Hank says our best season. A flood of dates came in after the Arkansas Derby and we are booked solid for next year too.

The morning following the dinner at Mr. Goldman's, Papa and I go to the bank and sign papers and deposit money in the TJ Dairy Company account. Mr. Goldman takes care of the paperwork and works out bids to begin construction of the plant. Papa and I know nothing of such details. We have dreams of the end results but lack the technical know-how.

We feel our partnership with two expert businessmen to be very fortunate for us. As Papa puts it, "Very fortunate indeed!"

I have a terrible time trying to get through one day at a time. Seems my mind runs in a constant turmoil. Rachel has been very quiet, hardly says anything since our night at Mr. Goldman's.

On our trip to deliver milk and eggs after about a week, Rachel says in a low voice, "Sonny, I've been with you nearly constantly for a year now. The saying I've heard or read somewhere, 'Familiarity breeds contempt,' is certainly not true in my own case. But there's something about you. Something mysterious.

You're not quite 17 years old, yet you have a knowledge and wisdom way beyond your years. Grandma Annie and I discuss it. She says you've been this way since you came here at twelve years old. She thinks maybe you hear voices. Do you ever hear voices?"

Stricken with hearing this I nearly lose control of the truck. I feel some upset at Grandma and Rachel talking about me. In a louder than normal voice, I say, "Ya'll think I'm some kinda spooky, idiot freak what hears voices?"

"Now, Sonny, calm yourself down. Think about it for a minute. Go back over the last four and a half years. We think maybe you've been blessed with a mysterious good spirit that directs you to do good things."

I calm down and sorta in a trance-like state of mind begin to think. I have been having dreams. Sometimes I can't remember them when I wake up, but sometimes they are so clear I can remember every detail. Dreams that are like some sort of instructions. Sometimes I have to work the dreams out in my mind.

Some dreams I never do work out. These dreams only occur once in a while, not very often. Most of the time I never have any dreams at all when I sleep. I tell Rachel all this in a low voice.

"Did you have dreams about the dairy plant?" she asks.

"Yes, I did. There are still things I'm not clear about."

"Did you have a dream of winning the Arkansas Derby? And the money?"

"Yes and I have a muddled dream about how to divide the money and how to invest my share in the dairy company."

"Sonny, have you had any dreams about our future together?"

"Yes, but it is so jumbled, I can't figure it out. I know there is a long separation in the dream."

"Have you ever had any bad dreams?"

"No. Never. Most are very pleasant, some so confusing I forget what they are about."

"Sonny, do you believe in angels?"

"They must exist. They're spoken of in the Holy Book numerous times."

Then I speak up rather loud. "Rachel, such talk as this makes me uncomfortable. You're the only person I've told of my dreams. Please don't mention it to Grandma or anyone else. Let's not talk of this again. I lack the words to explain it."

After two or three minutes of silence, Rachel says, "Watch the road," then leans over and kisses me on the cheek. "I promise it's our secret."

After unloading the milk, we go to the market area a short ways from downtown to unload the eggs. A group of farmers are standing around talking. I remark that the flying red horse is the reddest red, so red it makes all the downtown area have a reddish glow.

One man says, "Yeah, we calls it baboon red."

"I ain't never seen no baboon, but I sure didn't know they was red," I say. "I thought they was like a big monkey brown colored."

He spits out a stream of tobacco juice, looks at me, and says, "Boy, ain't you never been to no zoo? You must be from so far back in the sticks you ain't never learn't nothing."

"I reckon so," I say. Several years pass before I understand what he means.

I start going to the training track again to refresh TJ's gate manner and to run with some competition. Asa and the boys greet us with much joy, laughter and petting of TJ. Pats on the back for me, a lot of "Thank you's, 'preciate that for the bonus money."

"We all rich now," Asa says, "And we ain't forgetting what caused it. This little old brown hoss got more personality than any hoss I ever been around. I ain't never seen a hoss with so much fire in him, yet gentle as a kitten. I believe a four-year-old kid could be safe with this hoss. Most hosses ain't very smart but this one got plenty of smarts in him. He's a pleasure to work with."

Hearing this makes me feel good. I love my TJ and it pleases me to hear nice things said about him. The next week goes by real fast, mostly repeating the things we have done before the Arkansas Derby.

The farrier or as we called him — the "hoss-shoe man" — comes out to the farm to trim the hooves and shoe all the horses on the place. He has a truck and trailer rigged up with butane, anvil and all the things needed for his work. I round up Ruth, Esther, Bathsheba, Laudie and Maudie. We go to the old Jones farm, Woody and Saree's, to the corral attached to the barn.

The horse shoe man, Mr. Morris, says, "No need to shoe 'em. Just trim their feet. They is some growed and splayed out." A good size pile of trimmings is left when he finishes.

Mr. Morris works nearly through the third day when a big black cloud comes up and it starts thundering and lightening something fierce. All the lights go out. Mr. Hank goes over to a small barn, goes in and we can hear a faint humming noise from the barn. I ask, "What did you do to get the electricity back on?"

"When this place was built before I came here," he says, "they installed diesel electric generators for electricity. Now that we are connected to the rural co-op electric company, we use it for standby power."

How amazing, how interesting, I think. *If I ever build a house, I'd like to have such a system.*

It commences raining. The rain puddles in the lawns and the gutters pour water out of the drainpipes. Mr. Morris says, "This rain reminds me of a hoss shoe I've made for muddy conditions." He goes out to his truck and comes back with a hoss shoe to explain to us what he has invented.

"You know, baseball, football, soccer and track shoes all have cleats for traction so the athletes won't be slipping and sliding and losing their balance. Even in a sissy game like golf, the players have cleats on their shoes."

We examine this shoe closely. Sure 'nuff, it has little cleats all around the shoe's perimeter. Mr. Hank asks if the shoe has been tried and proven successful. Mr. Morris says, "No, it's just an idea and theory."

"In nature," Mr. Hank says, "horses don't even wear shoes."

"A few thousand years ago, men in nature didn't either," Mr. Morris replies.

Mr. Hank laughs. "Make us up several sets. Measure TJ's feet exact. We'll try to be prepared for any conditions."

Uncle Joe, Grandma and Grandpa put their feet down and forbid me to make any more milk and egg deliveries. I fret some. I feel I'm needed. I like to think I hold up my end.

Uncle Joe points out, "You going off to A&M this fall anyway. You have to get used to the idea we gonna manage somehow. We can hire help if need be. You can trust your ole Uncle Joe to take care of things. You clear your head 'bout this part of the family operation. You think about the race and what comes after." I think about this and know my Uncle Joe is right.

The time draws near for making preparations for our trip to Churchill Downs, near Louisville, Kentucky — the greatest race in the world for three-year-old colts. Can it be possible that a little under-sized three-year-old brown colt and his 16 year old owner/apprentice jockey from East Texas are going to Kentucky for a chance at all the glory? As Mr. Hank remarks, "Sonny, when you have dreams, you sure dream big."

We make travel arrangements similar to the Arkansas trip. Mr. Hank, Rachel and I will be in Grandpa's pickup pulling TJ's trailer. Mr. Hank isn't taking any other horses to the Derby so he can focus on TJ. Asa begs to go along, riding in the trailer with TJ. I like this 'cause TJ likes company.

Mr. Hank uses his directory of horse farms all over the country to telephone and make arrangements for lodging for TJ for two nights on our route to Churchill Downs. Much to our delight we are also invited to stay the night at the two stops. It seems horse people stick together and love visiting and talking to other horse people. This is before motels line highways and just about all overnight lodging happens in downtown hotels with no place for horses.

Uncle Joe, Grandma and Grandpa are coming right behind us. To give TJ time to settle in, we plan on being in Churchill Downs about seven days before race day, which comes on on May 9th this year.

Uncle Joe calls Ben Tuttle to see if between the three brothers, they can help out while we are gone. Makes Ben most happy. "Me, Tom or Charlie — one there early every morning. Tell Miz Annie we know all about chickens and turkeys and we shore know about milking cows."

Mr. Hank, at the last minute, puts a couple sets of Mr. Morris's cleated shoes in the truck as well as a tarp to keep the rain off our things in case it rains. As we are loading TJ along with oats, hay and water, saddles, bridles, blankets and everything we think we might need, Woody comes up to me. He seems so somber, not like himself.

He looks me right in the eye and says, "Mista Sonny, the whole church congregation be praying for you and little TJ. That may not sound right, but the preacher say in this case, the Lord will understand. Count on He be knowing 'bout you." All I can do is put my arms around Woody and give him a hug. I turn and leave without saying a word.

On the way to the road, we stop at the house to give our farewells and promises. They will be following right behind. I can sense a little fear in Mama and Papa. I start in to laughing and commence to singing, "Give Me That Old Time Religion." Smiles break out and we start our journey to Kentucky.

Our first night, we stop in Monroe at Monroe Horse Farm of Arkansas. Two brothers own the farm, a beautiful place nestled in a range of hills about ten miles off Highway 67. They greet us with the usual good old southern hospitality. When TJ backs out of the trailer, they are all eyes. TJ is shining and beautiful, his little ears sticking up.

Mr. Monroe says, "He is one beautiful hoss, perfectly proportioned, maybe a little on the small side." Later we talk of bloodlines, breeding and mention is made of Gallant Hood and TJ in the future — a very enjoyable visit. Mr. Hank and the Monroes know one another from various race meetings. Rachel, Asa and I mainly just listen.

One of the Mr. Monroes comment that he has seen the Arkansas Derby. Nearly everybody has written and called TJ's win a fluke. Can never happen again. "I was there," he says, "and it looked to me like little TJ just flat out beat him. Didn't look like no fluke to me."

He says the great Warsaw has run two more races since the Arkansas Derby and has won them both easily. He is the big favorite in the Kentucky Derby. How can that be? We beat him. I can't understand this. Looks as if we should be favored over Warsaw.

I've cleaned out the account at the bank and Uncle Joe has the money. We are going to do the same as at Arkansas, but with $10,000.00 this time. Uncle Joe argues about putting up his share of the money, but I say absolutely not. It is mine to lose. I can't stand the thought of Uncle Joe or Grandma risking their money. The risk will be mine alone.

Uncle Joe cries out, "You share the winnings, why not the risk?"

"Uncle Joe, that's just the way I want to do it." This is fairly firm for me.

Uncle Joe says, "You shore make it hard for a feller to understand you sometimes. You been calling all the shots. I'm gonna be playing backup. So far, we been winning. Let's keep on like we been doing."

I laugh real big and say, "Uncle Joe, we sure can't break up a winning team."

Uncle Joe hollers out, "I'm a natural born team-winning man!'

I get to studying on Warsaw being the favorite, since he lost in our Arkansas Race. It is called a fluke win for TJ. Maybe the odds will be long. I have to get such thoughts out of my head. Bad thinking always connects with this predicting and I become some uneasy for allowing such thoughts in my mind.

I justify, right or wrong, that my conscience be clear on this. Any winnings do not harm any individual or group of people. They seem to come from some unknown source. What the money is used for only counts any way, but I never can get it completely straight in my mind. I depend on my feelings inside.

Asa and I insist on sleeping on cots in TJ's nice spacious stall. We feel that him being in strange quarters will be easier with some familiar comrades. The next morning we load up to continue our journey. After much handshaking, "Thank you's, see you at the Derby" farewells, we head on out for our next stop in Tennessee.

I share the driving chores with Mr. Hank. We drive leisurely and carefully. We know we have a valuable cargo to be conscious of — ourselves, our hopes, and mainly TJ.

When we cross the Mississippi River going into Memphis, I look down off the bridge at this mighty river. For some strange reason, I feel a slight fear. It is such a huge river. I've never even imagined how awesome. I am glad when we're across. We make frequent stops on side roads to stretch our legs and walk TJ around some, and feeling no anxiety up to now, I just enjoy the scenery.

A couple of hours out of Memphis, we begin to see a lot of hills with pretty little valleys tucked amongst them. Texans love Tennessee. This state sent Texas Sam Houston, Davy Crockett, and if you read the rolls of the Alamo, Goliad and San Jacinto battles, you'll see more men from Tennessee than from any other state. Plus it is a state of great presidents and military heroes with Andrew Jackson, Alvin York, a state of volunteers and great American heroes.

We go on through Nashville and near Gallatin we find our friendly horse farm people and lodging for the night — one more day to Louisville. It is a repeat of our first night. TJ is examined very closely, pedigrees are discussed. There are a few horses on this farm with pedigrees back to some of Andrew Jackson's race stock.

We use their training track and everyone watches as we go around a couple of turns, all the comments complimentary. TJ loves all of this, nickering and talking to the other horses. We have really entered horse country. I am proud of my little TJ and it pleases me to hear nice things said about him.

We load up the next morning, say our thank you's and farewells. We are on the final leg of our journey to Louisville. As we pull out, we hear a lot of "Good lucks, hope to see you in the winner's circle, and see you on your return trip." Southern people are so gracious. We leave feeling good.

Chapter 16

This afternoon, May 1st, we arrive at Churchill Downs Racetrack, just a few miles east of downtown Louisville. The Saturday races are in progress and we can hear loud cheering, more like a big roar.

We go around back to the stalls and enter through a manned security gate. A guard checks our papers against a sheet of permitted entries, tells us what stall is assigned to us and gives directions, most courteous and helpful.

We unload TJ out a ways in an area set aside for loading and unloading. We are the only ones unloading. Asa leads TJ around some and we go looking for his stall. The stall area and separate exercise track are about half a mile from the main racetrack.

We find our assigned stall, commence unloading gear, set up a cot in TJ's stall for Asa, set out oats and hay from home for TJ's feed not taking chances on him eating something not exactly like he is used to eating. TJ seems a little curious and nervous with the noise and people and horses all around us.

We get everything squared away and head into Louisville to the Blue Grass Hotel about 20 minutes from the track. Asa refuses to stay in the hotel choosing to stay with TJ instead. I am happy about this.

Our hotel arrangements are a suite with two connecting bedrooms. Each bedroom has two beds. Mr. Hank and Rachel stay in one bedroom and I stay in the other until the rest of the family arrives, then Uncle Joe will room with me. We expect them Wednesday evening.

Mama, Papa, Grandma, Grandpa and Uncle Joe are coming in the Cadillac. I bet Grandpa enjoys this trip since a Ford getaway car isn't near as comfortable for a long journey, not like the big heavy roomy limousine-like Caddy.

After checking in, we go down to the dining room for supper. Rachel and Mr. Hank order the house special, Kentucky ham steaks. I have a tomato and lettuce salad with a little dab of tuna fish. I try one bite of Rachel's ham. It has a real good flavor but tastes quite salty. I notice they are drinking lots of iced tea.

We carried Asa a big box of various vittles and a supply of drinks for his ice chest. We also have a big two-quart thermos of coffee filled for him. He has a radio. I like his quarters better than the hotel. A shower and restroom are a short distance from the stall for the grooms and exercise boys.

The next morning, Mr. Hank has me up at four a.m. for TJ's exercise run. By five-thirty, the weather starts getting a little gray around the exercise track. TJ feels good. Mr. Hank tells me to let him go for a mile. He pulls his stopwatch out and waves at me to go. When I come by him, he gives a thumbs-up sign. He seems real happy but won't tell me the time; just says everything's fine. We leave Asa walking TJ, then go back to the hotel for Rachel.

Mr. Hank says we'll be driving over near Lexington about 80 miles east of Louisville to visit his relatives. We drive through the heart of the world's finest horse farms, mile after mile of white board fences and grass so green it looks blue.

Mr. Hank explains it's blue green due to limestone-based soil, most nutritious grass for growing horses. He also mentions that limestone-based water produces another famous Kentucky gift, bourbon. I silently think, *A product the world don't need.*

We turn off the main road winding through beautiful country for ten miles then drive down a lane to a spread out collection of barns, sheds and paddocks of white fences. A sprawling, long red brick house sits in the middle of all this. We pull up next to the house and people come flying out hollering, "Brother Henry, Uncle Hank, Cousin Rachel!"

All kinds of hugging and kissing go on, this being the way of Southern people. Mr. Hank introduces me around. I can see eyes shifting from Rachel to me and from me to Rachel. I know what they are thinking.

Mr. Hank explains, "Sonny is owner and jockey of our entry in the Derby. I'm supposed to be the trainer. Sonny is my partner's son from back in East Texas. He's nearly 17 years old and raised his colt from the day it was born. It's a long story."

I hear one of Rachel's cousins ask, "Is he your feller?"

"Could be," she replies.

Mr. Hank's sister, Bessie, looks fortyish; his brother-in-law Adam, appears tall, skinny, with dark hair and complexion, and there are six kids, ranging in ages from six to sixteen. Adam raises horses for sale at the Lexington auction but he doesn't race any of his stock. "Too risky," he says. "Good way to go broke."

We have a big Sunday dinner with fried chicken and more Kentucky ham with all the trimmings. I eat a small helping of collard greens and a dish of English peas with little onions mixed in. I have to explain my weight situation. They are most sympathetic. We leave late in the afternoon loaded down with lots of good vittles.

While we are leaving, Adam says, "We won't be coming to the Derby this Saturday, the traffic and hassles are such that it's easier to listen on the radio. The way the race is called and described is about as exciting." He says they'd be praying and rooting for us, but I have a strange feeling he doesn't expect us to win.

As we load up to head out, a pretty girl of about 15 comes up to me, gets right in my face, and says, "I bet you'd like to know what my name is."

Rachel comes a flying from around the truck, grabs my hand and jerks me nearly down. "Betty Jo, he don't care nothing 'bout what your name is!"

Rachel acts some mad about it. I'm embarrassed and sure baffled. As we are going down the road back to Louisville, Rachel says, "How dare that hussy Betty Jo flirt with Sonny like that!"

"Why would any pretty girl flirt with me? I shore ain't much to look at."

"You have no knowledge of women," Rachel says. "You're so pathetically naïve you wouldn't know anyway."

"You're shore right about that," I say. I know nothing of women. Mr. Hank starts laughing. He laughs and laughs nearly all the way back to Louisville.

The next three days I exercise and pet and personally see to TJ's feed — white oats, alfalfa hay with a little dribble of strap. I fix him a small salad of chopped up carrots and apples. He's in perfect fettle.

Wednesday late afternoon, Mama, Papa, Uncle Joe, Grandma and Grandpa arrive. I know my mood and outward appearance reflect on their moods, so I smile all the time even while I churn with nerves inside.

That Thursday morning as I make a lap around the exercise track I see the great Warsaw and Eddie Palomo. We pass each other on the track. Eddie calls out, "Hey, Sonny, you and little TJ look mighty fit."

We lead our horses back to the stall areas exchanging talk about how the big gray has won two big stake races since Arkansas. His record is 10 wins, one loss. "What a record!" I say. "TJ has only one win."

There are two men and a woman standing off to one side as we are going to the stalls. Eddie says, "That's the owner and his wife, Mr. and Mrs. Gabrowski and Warsaw's new trainer, Jubal Mullur. The other trainer is sick in bed with ulcers."

I can sense he doesn't care much for the new trainer. We walk up to them and Eddie introduces me. I shake hands with Mr. and Mrs. Gabrowski. They look to be in their 60's and speak with strong accents and have very dignified manners.

All at once, in a fairly loud voice, Jubal says, "So this is the little runt of a horse that messed up Warsaw's perfect record. This great horse will probably never lose another race. No other horse is even close to him. I hate to think he was beaten by a fluke or maybe a doped-up horse such as this one." He jabs a finger at TJ.

Stunned and speechless for a minute, I finally speak up and say, "Mr. Mullur, that's the most terrible insult I've ever heard. What's wrong with you?"

He replies, "Ain't your daddy a vet and a human doctor?"

"Yes," I say.

"Well," he answers, "that explains it. He has a secret dope that is not detectable in the saliva test."

Mr. Gabrowski says, "Jubal, that's far enough. You can't use language like that. I insist you apologize to young Mr. Quinn." Jubal sticks his hand out grinning. I notice he has a big hand to go along with his size, about six foot two and 200 pounds.

I don't really want to shake hands with him. I don't like the sly look on his face and what he said was beyond shaking and no hard feelings. With great misgiving, I stick my hand out. He immediately grasps my hand, extra firmly, and says, "No hard feelings."

I detect a slight whiff of bourbon coming from him. He starts squeezing my hand very hard. I have strong hands, what with picking cotton, gathering corn and toting milk cans. Farm work makes for strong hands. But he grips my hand in such a way that I can't use my hand strength. He grins like the devil and commences to really bear down.

I calmly look him in the eye and say, "Mr. Mullur, you are hurting my hand. Please let go." He grins a little wider and really comes down on my hand with all his power.

I yell out, "Let go of my hand!" All at once, I get mad and something in my mind screamed, *Bite!*

I bend over, get his wrist in my teeth and really ground down hard. He lets go of my hand, lets out a mad shout and backhands me right in the lips. I feel my lips burst. I stand stunned for a couple of seconds.

All at once, a khaki and blue blur comes flying between us. It is Papa. He strikes Jubal with the flat edge of his hand right in the throat then smashes him with his elbow directly in the nose. He smashes Jubal again right below his right ear with the flat of his hand and then kicks him in the privates. All of this happens so quickly it is like a dream, yet I can see it clearly. Jubal is on the ground gagging holding his throat.

Mr. Hank has his arms around Papa saying, "Hold up, hoss; easy, old hoss; calm down, hoss."

Papa's blue eyes blaze like they have some kinda inner fire behind them. Papa calms some and turns to me. He whips out his handkerchief and starts patting the blood off my lips. He looks in my eyes real close and says, "Sonny, you feel all right?"

I am so full of emotion, not from the busted lips or hand, but for Papa. I am crying a little bit — I can't keep from it. "Yes sir, Papa. I'm okay."

Jubal, all bent over, gags and stumbles off toward the stall area.

Mr. Grabrowski says, "Mr. Quinn, I regret this very much. I assure you I had no knowledge Jubal was like this. He replaced my regular trainer, but after Saturday's race, he will no longer be in my employ — perhaps not in any owner's employ. I intend to report this incident to the racing commission. Please accept my sincere apologies."

Papa responds, "Apology accepted. Sometimes you get a bad one. I suspect whiskey has clouded his actions."

Mr. Hank starts smiling and says, "Hoss, that action just now reminded me of that time in 1918 when those four Germans jumped in our trench in the Argonne. You were something then and you're something now. First time I called you Hoss since then."

Papa replies, "And I hope it's the last time you have occasion to call me Hoss."

I stand in a state of awe. I had no idea my gentle kind papa, when aroused, can be so fierce. I've never seen a wolverine, only read about them, but I have a silly thought flash through my mind. Papa is like a wolverine, small but very powerful.

Papa speaks up and says, "Don't say anything about this to the family, only upset them. Sonny, you can tell a small harmless story about running into a post or something about your lips."

"Yes sir, Papa."

That night after we go into our bedrooms, Uncle Joe tells me he has the $10,000.00 in his shoes in $100.00 bills. He can barely hobble around. "I ain't taking no chances on pickpockets," he reports.

He has a rolled-up racing form in his hip pocket. He takes it out and starts reading out loud, "Warsaw is the odds on favorite three to two. Comments are 'Unbeaten, except for a fluke loss in the Arkansas Derby. The jockey didn't ride smart and maybe he didn't feel well.'

Down the sheet to TJ the probable odds are 25 to one. Comments are 'A fluke win, a lucky win with a 16-year-old apprentice jockey. Beginner's luck. Horse too small to be much of a champion.'"

I think about this for a few minutes then tell Uncle Joe, "TJ don't know he's small. He thinks he's as big as any horse."

"You got that right, Sonny, and you and TJ got something no other horse and jockey got — each other," he says. "I notice in this here paper that it's supposed to be raining Saturday and there could be sloppy track conditions. That could be a great equalizer."

Friday morning after TJ's run, Eddie Palomo comes by the stall. "Sonny," he says, "I ain't riding Warsaw tomorrow. I had it out with Jubal. He looks terrible. Your papa is something. I ain't never seen the likes before. Jubal has his nose in the bottle. I told him I was sick with the flu and unable to ride. He's replaced me with a young, tough, smart-aleck jockey named Bobby Perez. I notice your gate position is number seven, and Warsaw's number eight."

"Be careful. Let him go on ahead of you. Don't let him stay behind you or beside you. Warsaw outweighs TJ by 400 pounds. He might try to knock you down. He's clever and tricky. Jubal's muttering threats. I wanted to warn you. Be extra careful." I shake Eddie's hand and thank him.

He says, "Nearly everyone in this racing business is pure gentleman, sportsman. The bad ones don't last long. It's practically a 100 percent pure honest business. Now and then the pressure gets to some of them and I think it's got to Jubal. He's turned to whiskey for comfort and unless he gets hold of himself, he's done for."

Eddie finishes saying, "Good luck, kid," then walks away.

I tell Asa not to let TJ out of his sight — not for one minute. "Get you a bucket in case your kidneys or bowels act up and lock the stall down," I advise. He assures me he will guard TJ with his life. I think we are being overly spooky and Asa is a little dramatic.

That afternoon it starts thundering and lightning. The rain comes down in sheets. By six a.m., it still rains. Mr. Hank gets his tools and the set of shoes with the little spikes on them out of the truck then pries TJ's shoes off and nails the mud grip shoes on. We saddle TJ in the pouring rain then make a run around the exercise track.

He doesn't slip or lose his balance one time. Mr. Hank comments, "Hmmm, could be we got something here." I explain every single move TJ makes and Mr. Hank seems happily satisfied.

The dawning of the 62nd running of the Kentucky Derby arrives. Sadly, it pours down rain, gloomy, dark clouds hanging low to the ground. Not much of a dawning. At nine a.m., Papa, Mr. Hank and I go by cab out to the track. The race is scheduled for three p.m. We hope for a break in the weather. Possibly clearing off in the next six hours. There is nothing to be done, only wait and see.

The day races before the Derby are to start at noon. They are canceled due to dangerous conditions they might create before the big race. There are twelve horses entered. Our position is our old lucky number seven. I see Warsaw's spot, number eight, right next to me on my right. These are all high quality horses. Anything can happen. I don't want to focus all my attention on this one great horse. I don't want to focus my attention on any horse other than TJ.

About one p.m., five or six of the owners go to the racing commission and ask for a one-week postponement of the race: the main reason being that conditions are too dangerous for such valuable and expensive horses to run. No mention about danger to the jockeys.

The commission emphatically says, "No Derby has ever been delayed, postponed or canceled in the previous 61 runnings, and it isn't about to start now. If a top-notch thoroughbred can only run on a dry fast track, something might be lacking in such a horse." Three of the owners scratch. That leaves nine.

By two o'clock, only a light rain comes down. Asa leads TJ out. Mr. Hank inspects his shoes and feet closely. Mr. Hank says, "Sonny, start your dressing and do your mental preparations."

We weigh in. I am allowed five pounds for being an apprentice. We weigh in right on the mark: 121 pounds. The other horses are carrying 126 pounds. I am the only apprentice in the race. Probably no other trainer would have enough confidence in an apprentice. Not only an inexperienced jockey, but I've only ridden the Arkansas Derby.

At the weigh-in, I look at Bobby Perez, Warsaw's new jockey. He is a young, happy-faced man from Panama. Slightly dark complected, he looks plenty capable.

We lead TJ around a viewing circle to let people see the horses. The stadium is full, a big sea of umbrellas. I see all the family near the finish line in a railed-off section reserved for owners.

Time comes to mount up. Mr. Hank helps me board and says, "Sonny, you might consider keeping TJ on the far outside, out of the sloppy going near the inside rail. The distance will be longer, but the possible better traction could more than compensate."

As we parade in front of the grandstand, heading for the starting gate, a band starts playing "My Old Kentucky Home." I think, *What a sad, haunting, wishful song. A beautiful melody.*

The track is sloppy with puddles and puddles of standing water that has not drained off. The rain barely comes down, though black clouds are hanging low. I notice most of the horses have glass shields fitted over their eyes. All the jockeys have goggles, me included, to keep the mud and water out of our eyes.

I slow lope TJ around behind the starting gate to warm him up some. He has real fine gate manners, no problem with the gate. I can feel him ready, like a wound-up spring. He knows something is coming.

As we approach the gate, I pray, *Almighty Father, Jehovah, I ask Your blessing. Thy will be done. Thy will be done.*

The bell clangs and we're off. We are pretty bunched up at about the one-eighth pole when Warsaw bumps us. TJ goes down and slides into two horses that also go down. I can hear a huge groan from the stands.

I feel TJ on my left leg. The track is so soft and muddy I just feel my leg sink into the mud. I don't think I'm hurt. TJ scrambles up. I get free of the saddle. TJ starts running and I reach out and grab the left stirrup. He panics. He drags me right in front of the huge crowd. I holler, "Whoa TJ! Whoa! Stop TJ!"

I hear a piercing scream, "Sonnneee!"

I know it's Grandma. I hear Uncle Joe's roaring voice screaming, "Let go! Let go!"

Everything happens so fast it's a blur. I hang on for dear life, begging TJ to whoa! I guess TJ feels me out of the saddle as he drags me. By a miracle, he slows to a trot. That lets me run alongside him and I vault up and onto his back. I get my feet into the stirrups and see I've lost my boots and socks and my toes are bleeding.

The second I get seated, TJ takes off like the furies. For the first time, he seems out of control running away with me. I jerk a couple of times on the bridle reins hollering, "Easy, TJ! Easy, boy!"

I know we won't last a quarter mile this way. I lean over and start patting TJ alongside the neck talking to him. He settles into his stride — not his regular long floating stride — a hard driving stride. He really digs in. I think, *TJ is sprinting. He can't hold this pace*. We still have nearly a mile to go and I can see the other horses about 50 lengths ahead.

TJ goes faster and faster. I've never in all our time together felt him run this hard and I become afraid for him. I see us closing the gap real fast. Without me doing anything, TJ runs on the far outside. I can see mud and water flying furiously from the horses in front.

As we make the run for the finish line, I see Warsaw pull ahead on the inside rail. At the pole before the finish, 220 yards, we pass the other horses. The only horse between us and the finish line becomes Warsaw. TJ not only maintains his hard sprinting run, he goes even faster. I think we might have a chance, a slim one, but maybe.

It feels like we're flying. About 20 yards or so before the finish line, I see Bobby Perez look over his left shoulder. Then he stands up in the stirrups and raises his right hand in triumph.

A clap of thunder lets loose and a lightning bolt sizzles down in the distance ahead of us. Warsaw breaks stride and lurches to his right as we flash by them across the line.

I have my hands full with TJ. It takes me more than half a mile to get him slowed down. He really has his blood boiling. We turn and start back toward the finish line and to the front of the grandstand. The other horses are already going off.

All at once, a bright shaft of light comes through the clouds and a rainbow forms. The most wonderful feeling runs through me. I feel peaceful and calm. I've heard the word "exhilarated" before and decided this is how I feel. I smile from ear to ear, nearly laughing, as TJ and I walk up in front of the tote board at the finish line. I see "Inquiry" and "Photo" light up on the board.

Bobby Perez is pointing at his goggles. He points at the sky and at the ground. The group of four men standing there with him are taking notes and talking amongst themselves.

After a couple of minutes, the Inquiry light goes off. Seems Bobby, blinded with foggy and muddy goggles, looked over his left shoulder and thought he had it won. But he didn't see TJ and me coming by his right on the far outside. He misjudged the finish line and the lightning flash caused Warsaw to shy to the right.

The Photo light goes off. The winner is number seven, paying $52.00 to win. I head to the winner's circle where a huge garland of roses is draped over TJ's neck. Flash pictures are taken. I am dizzy with happiness.

I look down and all I can see on Grandma, Uncle Joe, Grandpa, Mama, Papa, Mr. Hank and Asa's faces is pure sunshine happiness. I get off TJ. Rachel comes crying, kisses me on the cheek near my ear, and says, "My precious angel." I feel a shiver go all the way to my toes. I look down at my bare and bloody toes, but know everything still works perfect.

An excited, energetic-looking man breaks into our circle holding a big microphone. He shouts out a few words for "our radio listening audience." He sticks the microphone in Grandma's face and asks, "Mrs. Jackson, as half-owner, what do you think of your colt and grandson now?"

Grandma looks a little confused and hollers into the microphone like she uses a telephone, loud and with force, and says, "My grandson and this colt TJ are a miracle blessing, a precious gift from above."

The man looks a little confused at this reply, then hastens over to Mr. Hank. "Mr. Henry Ward, the trainer, ladies and gentlemen of the listening audience. Is this the greatest colt you've ever trained?"

"He's the greatest colt I've ever seen," says Mr. Hank. "No other colt or horse comes close. Unfortunately for me, I had very little to do with his training. The credit goes to Sonny. He trained him from the day he foaled. They trained each other."

The radioman moves over to Mama and Papa. He introduces them to the radio listeners as Dr. and Mary Quinn, parents of Sonny Quinn, then asks, "What about the ride your son just made?"

Papa replies, "I give the usual parent answer, we're proud of our exceptional young son. He's tenuously worked and trained TJ and himself for this greatest of races. It didn't come easy for him."

He turns to me and asks, "As half owner with your grandmother, what are your comments? Do you dedicate the race to her, or your parents?"

What a strange question, I think to myself. *Am I supposed to say yes? Is he putting words in my mouth?*

"No, sir," I say. "I won the race with my little TJ. We won it for us. It's a promise and a dream we've had since his birth. We appreciate all the encouragement, support and prayers of everyone," I add.

He moves on off. There are flash pictures being taken. I suddenly become conscious of being muddy from head to toe, cap gone, busted lips, bare bloody feet. I reach over and take Papa by the hand and ask, "Can we go now?"

Papa replies, "That's all for now. We're going to get Sonny cleaned up and into some dry clothes."

The purse is the largest in Derby history: $125,000.00. Uncle Joe had bet the $10,000.00. That payoff was $260,000.00 for a total of $385,000.00. Uncle Joe and Grandma take a check from the office of the betting windows in place of cash.

Papa has me sit with my feet in a pan of water with, I believe, peroxide in it. He tells me I'll probably hobble for a few days and gives me a pair of soft house shoes to wear.

The telegrams are pouring in — even one from Governor Alred of Texas, U.S. Texas senators, and U.S. Congressmen. The switchboard jams with calls. Uncle Joe gets some carried away and declares, "I ain't never seen the likes."

One phone call that I accept comes from Woody. He shouts into the phone, "Mista Sonny, we gloried and hallaleuja'd and praised the Lawd most all day Saturday. Our prayers for you and little TJ was heard. We all so happy we 'bout to bust. A whole lot of folks here love you, Sonny, we want you to know. We getting ready to give thanks most of the night and again Sunday. Saree making that piano smoke!"

I am happy and grateful for this call from Woody. I tell Woody, "I appreciate your telling me this. I'll see you soon. Tell everyone I said I love them too."

"I sho will, Mista Sonny!" he screams out.

I ask Papa and Grandma if they will make excuses for me and take the rest of the calls. I just don't feel like talking anymore.

"I'm having room service send up a small steak, potatoes and salad for you. Don't overdo it. For a few days, eat small portions. After you eat, I want you to go right to bed. I'll see you aren't disturbed," Papa says.

Chapter 17

Sunday morning, May 9, 1936, my eyes pop open. I know it to be a few minutes shy of four a.m. Months of starting the day at four to work with TJ has caused a built-in wake up, no alarm clock needed. I can hear Uncle Joe in the bed next to mine softly snoring.

The day after. Is it a dream? My thoughts go to the race. This is no dream — it has really happened. Is this the top of the mountain? Is it downhill from now on? Will there be higher mountains to climb? Thy will be done.

I give thanks for all my wonderful blessings. Why me? I have no clue. I pray and give credit and gratitude. I pray for future guidance and direction. I throw my legs over the side of the bed to head for the bathroom to bathe and start my day. My cheeks are wet.

I adjust the shower and step out of my underwear. I've always slept in my underwear. "Pajamas" is only a word I've heard. None of the men in my family wear anything other than their underwear to sleep in.

There stands a full-length looking glass clamped onto the bathroom door. I've avoided looking at myself. I know it will not be a pretty sight. This morning I do. I've become so skinny it alarms me. My head looks way too big for such a skinny body. I'm all head and eyes. I stand five foot nine, maybe five foot ten, and weigh only 115 pounds. Months of existing on black coffee, dry toast, and as Uncle Joe calls it "rabbit grub," has me in pitiful shape.

My racing days are over. Never again. I decide, and starting this morning, I will eat, eat, eat. I walk up the hall to the hotel's all-night coffee shop for breakfast. I glance at the clock — fifteen minutes till five. There's no one in the coffee shop except Rosie, the waitress, a large, pleasingly plump, red-haired woman. Her name's embroidered on her green uniform.

Rosie has her elbows propped on the counter reading the front page of the morning paper. In big block letters with a large picture, it screams out, "Long Shot Thomas Jackson Wins Derby."

Rosie glances up at me and says, "The usual: dry toast, black coffee." After a week of this, Rosie knows what I order.

"No, ma'am, Miss Rosie. I want two fried eggs, over easy; four slices of bacon, crisp; hash browns; a side order of corn grits; biscuits — if you have them — with lots of butter."

She looks me right in the face with a puzzled expression, "Run that by me again," then all at once, "Ain't you Sonny Quinn?"

"Yes'm, Miss Rosie. That's me."

"Lordy, chile!" she screams as she runs around the counter and grabs me and pulls me off the stool and smashes my head right between her big bosoms. She squeals, "Lordy, I was at them races yestiddy. When I seen that little ole brown pony with his number seven walking to the starting gate, I had a sudden rabbit foot hunch. I bet a whole double sawbuck on the nose. I got more money than I ever dreamed possible. I ain't never had this much cash money in my whole life!"

Miss Rosie squeezes me so tight against her big feather pillows I near about suffocate in a fragrance of Oxydol soapsuds, lilac powder and sachet. I struggle and holler, "Miss Rosie, I can't breathe!"

She lets go, snaps her fingers, does a little jig, sings "Do Da, Do Da, Run All Day," then runs over to the kitchen and screams my breakfast order into the cook.

"Miss Rosie, what's a double sawbuck?"

She hollers, "Twenty whole dollars!"

Miss Rosie stares at me the whole time I eat breakfast. As I finish my coffee, Rosie asks if I'm going to Baltimore for the Preakness. I tell her TJ and I have run our last race. We're going home, back to East Texas.

"I can tell you are a fine young gentleman and I wish you lots of good luck in the future. I will never forget you."

"Thank you, Miss Rosie. The same to you, and I will always remember what a smell-good elegant lady you are."

"You ain't paying for this here breakfast! My treat with pleasure, you hear?" As I go out the door, she calls out, "Good bye, Sonny!"

I stop in the lobby and buy a newspaper. Sure enough, the front page shows a picture of TJ and me. I have toweled the mud off my face. It is a good likeness — idiot-looking with a silly ear-to-ear, wide-open mouth that could be a smile. TJ's little ears are up. He looks right into the camera.

I read the story:

May 9, 1936. Long shot Thomas Jackson wins! In the annals of Kentucky Derby history, this race finishes first in the unbelievable bizarre finish in this greatest of all supreme horse races. In covering 32 previous derbies, no other race comes close.

Knocked down at the start, in a three-horse spill, the young little brown colt and his tenacious 16 year-old kid apprentice refused to stay down. Somehow they managed to get up and back into the race. With a mile to go in the slop and puddles of water, Thomas Jackson, in a hard driving sprint on the far outside, made up 50 lengths on the leaders. He tore down the track throwing mud behind like a runaway steam shovel.

On the turn for home, into the backstretch, he passed all except Warsaw, who looked to have the race won. Bobby Perez, Warsaw's jockey, with his goggles fogged and covered with mud, thought he'd won the race but misjudged the finish line. He stood up in his stirrups as Warsaw broke stride. Thomas Jackson thunder bolted to the finish line on the far outside. Perez said later that he never saw Thomas Jackson; he was looking over his left shoulder.

Here comes the bizarre part: a clap of loud thunder and a lightning bolt streaked to the ground. Warsaw shied sharply to his right just before the finish line. Thomas Jackson flashed across, the winner by a head.

I will always believe this race was pre-ordained. I will always be convinced this young boy and his little brown horse had help from above. It was meant to be. There will be jubilation in East Texas, all over Texas, for days to come. These two young champions did their state proud.

The story goes on in more detail, but I begin to feel uncomfortable. It seems to be glorifying to TJ and me. I know — perhaps TJ somehow knows — who is due the credit for our win: God.

The story goes on about Grandma and me raising TJ from a colt, about Papa and Mr. Hank being partners in the horse farm. I don't know how reporters find out such things. No matter. I am full of happiness.

I drive up to the security gate at Churchill to go see about TJ and Asa. The security guard comes out to the truck wanting to shake my hand and congratulate me on winning. He acts so overly nice I wonder how he's act if I had run last. I know people love winners. How about the losers? I try to pay more attention to losers than winners. Maybe I'm different.

I think back to Field Town, my race with Big Red, Mr. Jean Manseur, the Arkansas Derby, the big race yesterday — the Kentucky Derby. I am grateful I've won. But what a fine line exists between winning and losing.

I go to TJ's stall and rattle the door. Asa opens it, starts smiling, and reports everything "hunky dory."

I've stowed a sack of dried apples in the pickup and have some in my hand for TJ. He comes sniffling and kinda butts me with his head. Asa says they've slept well. Believes the shoes TJ has on make him a little uncomfortable, kinda like wearing track shoes.

I brush and pet TJ when Mr. Hank comes in. He pries TJ's shoes off and paints his feet with some hoof sealer, then decides to let him go barefoot for a while. I tell Mr. Hank I'd like to get an early start for home the next morning after we finish up all of our business. He asks me about the Preakness.

"No more races," I say. "We're going home."

"Your decision."

Seems no one wants to hear, "No more races."

Rachel, Mama and Papa come out to the stall area about nine a.m. with a bushel of telegrams of congratulations. Rachel agrees to write thank-you replies and sort them out for my personal comments.

Papa has made seven p.m. reservations at the hotel dining room for a celebration dinner.

I walk TJ around the track a couple of times. Lead, not ride. The track is still churned up with lots of water and mud. TJ has no shoes on and I don't want to take chances on an exercise run. Being Sunday, there isn't much to do. Just about everything is closed. I stay out at the track most of the day to keep away from the ringing phone and reporters requesting interviews.

I can tell everyone wants TJ and me to plan other races. I have troublesome problems in my mind about this.

That evening we are all in the suite waiting to go to our celebration dinner. Everyone gets all dressed up and looks good. Uncle Joe with his big strong voice declares, "TJ is just like a natural born gold mine. We gonna have more money than a show horse can jump over 'fore he's through."

My heart starts fluttering, then I jump up out of my chair and cry out, "You don't understand! TJ is a special gift for me. He has a soul and spirit! He has love. He has changed all our lives. Gold is just dead metal. TJ and me are one. I can't explain. I can't make the weight. Something inside me tells me no more races. We're through. We quit as winners, in great triumph. Think a second about the lightning flash. The rainbow. What we overcame to win the Derby. TJ is going home to retire as a papa horse. I have to prepare to leave for school in three months. I tell all of you, our racing days are over. Be grateful that we had this gift of love."

Total silence for about a minute, then Uncle Joe says, "I got a natural born big mouth, and a natural born big foot to stick in it. You and TJ is worth more than all the gold ever."

Grandma speaks up, "That's settled so let's hear no more 'bout it. Whatever counts with Sonny counts with me."

Papa starts laughing, saying, "You set my mind at ease. I can quit being in a state of turmoil about your weight. Let's go for dinner and leave for home in the morning."

Grandpa mumbles, "Wonder can I get me a mess of collards with that there Filly Miggins steak?"

We leave for home about six the next morning. Mr. Hank, Rachel and I pull TJ's trailer, Asa rides in the trailer with TJ. Grandma, Grandpa, Uncle Joe, Mama and Papa drive on ahead in the Cadillac. They will get home two days ahead of us.

We plan on the same stops going back as we have coming to Louisville. We have a hero's welcome at the first stop. When Mr. Hank tells them we're retiring TJ to stud, everyone starts examining pedigree records, books, charts, discussing price, dates and so on. I get Mr. Hank off alone and ask him if he would take charge of all this as I have no knowledge of such things. I tell him I'll appreciate it that we work something out. "It will be a pleasure," he says.

The other overnights are about the same. Then we're on our final stretch for home. We have about 300 miles left. Mr. Hank drives. "Sonny," he says, "I booked TJ for 15 appointments, charging a reasonable fee. We have the undefeated Derby Champ here. Surprisingly, I booked Gallant Hood at a much higher fee since he's proven himself with this one great colt. You adjust fees depending on what the offspring do."

As we are rolling down the highway, I say, "Mr. Hank, I been studying on a business proposition for us. I have to clear it with Papa. I don't see any problem there but I have to clear some of it with Grandma, about TJ's stud fee."

"If we could keep things sorted out, it's all in the family. What I'd like to do is put up $25,000.00 then you select some good brood mares, and you and I go partners. You study on that some and tell me what you think. I'd like Asa to be TJ's personal groom and if you can see your way clear, you make TJ's appointments for the future."

"Grandma gets half, the other half we can put in our partnership. I feel we can keep it sorted out."

We drive on in silence for about 20 minutes. Rachel sits up kinda stiff. Mr. Hank reaches over with his right hand. I reach with my right hand. We shake. He very solemn-like says, "We got us a deal, partner."

Rachel starts laughing and says, "Papa, you had me worried there for a minute. Like Sonny said, it's all in the family. I know it will be good. And Asa thinks TJ is almost human. He'll be happy to be TJ's special groom."

It's near dark when we pull down the lane to the house. Dog barks a friendly welcome. The Belle nickers frantically and TJ answers. All the lights are on as TJ backs out of the trailer. Asa says, "I'll rub him down good and feed him. Get him settled in for the night."

We go into the kitchen where Woody, Saree and Aunt Willie are beside themselves, deliriously happy. I have never seen such a happy mess of people. Aunt Willie, Saree and Grandma have supper ready. We have a table full of good East Texas vittles. We eat and laugh for nearly two hours. The telephone rings so much we have to tell the operator to report our phone out of whack.

The next morning while Uncle Joe makes the milk run and Grandpa helps Woody with the milking, Grandma and I are finishing up breakfast. Grandma hands me the two checks from our winnings and the purse.

"Sonny," she says, "It's over my head what to do with this much money. You take care of it the way you see fit."

"Grandma, I'm gonna give some of the money to places where it's needed. I'll make a fair division for the family. Will my decision cause any bickering?"

"No! What you decide will be agreeable. You have my word on it."

"Then I'll head for the bank, make a deposit and do the dividing."

On the way to the bank, I stop at the big house and pick Rachel up. When we walk into the bank, Mr. Goldman and all the bank workers let out a big cheer. Mr. Goldman leads us back into his private office, then sends for coffee and cinnamon rolls. He acts so happy he can't make much sense. When we finally get settled down, I pull the two checks out and say, "I need to deposit these checks and then write a few."

He stares at the two checks so long I start thinking he's had some kinda stroke. "Sonny," he says, "This is a staggering amount of cash money — more than in this whole county. The good or bad thing is, you don't even know what this means. The checks are certified so you can write on the account at once. Would you like for me to make out the checks for you?"

"That would be nice. I ain't never wrote many checks, at least not big ones."

"Do you have a list?"

"In my head."

He gets a pencil and paper, then says, "Tell me who and how much."

"There are five churches in town, including the Colored Baptist Church: $10,000.00 to each one. To Booker Woods — Woody - $40,000.00. Two checks: number one, $25,000.00 to Henry Ward; number two, $10,000.00 to Asa — I don't know his last name, just put Asa on it. To Uncle Joe, $80,000.00; to Grandma and Grandpa, $80,000.00. Then $80,000.00 to me, and any remainder to the farm account."

"I'm going to build a decent house and hire a good couple for the farm, the woman for the cooking and housework. Grandma was never much of a body for inside work and Aunt Willie and Uncle Joe are moving into their new house. I want the man to mainly help Grandma with her chickens and turkeys and garden around the place. We pay good wages so I think we can find us a good couple. The rest we can use for what else is needed on the place."

He studies the list for what seems like a long time, then jumps up and says, "I'll get these machine printed. Be right back." I look over at Rachel. Her eyes are big and shiny. She smiles.

When Mr. Goldman comes back with the checks, I ask him to pass out the checks to the churches. I know there will be a lot of carrying on and such things embarrass me. "With the greatest of pleasure," he says.

"Now, Sonny, I want to tell you about our milk plant. The dirt is flying and we're ahead of schedule. We expect to be in limited production by October. I've had some booklets printed up and mailed out to all the farmers in the county about buying their milk. We'll send trucks, pick up the milk. I've offered capital for dairy cows. Everything is working out very well. I'll keep you informed. If you have time, maybe you'll have some input on any ideas," he finishes.

Chapter 18

When we leave the bank, I give Rachel two checks — the one for her papa and Asa's check. "Tell Mr. Hank the $10,000.00 for him and Asa are winners' bonuses. The $25,000.00 is for our brood mares."

Rachel says, "Papa and Asa will be very happy. I know why you want me to give these to them for you."

We go across the street to visit Mr. Dillard and Billy Joe. They make over us with a lot of foolishness. When we start back for the Cadillac, a large group of friends and neighbors are standing on the curb. They start hollering, "Congratulations! Way to go! You and little ole TJ showed 'em!" I become so flustered it takes nearly 20 minutes to get away.

I give Grandma her check and Uncle Joe his and Woody's checks. Uncle Joe grabs me and starts hugging me and bellows out, "Sonny, Mama be right. You got a natural born angel on both your shoulders. I gotta be careful when I give Woody his check. He gonna get them palpitations of the heart."

I tell Grandma there will be a crew of carpenters out tomorrow. I've already gone by the lumberyard. I explain to her about needing help since Aunt Willie will be leaving for her new house and I'll be going off to A&M soon. She just smiles and says, "Good thinking, Sonny."

A car horn honks and Dog starts barking. We go to the door. It's our mail rider Mr. Tom with near about a bushel of mail. Mr. Tom declares, "This 'peers to be fan mail. You need to set a five-gallon lard bucket out by the mailbox. I 'spect this is just the starting of it."

He's right. We have so many requests for autographed pictures I have a man come down from Dallas and take a picture of TJ and me. On top of the picture I have printed "1936 Kentucky Derby Winner, Thomas Jackson." I have a rubber stamp made for my autograph that reads, "Best Wishes, Sonny Quinn" and stamp it in the right hand corner of the pictures.

We order 2,000 pictures. Most of the requests for pictures have a dollar in them. The ones that don't, we send anyway. Rachel and I are working 21 hours a day just taking care of the mail. I answer every single one. I mail five pictures to Mr. Jean Manseur over in Shreveport, writing "My Dear Friend" on the pictures.

One of the letters has what you call an endowment contract for a breakfast of champions cereal. They offer $500.00 a year for ten years to use TJ's and my picture on the box. I have the money part made out to Grandma. A bread company that makes light bread called Bread of Winners offers the same deal. I make the money part out to Grandpa.

When I tell Grandpa it will give him some money for his rocking chair and a chest of whittling tools, he laughs real big and says, "I ain't studying on no whittling tools for a long, long time. Maybe not ever."

The big one comes in from Ford. All I have to do is say, "I haul TJ in a Ford Truck, and use Ford and Son tractors," which is true. They pay $1,500.00 a year for ten years. I make that money out to Asa for his wages for being TJ's special groom.

There are others, but these are the only ones I sign for. Seems as if fame is not so fleeting in our case. People love that a little small colt and a 16 year-old kid won the Kentucky Derby. People love to see big underdogs win.

I get a personal call from Governor Alred asking if I will take TJ to Dallas for a week for the biggest event taking place, the Texas Centennial Celebration — Texas's 100th year of independence. How can I turn the governor down?

We load TJ and Asa, then Rachel and I head for the Texas Centennial up at Dallas. We stay ten days. Twice a day I ride TJ around. The Livestock Pavilion seats about 5,000 people. They clap and cheer and whoop and carry on. TJ seems to like it. People line up and pass by to look at him.

They have a sort of special enclosure bunkhouse with a kitchen and dining room. Asa, Rachel and I take turns staying with TJ around the clock. When we get home, a personal letter from Governor Alred comes thanking me with some other foolish talk about our service to Texas, honor to our state, and so on.

The summer goes by in a frantic blur. Papa commissions a well-known artist to paint TJ and me, which he paints from a photograph. Papa proudly hangs it in the foyer of the big house. All this fame wears me to a pleasant frazzle.

In two weeks, Rachel and I will be off to school. Rachel, for some reason, has a touch of sadness about her. I become some puzzled since I'm happy as a bull goose. The mail has slacked off some and Mama says she'll take care of it when we leave for school. The newspaper people have quit coming around and we are gradually getting back to normal.

I've been having this troubling dream over and over. Recurring I think is the word. One day Rachel and I are having coffee, just us two, and I tell her about my dream. I have it sorted out except for one part. These dreams are always jumbled up so I have to figure them out.

"TJ is old, has a lot of gray in his face around his muzzle and eyes. His whole face is near 'bout gray. Then a young colt that looks like he looks now — I figure his son — named Stonewall. He wins a bunch of big races. Now here come the part I can't understand. He has a young woman jockey. Black hair. At first, I think it's you, but this young woman has big blue eyes. Probably nothing to it. It's way in the future anyway."

Rachel says, "I sure don't believe in any kinds of crystal balls or wishful make believe — except in your case." She lets out a laugh, then asks, "What are your dreams for us?"

"I ain't had no dreams about us yet," I say. "A puzzling long separation, parted by a vast distance of water; an ocean, I assume." I see a look of sadness in her eyes. I never am much good at figuring out women.

My birthday comes. I turn 17. I stand five foot nine and a half inches tall and weigh 135 pounds. I wish to get to maybe five foot ten and 140. I do in time, which is as big as I ever get. Nobody makes any big fuss over my birthday. We have a cake and sing "Happy Birthday." My family knows I'm shy about being fussed over, so they spare me.

Mr. Jean Manseur calls. He wants to honor us with a big barbecue the Saturday before I leave for school. I have a lot of friends at Field Town and Mr. Manseur is one of my best. I tell him Rachel, Papa and I will ride the horses over; Grandma and Mama will drive. They are both good drivers, unusual for this time. Grandpa and Uncle Joe can't make it. The milk business is a seven-day-a-week job. I don't believe they want to go anyhow.

On Saturday, the last week of August, 1936, in Field Town, Papa, Rachel and I arrive about 11 o'clock. We ride slow and easy 'cause of the heat. We hear music, smell hickory smoke and it sounds like people are already commencing to have fun.

As people see us ride up on those three beautiful thoroughbreds, Gallant Hood, the Belle, and TJ, they begin cheering. Seeing the Kentucky Derby winner in the flesh gives them something to tell their grandkids about. In the distance, I see Mama and Grandma with Mr. Jean Manseur. When he sees us, he comes a running, screaming, "Sonneeee!"

He laughs and carries on like a madman. He practically drags me off TJ and starts kissing me on the cheeks. That's the way of Cajuns. He is wild-eyed and smacking Papa on the cheeks and hugging and kissing everybody he can reach.

Everybody doubles up laughing. Somebody screams, "Calm down! Control yourself! Easy!" It is Mr. Manseur. All swole up and prideful, he parades us through the crowd. So happy for us he cries and laughs at the same time, saying over and over, "This one the best day of this ole Cajun's life."

"Sonee," he says, "I tell you surefire 'bout people with the French blood in 'em. Dem people is what you call feeling. Your Mam'selle Rachel, she got the French in her. You remember that."

There are a good many musicians, some playing Cajun music, some East Texas hillbilly. There are washtubs of iced-down sody water, tubs of bottles of Jax and Texas Prize beer, some cases of moon pies and barbecue cooking in several pits in the ground.

We find shade for TJ, the Belle and Gallant Hood. Mr. Manseur puts one of his men to guard them to keep the rambunctious boys from trying to get on 'em. The music and eating go on and on. We are sitting in the shade with full bellies watching people have fun. Must be eight or nine hundred folks.

Mr. Manseur tells me, "Sonee, I bust dem bookies out all over. Some down in Cuba. I'm gonna sweeten you and Mam'selle Rachel's wedding gift. I ain't saying how much. You will be surprised the day you take the vows. The luckiest day ever was the day you beat my Big Red.

"Ah, Sonee, I have a most delicate matter to discuss wid you in private. Come, let's you and Papa Doc walk over here away from the ladies.

"I have come into possession of two most beautiful long-legged ladies from Kentucky. One is of the red hair, one if of the brown hair. Very highbrow from the best of families. I would like to make their acquaintance with Mr. TJ next February or March, when love is in the bloom. Can we arrange such a rendezvous? TJ would be delighted to make their acquaintance."

"It can be arranged," I say.

"Merci beaucoup," he seriously replies.

We finally have to leave. Mama, Grandma, Papa, Rachel and I are standing with Mr. Manseur. He looks at all of us, turns to me and says, "Sonee, you one lucky boy to have this family. I love all of you. Au revoir," then he turns and walks away.

The last week at home before I leave for A&M goes by at a frantic pace. I get excited about new friends, which fraternity to join, really excited about being in the Cadet Corps, dressing in military-style uniform. I am full of self confidence.

Grandma tells me not to fret about the farm, but I can see the anxiety in her face. I promise her I'll call at least once a week. I know she's really some upset at me leaving. College Station is only 100 miles away. If need be, I can come home on a weekend. There will be two weeks at Christmas, spring break and three months in the summer.

"I want you to have schooling," she says. "I just feel like I'm losing you. Be sure and go to church every Sunday, you hear?"

"Yes'm, Grandma. I'll be sure to do that," and I do.

Papa wants to talk to me. We go into the library at the big house and Papa says to be on guard about drinking alcohol.

"Don't get into any kind of habit using vulgar language. Don't go to Laredo with any of the boys. Keep yourself pure for Rachel. Don't be playing poker or shooting craps. You probably don't know it, Sonny, but you've led a very sheltered life in most ways. And call me once a week."

Then laughing, he adds, "I know you won't need any money. Just call as it would please me if you need any advice. That's what papas are for. I need to steer you around the pitfalls of a young innocent man's life."

"Sonny, have you told Rachel how you feel about her?" he asks.

"No sir, Papa. She knows."

"Take your Papa's advice and tell her anyway."

We talk and talk. Papa does most of the talking; I do the listening. The way it should be.

Rachel will be in school at Texas Woman's University at Denton, about the same distance from home as me. She plans on being a nurse. Nursing and teaching are pretty much the two main studies for women in this day and time.

College Station and Denton are about 150 miles apart.

The Sunday morning before time to leave on Monday morning, I have a hard time sleeping. The weather is so hot we're all sleeping on the sleeping porch at Grandma's. Rachel sleeps at the big house.

I hear Uncle Joe get up to load the milk cans for the run to Dallas at two a.m. I help him load. After a while, about four a.m., I trot up to the big house, go in the back door into the kitchen, turn on a light and start making coffee.

I sit at the kitchen table drinking my coffee when Rachel walks in. Her hair is tussled, she has on a bathrobe and is barefooted. She has a sorta sleepy look about her. "I thought I heard a noise," she says. "I haven't been sleeping well lately."

She pours a cup of coffee and sits down directly across from me. Her mouth turns down and her eyes have a sad look. I ask, "Something wrong? We leave in the morning."

She looks me direct in the face and says, "Look at me, don't look away. You speak to me of our house we will build, our farm, our horses, our children and our future. Our this, our that and yet you have never spoken of how you feel about me."

She looks right in my eyes and says simply, "I love you, Sonny."

My insides are churning. After a minute, I say, "Yes, I know. I feel it." I look her in the eyes and said, "Rachel, I love you."

After a minute, she says, "I know, I can feel it."

She stands up. Tells me to stand up. "Put your arms around me and hold me."

I am surprised to see she is about as tall as me — first I've noticed. I put my arms around her and she lays her head on my shoulder. She pulls her head back, looks into my eyes, and then closes her eyes. I kiss the left eye, the right eye, each cheek, then a soft lingering kiss on her lips.

A river of tingling jolts run through me, then a flood. I have some kinda strange feeling going through me. My head swims. I hear Rachel. "Whoa! Whoa there!"

I snap out of it. She steps back with a wild proud happy look on her face. She laughs real pleasant like and says, "You know something, Sonny? The day we take our vows, I'm gonna give you plenty love with beaucoup, mucho amour gusto, all you will ever want. You sabby?"

"Si, I comprendo." And she does.

Rachel and I graduate in May 1940. We take our vows the first week in June. We are barely 21, young, full of optimism, hope and love. We buy a new Cadillac to motor around the country for our honeymoon. An architect finishes up our home.

Our first stop is Dallas. The Adolphus Hotel. We never, I'm embarrassed to say, leave our suite for three days. I founder my fool self. Copius!

Then in November 1940 our world comes crashing down with notice of activation of the 36th Division. Grandma says we're being tested.

Mary Annabelle is born April 1941. Our last time together is an August weekend in 1942 in Norfolk, Virginia, where I am preparing to sail for North Africa. Our separation lasts three years and two months.

CHAPTER 19

~~~

October 1945

I don't sleep. I have my eyes closed and dream, remember. The bus driver calls out my town. I glance out the window as we pass the TJ Dairy Company. It looks to cover 15 or 20 acres, the dairy center of the southwest. There stands a bronze statue of a horse at the entrance. First I've seen it. I know it is TJ. Most statues are of dead things. TJ is very much alive. He's coming on 13, in his prime.

As the bus comes to a stop, my heart flutters. Happiness and joy in my family always brings tears, tears of joy. I am the last one off the bus. I can see Rachel and the family as I step down. Rachel comes flying, kissing me all over my face, crying, "Oh! My precious husband."

I kiss her and hold her tight, saying, "We will fall in love all over again."

"Not again, just deeper," she says. "There's no bottom."

The family acts courteous standing back and letting Rachel and me go first. They kinda line up and I feel a pull at my hand. I pick up little Annabelle who looks into my face and says, "You are my poppy. Come home to stay always." I kiss her on the cheek and she smiles showing her little baby teeth.

As I am looking at my baby, I have a strange sensation. Black hair, startling blue eyes — a stab of memory hits me deep inside. The dream in the summer of 1936! I look at Rachel. She smiles and says, "Yes, I know. She's the one." This happens in about 30 seconds.

I go to Mama and Papa. I kiss Mama, then Papa puts his arms around me saying, "Sonny, we are so very proud of our son."

"Thank you, Papa. You and Mama have always been my heroes."

I hug and kiss Grandma telling her I appreciate all the boxes of socks and rosebud salve she has sent over the years. Saved my feet. "Grandma," I say, "You have always been my inspiration."

I hug Grandpa, tell him I love him. He is smiling saying, "I got a colonel, my grandson, and a general, my son-in-law doc in the family. I was just a top sergeant."

"Grandpa, you will always be the commanding officer of this family," I say, adding, "I hope you order yourself to cook a rump roast soon." I'm trying to express my love the best I know how.

I hug Uncle Joe, kiss Aunt Willie on the cheek, and tell them I love them. There are seven kids lined up — two sets of twins. I say, "Uncle Joe, you practically have your own softball team."

Aunt Willie hollers out, "I never did get fixed!"

One of the older boys says, "Colonel Sonny, will you tell us some war stories?"

"Later. I have you some souvenirs in my bag." He whoops.

I go to Woody and Saree. I hug Woody, kiss Saree on her cheek and tell her I appreciate all her cakes and cookies over the years. Woody is smiling real big saying over and over, "Praise de Lord!"

Saree says, "Soon as you get settled in, you and Miz Rachel come to the house. I been baking some pies."

"I was always partial to your pies and I would appreciate a few songs from you."

She laughs and says, "You got it, anytime."

Mammy BB hugs me, looks me up and down, and says, "Lawd, Mista Sonny! I got to put some meat on them bones."

I laugh and say, "Mammy, you are helping to raise the third generation of this family, little Annabelle. We are better because of you."

She laughs and adds, "Peach cobbler and rooster coffee for dessert tonight."

Mr. Goldman, Mr. Dillard and Billy Joe are next in line. We hug and shake hands. Billy Joe says, "Sonny, if it wasn't for you, I wouldn't be here. Remember at the Rapido River?"

"That goes two ways, Billy Joe. Remember at Salerno? We looked out for each other."

Mr. Goldman says, "When you are squared away, you and Doc, Miz Annie, Dillard and I will have a stockholders' meeting. You'll be pleasantly surprised."

I miss Mr. Hank and Asa, thinking maybe they didn't know I was coming today. Then I think I hear a clop, clop. I look over my shoulder and Mr. Hank and Asa are leading TJ and the Belle, all saddled, toward us. I step away from everyone as they come up.

TJ stops, sticks his little ears up. The Belle acts skittish. I walk up to TJ, put my arms around his neck and kiss the side of his face. I blow in his nostrils. He begins snuffling, butts me in the chest, lets out a low nicker. Belle nickers too.

Mr. Hank and Asa laugh. Mr. Hank hugs me. Asa hugs me too and says, "We thought you and Miz Rachel would like to ride home."

I am so happy this moment I think, *There can't possibly be a more perfect world.*

Rachel rides the Belle and I on TJ start down the lane to our big beautiful new home — when I stop. Rachel turns and comes back with a puzzled look on her face. "Are you all right?"

"Rachel, is there anything on my shoulders?"

"No, I don't see anything. Why?"

"I felt and heard a flutter of wings that I thought could be some pesky mockers trying to roost on my shoulders."

All at once she smiles real big. "Sonny, I believe it's your angels roosting on your shoulders."

The End

Printed in the United States
146491LV00001B/11/P